D0651593

Barbara Esstman

Night Ride Home

Harcourt Brace & Company
New York San Diego London

Library of Congress Cataloging-in-Publication Data
Esstman, Barbara.
Night ride home/by Barbara Esstman.—1st U.S. ed.
p. cm.
ISBN 0-15-100288-6
I. Title.
PS3555.S69N54 1997
813'.54—dc21 97-9305

Text set in Centaur
Designed by Linda Lockowitz
Printed in the United States of America
First U.S. edition
F E D C B A

To 'Naldo, from Rosie,
and for Bryan, Beth, and Mark.

Some things I wanted to tell you,
Some things that might have been.

Thanks, as usual, to
Miriam Altshuler and The Group,
especially Jody Brady; and to
Mike Esstman for
continued child support.

Being sacrificed is a way to go home.
He who loses his life shall find it.

—JOSEPH CAMPBELL

LaCote, Missouri

Spring 1947

There is no space wider than that of grief,
There is no universe like that which bleeds.

—Pablo Neruda

from "Point" by Pablo Neruda

Chapter One

Clea Mahler

My brother Simon died with his eyes open, staring blue into the sky. Out of the corner of my eye I had seen him fall, but at first when I turned I thought he was joking, splayed out like a snow angel in the grass. No blood, no marks on his body. I didn't believe he could be hurt, let alone dead. My mother's mare, Zad, the gray Arab he had been riding, turned back, nuzzled his hand, and snorted. Then the morning pulled tight and held so quiet that I could hear the horses breathe and shift and rustle.

"Simon," I said.

My little gelding tossed its head and mouthed the bit.

"Simon," I said again, angry that he would frighten me. It would be just like Simon to pretend for a second that something was wrong, just to get me to laugh in relief a minute later. Then I went sick deep in my belly that this might not be a trick.

"Simon, stop it," I said.

When he wouldn't answer, I dismounted but stayed a few steps away, afraid that he would leap at me or grab my hand. When I finally worked up the nerve, the warmth of his skin made me jerk back. His head rolled sideways as if he had turned to tell me something.

I knew in that instant he was dead. I mounted and kicked the bay hard, riding low over its neck with my legs banging and its sides lathering. I could not find its rhythm and gripped the edge of the saddle for balance. What I thought about then was not that I might be thrown and killed, as apparently had happened to Simon, but that my fingers pressed between the blanket and ridge of the horse's back were warm in that space between its shoulders.

The day broke into odd pieces: Black mane whipping and green grass blurring. The stripes of the saddle blanket, and the bright, hot air like a solid through which I was only dreaming I made my slow, thick way. And always Simon's blue eyes staring down from the sky and up from the ground and out from inside me.

When I came galloping up from the low fields with Zad trailing behind the way she always followed like a dog, my mother, Nora, stood up from the rosebushes she was pruning, her hand shading her eyes. Then she ran, her head back and fists pumping like a sprinter. She got to the gate before I could unfumble the latch and stood with her hands against the bay's rump and withers as if trapping me in her arms for just long enough to see if I was all right.

"Where's Simon?" she asked. "Did Zad throw him?"

I nodded yes, and she grabbed for Zad's reins. As she mounted, one foot in the stirrup, Zad turned in an excited circle around her.

"Get help." She slapped the mare's haunches to knock it out of its turning and threw her leg over its back.

I watched until she disappeared down the trail at the edge of the pasture. Then I left the gelding in the paddock and ran to the house to call my father, Neal, at work, and the feedstore, where Ozzie Kline, the hired man, had gone. My voice was shaking so I could hardly give the operator the numbers or explain clearly when I got through.

"Stop blubbering, Clea," my father shouted. "Is Simon hurt?"

"Yes," I told him, afraid to say more and make it certain.

Ozzie arrived at the same time as my father with the doctor, driving fast down the lane one behind the other. I'd saddled each a horse. My father hesitated a second before mounting his, but he followed silently as I led the men down the bluff. I rode at a fast trot down the middle of the trail so none of them, especially Ozzie Kline, could come even with me. As we came out past the tree line, I could see my mother as she leaned over Simon, her body shielding his. I could only think of a photograph I'd seen of a Civil War battlefield, with bodies arranged like frozen dancers in beaten-down grass, arms flung out and backs arched against the sky.

The men rode past me, and I reined in the bay. I wouldn't go near Simon, though I watched the doctor pass his hands over the eyes to close them. I turned my horse to face the river, hidden down the slope of its banks at the edge of the pasture, my back to the men, whose voices sounded like the baying and yelping of pack dogs.

But I had already seen too much and remembered too clearly: Simon and I on our way to the river to see how high the last rains had brought it and how it was leaking over its channel into the lowest spots of the bottoms land. Simon asking questions I didn't want to know the answer to and then staring up at me from the grass.

My father had told my mother that this year the water would reach the house and make us sorry we lived on the floodplain between the Missouri and Mississippi Rivers. He'd also told her not to let Simon ride Zad, that she was too spirited. But my mother didn't listen any more than Simon to what she didn't want to hear.

My father was right about Simon riding Zad, but for the wrong reasons. It was not Zad's fault. She had stumbled over the rock and slid on the wet ground. I'd heard her hoof strike with a hollow ring and turned just in time to see her knees bend as if she was dropping to prayer. It wasn't her fault, but Simon's for riding with the reins loose and one knee up on the saddle, even after I'd warned him that the trail was slippery.

Simon was older. He'd defend me against anyone, even when I didn't want him to. If a boy called, Simon questioned him like the gestapo. If one asked me to dance, he circled around us like a bouncer. But here, between Simon and me, I was fair game, and he rarely missed a chance to prove he was the better rider, the only one besides our mother allowed to ride Zad.

I was suddenly angry at her for giving him this privilege and with him for showing off and even with Zad for falling. I couldn't believe that Simon, always so perfect and good at everything, had made a mistake. My whole life, he'd been with me. Always two years smarter and more experienced, always willing to share what he'd found out. How could he be gone forever?

The black roofs of my house and the barn rose through the treetops on the ridge, above the trails leading down the bluff to the flatlands. The pasture was knee-deep with grass and flecked with buttercups. Ahead of me was another line of trees that divided this from the drop-off to the river. By the river below the house was a cabin where Simon and I went together to be alone and talk.

The farm was my great-grandmother's, the place my mother's family had lived for seventy years. The same as it always was, except for my mother's wailing, the kind of crying animals make at night.

The sound sputtered, then stopped. I couldn't help myself from looking back over my shoulder. Simon was curved belly down over Zad's saddle, and Nora, walking beside, held the reins with her palm cupped over his head to keep it from bobbing. Ozzie Kline walked beside her and led his horse. My father and the doctor rode on either side like an honor guard.

Simon's fine, straight hair flew out with every step, in unison with the horse's mane. I thought of how his eyes had been so blue and open, and I kicked the bay hard and rode past to the trailhead and on up the bluff. A few times the horse stumbled, and I dropped down slightly. The outside of me seemed to fall faster so that my heart bruised itself against the bones of my chest, and I realized this sensation was the last Simon felt before his head hit the rock. Then again I slid my fingers under the edge of the saddle, though Nora had told me a hundred times that how I held the horse between my legs was what kept me with it.

She had taught both Simon and me to ride, starting us as babies barely old enough to sit in front of her on the saddle.

The horses were hers, and my father hated them and the time she spent on them. If she had listened to him, Simon would be alive.

I kicked the bay again. It huffed and snorted up the steep trail and through the gate. I slipped off, ran clinging to its sides for a few steps, and then hauled back on the reins. The bay dug in and stopped, swinging its face back to watch me. I pulled the saddle and bridle off, leaving them where they fell, then slapped the horse on the rump. Not slapped. I brought my fist down and hit as hard as I could at the end of its spine.

I didn't seem to hurt it. It plunged forward, then wandered off a few steps and dipped its head to rip a mouthful of grass. I walked across the remainder of the pasture which stretched forever before me. I trotted and finally ran to be sure I was in the house by the time the rest of them reached the barn.

My geography book lay open on the kitchen table, next to Simon's physics text and a spiral notebook with a half-finished problem. Less than two hours before he had laid down his pencil and said, "I'm sick of this. Let's go riding." I had been glad of the reprieve, but now I could not bear to look at the page that would never have an answer. I could not think that he and I would never sit together again, joking and doing our homework, talking about things we'd never tell our parents. Quickly I shoved our books and papers in our school satchels and went to my room.

Soon the ambulance rushed up the drive, spitting out chat from under its tires. It seemed silly to order an ambulance, but otherwise, how would Simon get to where he needed to go? Not propped in the passenger seat of my father's car or Nora's pickup. Not staring blue-eyed out the side window.

But I forgot they had closed his eyes. I lay on my bed,

pressing my face into the ridges of the chenille spread until the ambulance took Simon away. I pressed my eyes tighter against bits of image floating through. The bent knees of the mare. Her legs folding. Simon's eyes.

The draft from the attic fan banged my door shut, and when I ran to open it, swollen from the damp, it stuck. I yanked at it, panicky and afraid that Simon somehow was holding it closed. When I got a glass of water from the bath to rinse my mouth, I wouldn't look in the mirror, in case I might see him standing behind me. When evening came, I wouldn't go out of my room or to the kitchen, no matter how hungry I got.

The light stayed late, hanging pale and eerie in the first week of daylight savings. A little before dusk, my father returned alone. I listened to his car engine cut off, the solid closing of the driver's door, the bang of the downstairs screen, the sounds of his movement below me. If I had not been listening so carefully, I wouldn't have recognized the unlocking of the gun rack, the drop of shells into their chambers and solid click of the barrels latching in place.

I had thought what he might do, but it seemed as farfetched as Simon's dying. Yet he walked out and the screen slammed shut behind him. Then I shut my eyes, and the concussions of the shot smacked flat and hard against my chest.

But I could not keep myself from looking. The slit between the window frame and shade cut a narrow slice of yard. The mare lay as if sleeping, much like Simon in the tall grass, and as with him, I could not understand in my heart that she was dead.

I pulled the shades down and held the pillows over my head, sweaty and suffocating. When my father came to my door, I didn't want to talk with him. But sometimes the next day I refused to turn around. Other times I whirled to catch a glimpse of what might be there. I slept again with the pillow held tightly over my head and my body rigid, as if moving out of the space I had chosen would cause me to touch her muzzle or his hand.

When I dozed off, I dreamed of Simon riding her down the bluff, rocking with her stride, and her tail switching.

"Zad is the best ever, Clea," he laughed.

"Moe's good," I said, patting the neck of my gelding.

"Like walking is to flying. If you'd let me teach you to ride better, then you'd find out."

Through the leaves, the sun broke into dapples.

"Hey, Clea," he began, "have you ever noticed..."

He slung his leg over the pommel, the way he always got in a casual position when he was trying to work out a problem.

I couldn't speak to stop him. Simon and Zad fell again. My brother and all he knew slid out of reach.

The dream stayed close to the surface when I woke, and it seemed Simon and Zad had moved just past sight on the spectrum of light rays, their sounds now in the higher frequency that only animals can hear.

Three times that week before the funeral, the dog, lying with his head on his paws, raised up and tracked with his eyes what I could not see across the yard. Once he ran out, then stood baffled at not finding what he had gone to greet. The cats, too, suddenly waking from their naps, stared blinking into empty space as if they'd been spoken to by a figure there.

I barely saw my mother. She stayed at the hospital that first night, and my father brought her back the next day. She glanced at the paddock where the mare had lain, but Ozzie Kline had already chained up the body and dragged it off to the clearing near the river, leaving a smooth path away from the dark circle of blood. My mother could not have known what my father had done, but I swear she started as if the mare's absence told her all.

He took her upstairs to her room. In the next few days the doctor stopped by occasionally to give her a shot or more pills, and neighbors came to fix meals, delivering hers on a tray. I stayed in my room, pretending to read or nap, but sometimes crept down the hall to look through the half-open door, into the dimness, at her lying curled on the bed with her hair strung lank on the pillow like a sick animal's mane.

Yet right before a fresh dose of sedatives, she came loose and talked, then shouted. She did not sound wounded, as she had after finding Simon, but sharp and angry. When the sound of breaking came from her room, my father explained that the drugs made her woozy and she'd accidentally knocked over a glass or lamp. But to me, the shattering had force and aim and purpose, like target bottles exploding when Simon shot them off a rock.

As my mother became wilder, my father became more proper. I thought of them as a ratio then, with her lunging out in direct proportion to him pulling in, as if they had to constantly adjust the tension to keep a balance between them.

Two days after Simon died, my father stood again at the door of my room and gave the information he had to pass on.

Simon had died instantly from a blow to the base of his skull.

My mother was hysterical and had to be quieted.

My grandmother Maggie had finally been contacted and was returning from her trip in Mexico.

After three nights of visitation, the burial would be at the church grounds, not the cemetery on our land where my mother's family lay.

He never cried. Only once did his voice tremble, when he said Simon had "suffered no pain" as if that were bad news instead of good. I heard the whispers of the women who came to bring us food and clean the house, and the conversations of the men as they loaded up the rest of the horses the next day to take back to their owners or to auction, even my Moe. Neal Mahler in their eyes was a man to look up to, and my mother, Nora, was "not right."

At the visitations, I tried to be like my father, but could do so only by staying out of the funeral room that held Simon's casket and biting the inside of my cheek so hard that it bled. I locked myself in a stall in the ladies' room and cleared my mind of any images of my brother, any stories, any memories, because whenever I came near to these, I felt a cracking-open in my chest.

I was afraid that I might cry until I dissolved or broke apart into pieces too small to even see or pick up. I held very still so as not to jar the stillness and recited the Our Father over and over to fill my mind with its words only.

I stayed away from practically everyone that week, and all but Ozzie Kline left me alone. They spoke as politely as my father, never mentioning anything personal or real about Simon. They even avoided his name, usually saying instead, "I'm sorry about your brother." When my grandmother arrived, she put her arms around me, but I held myself stiff and she didn't try again.

But before Ozzie Kline left after the funeral, he hugged me so hard his bones poked against mine and I struggled to catch my breath. His scent was faintly like horses but also like a man newly bathed and come out again into the heat. He held tight and long until I was afraid.

"Take care of your mother for me," he said.

I pushed my hands flat against his chest, but he held on to me.

"Will you get your grandmother to help if Nora needs it?" he asked, shaking me hard. "Will you?"

Seeing his eyes red from crying was like seeing him naked. I twisted away from him and ran toward the house and did not turn when he called after me.

Several times each night during the next few weeks I jerked awake. I could almost tell the hours by my mother's cries, like those of a drowning person suddenly breaking the surface of water. I thought about what else my father might be capable of, beyond what he had done to Zad, and each day became like walking through a pitch-dark room where all the furniture had been rearranged.

I didn't know what else to do, but I never cried, not once. I didn't want my father to be angry with me, too. But I felt a huge space around me, so large I didn't believe anyone could ever touch me again, not even in a way that would make me feel just unafraid. But somehow that seemed safest. That emptiness was the only place I wanted to be.

Chapter Two

Nora Mahler

Simon's fingers were cold, and I chafed them between my hands the way I did when he'd come home from sledding. Then I pressed my fingers to his throat and wrists and laid my head against his chest, a distance swelling between us. Simon never older than at the instant of death and myself even then moving into the future where he was not allowed.

I panicked at leaving him behind, time pushing me forward into itself. I wanted to stop, if only for one last instant, but I could no more grasp minutes than I could have held an armful of river to stop myself from washing downstream.

I moved away from myself then also, heard my crying as if it came from another woman far off across the field. Neal pulled me to my feet and held me away from Simon as Ozzie and the doctor carried him to Zad and laid him over her. Neal wanted me to ride his horse, but I shook him off and took Zad's reins. As Oz fell into step beside me, he reached out to graze my arm with the backs of his fingertips.

"Nora," he said.

I saw this all happening below me, just as on the way to the hospital I saw my forearms scratched and streaked with garden mud, my hands folded in my lap with a line of dirt under each nail. I did not feel much at all. Not the pressure of gravity or air against my skin, but only a vacuum's weightless calm.

A doctor, not the one in the field, came to tell Neal and me that Simon was dead. He wore a white smock buttoned up to his tie knot and his thin hair combed primly across his skull. He pulled up a chair, and we huddled in a corner of the waiting room, our knees almost touching.

"The blow to the cranium," he said, "was very severe. Your son"—he looked from Neal to myself and then down at some papers—"died instantly."

He told us this very seriously as if it would be a bad surprise. I started laughing. I couldn't help it. How could I laugh at the news my son had died? But the laughter burst out and I could not keep my lips pressed tightly enough to catch it. I was not sure what exactly was so humorous. The pompous doctor and his dramatic ways? The superfluity of being at the hospital? The arrogance of modern medicine that no longer trusted us to recognize death by ourselves?

The laughter cut loose all that had been held together with hastily looped wire. It brought in great gulps of air where before I had been holding my breath so as to hear the beating of a heart. It sucked me down until I was caught within myself again. I stopped laughing suddenly and looked at the doctor and Neal staring at me.

"Of course he's dead, you bastards," I told them.

They blinked like retarded owls.

"What do you think you're doing?" I said more loudly.

So much came loose at once that it was like an avalanche inside. My joints unhinged and my bones turned liquid. I could not stop thinking. If the horse had not stumbled or the stone had been elsewhere or if Simon had caught himself a second sooner. So many bad lucks strung together and chances measured in inches and seconds.

In all the wide world, for all the miserable souls who would not mind the release of death, for all those who could die unmissed, why was it this child of mine, so greatly loved and full of promise, who was taken?

At first I didn't remember much of the rest—it came in small flashes as much as days later, like a drunk's memories of a binge. But when I woke in the middle of the night, I lay in the dark, so heavy with drugs that I could not work my way back into memory except with shards of image, disconnected and out of order. Of Neal holding my hands and the doctor telling me to get control. Of me trying to beat the men, to punch and hit them, until they responded in some real way to what had happened.

I switched on the light and swayed blind in the whiteness. I could smell it before I could see it—a hospital room with gray linoleum, slick under my bare feet. I pulled my gown closed in a fist behind me and careened to the desk where a small nurse with freckles looked up from her charts.

"Go back to bed," she said. "Doctor's orders."

"But I didn't say I wanted to be here." My tongue was thick and awkward in my mouth.

"You were in no shape." She got up and came around the desk toward me. "Not to mention that the pills we gave you should have knocked out a horse."

Another larger nurse came out of a room down the hall and hurried toward us as the first kept moving closer, talking low the way she would to a dog she wanted to slip a collar on.

"I want to go home," I argued.

But the bigger one lunged and pulled me to her, and the other threw her arms in a loop around my shoulders.

"Just be quiet," she said.

They held me up, pressed between their bellies and breasts, and danced me to my room, sometimes nipping my toes with the rubber edges of their nurses' shoes.

"You're in no shape to be running around tonight," the smaller one said, more kindly now that she had caught me. "Morning will be soon enough to talk about this."

"You can go home then," the second agreed.

The smaller one held me while the other smoothed my sheets. I leaned against the little one and let her lay me down. Then the other returned with a hypo and rolled me on my side. The alcohol was cool on my hip.

"This won't hurt," she said.

It did, but I didn't care.

"Don't think about a thing now," she said. "Just relax and let us take care of everything."

"That's right," said the other. "You can't do anything tonight."

I closed my eyes. The covers settled with a little breeze on my legs, the nurses' hands like moths above me. Their shoes squeaked around the room and their voices whispered in the hall. I tried to make out the words, but they ran together and were too much trouble to attend to. The warmth of the drug crept through me and I wondered if Simon felt as dark and drowsy. Or if he felt at all. I wanted to know so I could imagine him at any moment he came to mind, the way I had often done when he was at school or out with friends.

I wanted to be angry about what had happened to him and furious with Neal. But I seemed to be wrapped in cotton batting that kept me far from anything but whiteness. I tried to lift my arm but instead slid down toward sleep, letting the nurses care for everything, their voices now like mourning doves cooing in bushes after rain.

CHAPTER THREE

Neal Mahler

EVERY TIME I LOOKED at Nora, I thought about how I once hit a dog out on the highway, a black mongrel standing directly in front of my car. I couldn't have missed it without swerving in front of an oncoming truck or running off the road. I was sure I'd killed it, but it got up, its front legs braced and haunches swaying.

I pulled off and walked back. I don't know why I'd stopped in the first place or what I thought I was going to do. Habit, probably, from living with Nora who'd kill herself and everyone else in the car rather than run over a squirrel in the road.

The dog growled, drool and blood coming out of its mouth. Just then another car came over the rise and knocked the dog onto the gravel. It stared up at me with a gold eye so steady that I didn't realize for a moment when it actually died, and so I stood there like a fool.

In the hospital Nora gave me that same kind of look when the doctor was telling us the details of the accident. Just like that dog working to keep itself upright. She stood up so fast she knocked over her chair and swung her arms like she was clearing branches in her way.

Then she stood there swaying and looking at me as if our son's dying and God's will could all be laid to my blame. She was crying so hard by then we couldn't understand what she was saying, and when I tried to take her by the wrist and get her to sit down again, she twisted around like she was crazy. I told her she needed to get control of herself so she could go home and take care of Clea. "I don't care about Clea," she said. "I don't care about any of you."

Neither of us could do a thing with her, so a nurse got a syringe, and I pinned Nora's arm tight while the doctor swabbed the skin. She put her head down and butted against me, just like some animal, and as we turned, the needle broke off in her arm.

Then we got two attendants to help us hold her, but she didn't fight much after that. Just sat there looking from one of us to the other like she couldn't understand what we were doing to her. The doctor got a big tweezers and dug around with them awhile before he could find the end that'd snapped off. He gave her the shot finally in the opposite arm, and she was all right by the time I took her home the next morning. But when I got back from clearing up the most urgent matters at the office, she was upset again and giving the neighbor women at the house trouble.

The way she acted didn't change the fact of what had happened to Simon or that she had to be in shape to get through the funeral and carry on afterward. I knew he was her favorite. If I dropped dead in an instant, she wouldn't have blinked, but she couldn't do enough for him. It might have been the way he was born. A big baby, eleven pounds and something, and Nora kind of slight, especially when she was younger. The labor lasted into a second day, so long the nurses sent me home. By the end Nora and the boy were so beat up that no one knew for a while if either of them would live. Tore her up so badly that it was more than a year before we had relations again. But I think the fact they came so close to death made them special to each other. At least they decided that in their minds.

They were both crazy about the horses, too. Clea rode so as not to be left out, and I wouldn't go near the things. But Nora would stay on board all the time if she could, and even when Simon was a baby, she sat him in front of her on the saddle. I'd be angry with her then, but she'd hold on to him with one arm and pull the reins with the other to make the horse dance away.

"If you come closer, you might spook her," she'd laugh, and I'd back off.

When he was three, she got him a pony, so small I didn't know horses came that little. I'd told her I wouldn't buy him one, so she went out on her own with the last of the money her grandmother Grace had left her. That had always been one of Nora's problems, being left too much, the property and house and all, not to mention a little trust in her name that she drew from, and the income from boarding and training horses. She never needed to come to me.

She also didn't have to listen to my advice when she wanted to do something, like with that first pony. Simon loved it. He begged her all the time to take him riding, which meant circling around her as she held the lead. She said it was safe, but I told her how it could be if there was trouble.

"I'm not ten feet from him," she'd say.

I pointed out that unless she kept next to him with her arm around him, she wouldn't be close enough to do anything should that pony buck or toss him. She told me I was welcome to trot along right by his side, but I said that was her business and she ought to do it for his safety.

"Oh," she'd say, "what's mine is yours, but what's yours is your own."

"What's that mean?" I'd ask.

"Exactly what it says."

"Where'd you hear that?"

"From Grace," she said.

The grandmother again.

So Simon grew and the ponies in succession got larger until he worked his way up to a little pinto that she said was horse size. Nora never had the heart to sell the ones he got too big for and, after Clea was through learning, kept them all until they died, the last one just the year before. I told Nora it wasn't practical to feed that many animals we had no use for, but she said she liked to see them grazing out in the pasture. They looked pretty, she said, and they helped her remember Simon and Clea at all the ages they rode each one.

"Besides," she said, "I'm making enough from the other horses. I can afford them."

I tried to explain that the extra money would be better spent on stocks and bonds.

"Pretty expensive fertilizer you're investing in," I'd say, but she'd look at me crazy, like I'd just said something in a foreign language.

When those ponies died, I couldn't even get her to take them to the knacker's for a few bucks. She told me they had served us well and deserved a proper ending. If it was warm when one of them went, a guy with a backhoe came to dig the grave. He wouldn't take any money, but traded his services for his daughter's riding lessons. If the ground was frozen, Nora had him drag the animal off and burn it, then in the spring, scrape the bones into a shallow grave. I used to hate to be out in the yard and have that stench in the air that otherwise smelled so clean and crisp. Like breathing in rot, I told her, but she wouldn't listen.

"They're my horses," she said. "I paid for them and I take care of them. I don't ask anything of you except that you let me alone."

I argued that when Simon rode it became my business as his father, but telling Simon to stay away from horses was like living next to the candy store and forbidding him sweets. Besides, Nora argued, the better he rode, the safer he'd be. So Simon rode. When he was five and learning to jump low fences, he flew off and hit his head—Nora had to get up every hour during the night to make sure he didn't have a concussion. When he was nine, he fell off, broke his arm, and didn't get to go swimming all summer with the cast and all. When he was thirteen, a horse kicked him, and we thought at first his leg'd been fractured. Then at seventeen, a preventable death.

I almost saw it coming. Simon was one of those young men that everything's too easy for. He was handsome and well built, one of the fair-eyed blonds common on Nora's side of the family. He excelled in school without working, unlike Clea who slaves just to get by. He made friends instantly. Well, maybe not so much friends as followers. He slipped through life without a hitch and that over-ease made him careless. I couldn't make him believe that not everything was there for his taking.

But whatever I said was contradicted by Nora, and she said what he wanted to hear.

"Go on, do it, try it," she'd say. "I'll show you how."

He was a reckless kid, not like Clea who always had to be sure nothing would go wrong before she'd attempt a new thing. He'd trot off without a thought to talk with the devil, while Clea wouldn't go to her bus stop without knowing what time the bus was supposed to come and exactly what to do if it did or didn't. I never worried about her. From the time she was little, she was cautious, and Nora had to talk her into what she did do.

But Simon did whatever Nora suggested and a million things beyond that. It was only a matter of time until he caused an uproar in some way. The week before the accident, a friend dropped by the office to say Simon had been running my car over the back roads at ninety miles an hour. A few days later, another guy told me he'd found Simon and some girl by his tractor shed going at it. Their reports were just the latest in a long string, and the question was not whether Simon would eventually get in serious trouble, but if he would involve others and how many when it happened.

In a way we should have been grateful that it was only he who suffered. Not some innocent passengers in his car or an unsuspecting driver coming the opposite way, not some girl whose life was ruined because she got pregnant. The damage was contained, as they used to say in the war. The casualties were minimal.

I would have liked to have gone off by myself to sort it all through, but there was so much that only I could take care of, and even the few minutes I had alone at the office seemed stolen from my family. So I tried to concentrate on the living instead. After I left Nora at the hospital, I stopped by the office to get in touch with people. I asked my friends to call others, but by then many already knew. I called my pastor to reserve the church for the services, and the funeral parlor to tell them we'd be in soon to make arrangements. I tried to leave messages for Nora's mother, who was traveling and had given us an itinerary, but neither the foreign hotel operator nor the clerk spoke English. I shouted very slowly. "Wife's mama with you?" and "American lady, Missie Margaret Rhymer, come there?" But the connection was weak and crackly, and they didn't seem to get it.

I tried to set up everything that needed to be done. Nora was in no shape, and besides, making the arrangements was something I wanted to do for Simon. Something exclusive and special, unlike anything we'd shared when he was alive. I felt less helpless after that.

But as I was driving down Highway 94 to our place, I passed a carload of kids coming the opposite way with the windows down and the radio turned up loud. The boys and even one of the girls shouted and laughed as they went by, waving out the windows. I was angry that they had the long summer before them and insulted they could laugh and be silly on the evening Simon died.

In the fields beyond, animals stood quietly grazing. Dark shapes dotting the black-green pastures. Dumb animals. I passed a large herd of Angus like thick solid shadows and a small group of Charolais, shimmery white on the side of a hill. I wanted them all at the packinghouse and everything back in its proper place.

When I pulled up, the horse trotted over to greet me like some overgrown dog. Nora had taught her that, and she hung her head over the fence, tossing her mane and nickering as if I hadn't noticed her. I walked halfway across the yard between us. She looked at me, those big cow eyes, like she expected an apple or sugar cube. No different than a rabid coon that had to be destroyed to protect my family.

When I came back out with the gun, she was stupid enough to follow me out to the center of the paddock. She didn't try to run away, not even when I put the barrel against the side of her head. I did just what I'd seen Nora do. I said, "Stand, Zad," and raised my hand like an Indian saying, "How." She did exactly what I told her, and I shot her for Simon.

The score seemed more even then. I threw my clothes away, my white shirt and second-best work pants, but the blood rinsed off my shoes. After I cleaned up, I went to see how Clea was. Her door was closed. I asked if she was OK, and she called back to say she was. "If you need anything, tell me," I said. "Anything at all." I didn't know what else to say to her.

The next day, after we got Nora back from the hospital, she went wilder than she'd been before. She got so bad that the doctor and I discussed what we'd do if she didn't get better. I don't know what made her like that, the screaming and swearing, but I think that streak had always been there, that indulgence in her own feelings.

When I first fell in love with her, I liked it that she had a mind of her own. She was smart and full of spirit, but even when she got her way, she sometimes seemed angry and dissatisfied. I always told her she didn't know what she really wanted. She always told me I didn't understand.

After the accident, it took all my strength to get us through. But Nora seemed like fragile old china, all crosshatched with little hairline fractures just waiting to give. I felt the cracks forming and spreading, not only in her, but inside my chest, down the walls, and on toward Clea until everything was just hung together by the slimmest of holds.

The night after Nora came home from the hospital, I tried to hold her in my arms, thinking that if I could get her to keep still, she would stop. When that didn't work, I wanted to slap her. I'd heard about Patton doing that during the war. Some private started crying and screaming that he was going to be killed, and the general smacked him so hard the kid was unconscious for a minute. I didn't know what to do until the doctor got there. I'd never hit a woman, never. But I wanted to hit Nora then.

After the sedatives took hold again, I stood in the dark of our room and watched her sleep. The house was quiet, and she lay flat on her belly, arms and legs splayed out the way the kids had slept as babies. I hoped she'd be better after the funeral, and well enough to take care of Clea again. I wanted her to understand how I cared if she got well. How I'd do anything to make it so she could sleep quietly like this every night for the rest of her life.

CHAPTER FOUR

Nora Mahler

THE MORNING AFTER Simon died, Neal drove me home as carefully as an egg. As we passed horses grazing in small knots, I leaned my head against the window and stared at the faded paint of the barn, pinkish red in the sun. Before I'd left the hospital, a nurse had given me two pills I'd swallowed without thinking. I was left with only a vague sense of needing to comfort Clea, whom I remembered from the day before as a small figure sitting on her gelding, off away from where the men worked over Simon.

I got out of the car by myself. But Neal put one arm around me as if I were an invalid and cupped my elbow in his palm. I don't know exactly what gave him away. Maybe the pressure of his grip or how he hurried, almost lifting me up the walk and all the while talking too much about little things we needed to do around the house. I glanced to the paddock. If Zad wasn't too far out in the field, she came at the sound of the car and put her head over the fence. She didn't always come, so I passed off my unease at her absence to just a stray want. A craving to see a familiar creature beautiful and loved and untouched by what had happened the day before.

By the time I got to my room, I was so sleepy and heavy that all I wanted was to take off my clothes and lie down on the quilt. The room was close and stuffy, but Neal wouldn't open a window. Instead he set a fan on the dresser so it blew directly at me, swiveling from my head to feet and back again.

The women had stood in the hall and watched me go up the stairs—it was the custom in LaCote that the women gathered for every death, bringing food and staying to take care of what needed to be done around the house. Now Rose Hanson from two farms down fussed about, pulling the curtains and hanging up my dress. She tried to get me to roll over to the side of the bed so that she could fold down the covers.

"You'll be more comfortable," she kept saying, but I wouldn't move or answer.

"She's not herself," Neal told her.

I wanted to cry out that I was, but the weight of myself was so great that I could not resist gravity, not even to hold my eyes open. I slept like a stone then, so inert that even dreams were stilled. Neal had taken the clock so when I woke I could only guess it was late afternoon by the angle of the light and the smell of meat roasting from downstairs as the women prepared dinner. I lay dozing, my thoughts too slight to stay longer than a second. They came like doors opening and faces looking in. Simon dead. Clea alone. Something about Zad that Neal did not want me to know.

But I could not hang on to the complexities of these with my mind scooped empty from the sedatives. When Rose Hanson brought my dinner, I was hungry but had no appetite, certainly not for the beef broth that made me nauseous just watching the steam. So I spooned Jell-O, one green cube at a time, and held chipped ice on my tongue and ate the peaches and cottage cheese, slick and cold, while she stood watching.

"You'll need your pills after this," she said.

"They make me sick." I sat up straighter against the headboard. The food had given me some energy and cleared my head. I wiped my mouth on the napkin and on my way to the bathroom pulled back the curtain. I couldn't see the paddock from that angle, only the tractor with the chain hitch hooked up, parked next to the horse trailer instead of its usual place inside the shed.

I walked around the upstairs while she waited. Simon's and Clea's beds had been made and the rooms tidied. I closed his door but went into her room, picking up the odds and ends on her dresser, the jewelry and cologne bottle and small stuffed bear that suddenly seemed so dear. I didn't know where she was, if Neal had sent her to school or a friend's, or if she was out by herself somewhere on the property.

I finally locked myself in the bath, stood in the empty tub, and opened the frosted window that overlooked the barn and yard. Clea's little gelding and a pinto that Simon often rode were standing by the trough under a mulberry, and farther down the hill, colts there for training grazed in a bunch.

I splashed cold water on my face and held a cool washcloth to the base of my throat and insides of my wrists. I pulled off my rumpled slip, took a quick sponge bath from the basin, and ran a comb through my tangled hair. When I got back to my room, Rose Hanson held out the water and pills.

"I can't think straight with them," I said.

"It's not good to think at a time like this."

"It's always good to think," I said.

"I promised your husband that you'd take them," she said.

"How can you make a promise about what I will do?"

I sat down away from her in the chair by the window.

"He'll be disappointed," she said when she finally left the room.

Neal came in later, the women chattering at him all his way up the stairs. When I glanced at him in the doorway, I had one of those flashes that I sometimes did, that this man whom I had lived with for nearly twenty years suddenly did not look at all familiar, like some part of him kept hidden was now coming loose like a locust hatching.

But in spite of that, I was glad he'd finally come. I wanted him to hold me, let me rest against him, and start over. Instead he leaned against the bureau and folded his arms over his chest.

"The women say you won't take your medicine. How do you ever expect to get well if you won't do what the doctor says?"

Then we were like runners in a three-legged race who had started off badly and bloodied each other's ankles by stepping crooked.

From downstairs came the ping and rattle of women cleaning up, the regular off and on of water as they washed the dishes. I swallowed and wet my lips. I pushed the hair off my neck and turned so the fan could dry the sweat there.

"I'm not sick, you know."

"The doctor thinks you should take the medication until all this is over with."

"Until Simon is buried, you mean?"

"Until you're over what happened."

"Over?"

He didn't answer me.

"Where's Clea?" I asked him.

"She's fine," he said. "Don't worry about her."

"What does that mean?"

"Exactly what I said—fine."

"I want to see her."

"Will you promise not to upset her?"

"What do you mean?" I asked.

"Like yesterday."

I turned my palms up and shrugged.

"Take your pills and I'll get her," he said.

I almost thought he was joking.

"I don't need them," I said.

"You'll get upset again."

"I can't help crying for him, if that's what you mean."

"I haven't cried, Nora. I can't upset everyone around me, and so I don't."

"But I'm all right now," I said.

"We don't know that."

We went on for more than an hour until all I'd felt and done since Simon's death seemed chopped into pieces too small to recognize. Whenever I asked him about Zad, he said she was gone. When I asked where Clea was, he said again he'd get her once I took the pills.

"I'm going to look for her then," I told him, but before I could open the closet, he was behind me, one arm around my waist and his hand holding my wrist with strength that men must usually use only on other men.

"Listen to me, Nora," he said. "We have to get through this."

He tightened his grip, and I relaxed against him, my back

against his chest. This, in another version, was all that I wanted of him now, and for a moment I closed my eyes and relished being held.

"Take the pills," he said. "It'll be easier on you."

"All right," I said, "get them."

He squeezed me softly and kissed the side of my face. I walked around the room, pulled back the curtains, and stood by the window looking out at the tractor and chain hitch.

When Neal came back, I asked him about Zad again. He held out the pills and water.

"Take these first."

"Tell me first."

"You promised to take them."

"What happened to her?"

"Take a pill first."

I took one, held it between my cheek and teeth, and pretended to drink the water. Then I turned to look out the window and spit the pill in my hand.

"She died, Nora. Just dropped over."

"From what, Neal?" I turned back to him.

"Her heart gave out." He kept his eyes down and rolled the second pill between his fingers. "I didn't want to tell you, not with all the rest you have on your mind."

I stood there dumbly, watching the green pill rotate.

"She had a heart attack?" I asked.

"That's what the vet said."

"She was just standing there and died?"

"Apparently." He held out the second pill. "Now here."

I took it and asked him to get Clea for me. When he left the room, I stared out at the hitch. As a kid, I'd watched the hired men drag off our horses that had died or been put down.

They took them to a clearing by the river and burned them, and if the wind was right, we could smell the kerosene and smoke and flesh back up at the house. When I was very small, I hated the smell, until Grace told me that we could breathe in the horse and keep it inside us. She took me by the hand out to the yard, and we stood facing the river taking deep breaths. I liked that—to be able to take the horse inside me.

I wondered if Oz had buried Zad or burned her. But to think about her at that instant was too much. I hid the pills in the drawer of my bedside table—one had left a smear of green in my hand like the dye from a candy—and put on a blue housecoat to wait for Clea. I thought about going downstairs but didn't want to have to speak to the women. I picked up a novel I'd been reading two days before and opened to the marker, but it was one of construction paper and ribbon that Simon had made for me years ago, and I closed the book on it. I paced but couldn't stop myself from glancing out every time I passed the window. So I lay down flat on the bed with my hands folded over my breast and thought of Simon falling and Zad dropping and the rest of us following in sequence like prisoners before a firing squad.

The quiet brought all this to me, and I thought that perhaps I might want the pills anyway. I tried to think of good things, of Simon as a baby, his hands reaching for toys I offered, his first steps and the falls smack on his diapered bottom. Then that falling swung me back to his other falling, and I began to cry with sobs that stopped my breath.

When I heard Neal on the steps, I got up and tried to stop for Clea's sake. But the tears fell as if they were some independent phenomena, and Neal went on as if nothing extraordinary was happening. He took Clea by the shoulders and arranged her in front of me. I pulled her close and ran my fingers over the fresh skin of her cheeks and along the tips of her lashes and rim of bone around her eyes. Then I cried in relief at her presence.

I felt my ugliness—how swollen and raw my eyes, how tense and pinched my face. I could not stop myself from holding her too tightly, as if by digging my fingers into her arms and clutching her to me I could physically hold her in life. I wanted to tell her what I could do that would keep her safe with no question. But all I could think was that I had taught Simon to ride and let him go off on Zad not with worry but with joy.

"Oh, Clea," I said. "I don't want to let go of you."

"You need rest," Neal told me.

She rubbed my tears from her face, shrugged out of my hold, and backed off around Neal.

"I'm sorry," she said before she left the room, and Neal closed the door after her. "I'm sorry about what happened."

His hand rested on the black porcelain knob until after the latch clicked. The dark hairs on the backs of his knuckles were large and out of proportion.

"What if she blames herself?"

"Don't be silly, Nora. Why would she do a thing like that?"

"Still, that was hardly good enough to trade for a pill," I said.

"What do you mean?" He went about the room, pulling the curtains shut, and adjusting the direction of the fan.

"I barely saw her," I said.

"I told you, you can't upset people like this," he said, punching the pillows and laying one on top of the other. "This is all hard enough without making any of it more difficult."

He opened the closet and moved the hangers one by one down the rod.

"Do you own anything black?" he asked. "You'll need it for the funeral."

He whipped the hangers along as if he already knew he wouldn't find what he wanted there, as if he didn't like what he saw.

"I've asked a couple of the women to go shopping." He stopped long enough to check the label inside a suit jacket. "Size eight? I thought that was right."

I didn't know why that set me off. I did need something to wear. I couldn't even think of shopping. But I hated him for deciding on my clothes the way we would have to pick an outfit for Simon's burial. I had the strangest feeling that we had all died with Simon, and I was too exhausted and muddled to drag us back to life where we belonged. To even stop this confusion long enough to get our bearings.

I stared at the water glass on the bedside table, its clear cylinder so arrogantly present and set in its space. I picked it up, testing its weight in my hand, and threw it sidearm at Neal still pawing through my clothes. I didn't want to hit him, just startle him out of whatever he was doing.

I was in an awkward position, sitting on the bed. The glass hit against his arm and dropped to the floor. Neal looked down and then at me.

"What the hell was that, Nora?" he said.

I watched his mouth make the words and the muscles in his neck clench. I wondered at what made him move and talk, what was inside him that animated it all. I wanted to break him open to discover the cause, and then wondered if that was the problem between us—that he was whole and I was the one broken open like a button box to pick around in.

I got up, moving with the back of my legs against the bed to feel my way and not taking my eyes off him until I reached the dresser. The pink hobnail bottle was much heavier than the water glass and easier to aim. He ducked as it flew over his head, then dodged the matching jar that came at him spewing hairpins. These bounced and cracked, unlike the Wind Song that shattered and filled the room with musk.

I thought he would come after me, but instead he looked silly and surprised, then turned, crunching glass under his shoe, and slammed the door behind.

When the women came in to sweep up, I pretended to be asleep. When the doctor came to give me an injection, I let him. I wanted to be away from all this, if only for a little while. It was still barely light, and I thought the shot without the pills would just let me sleep. I moaned a little when the needle went in. I let the medication take me away.

At four A.M. I crept through the dark house, stopping at Clea's door. I wanted to lie next to her and hold her safe in sleep. But I no longer trusted that I knew how to do that, or that harm wouldn't seep through me to her without my knowing, the way it had with Simon.

Downstairs I became even more unsettled by how the women had rearranged the chairs they'd sat in, the things they'd used in the kitchen or dusted in the other rooms. As if they'd turned the house as strange and out of kilter as my feelings. I went out across the yard lit by the spot high on the barn and climbed the paddock fence. A stiff breeze turned up the white bellies of the leaves. I sat for a while, looking at nothing in particular, as if I could reconstruct what had happened by what was no longer there.

The parallel boards of the barn, looking more black than red in the night. The dark bundle of horses under a far tree in the pasture. A cat crouched on a hay bale, its eyes flashing gold as it turned its head. I passed over the dark circle twice, taking it for a shadow in the center of the paddock before realizing it was cast by nothing but itself. I got off the fence to look for tracks and found the broad smooth trail leading away between the chevrons of the tire prints.

When I swiped my fingers across the ground and held them to my nose, I imagined the rusty smell of Zad's blood.

As the lightning cut jagged across the clouds and the first rain pelted down, I ran for the house, afraid the wetness was not water but blood. The doctor came the next day and the next to give me more shots and pills. I slept on and off until the morning of the burial, and by that time I was sure all the horses were gone. My dreams were full of their sounds, which made my waking more profoundly silent. But I was tired of fighting Neal and hadn't the energy to care for them. It was just as well they'd been taken. It was just as well they were gone.

Chapter Five

Maggie Rhymer

On my first trip when Clea and Simon were babies, I went to Europe for two weeks and stayed three months. I left the tour that herded blue-haired ladies on buses to the Eiffel Tower or Tower of London or Leaning Tower of Pisa, then sent them for gondola rides before sending them home. Instead I rode the *Orient Express* to Istanbul and sat on Venetian piazzas like a character from Thomas Mann. I took a pensione in Montmartre and pretended the little shopgirl next door was La Bohème. I walked through London and listened for Anne Boleyn's ghost whispering to a French swordsman to make sure the first strike was clean. I went to all the places I'd read about while anchored to LaCote and relished being untethered in the world where I could be anyone I wanted instead of just Grace Hartson's daughter or Frank Rhymer's wife.

Neal nagged at me to take scheduled cruises or tours instead. He said they were more proper for a single woman and safer, but I liked following my own whims and getting to know the locals. To stay longer, I booked the cheapest passage, stayed with friends or rented small little rooms. Sometimes I taught English to earn my keep. I liked the men I met, too, the ones who for the length of dinner or space of a few days were sweet, fresh lovers, gone before their attraction began to turn brown at the edge. In this polar opposite of my earlier life, I found my balance.

During the month in Mexico I'd hardly thought of home, which seemed like a summer cottage locked up with sheets draping the furniture. I spent two weeks in San Luis Potosí with a family I'd met the year before in Rome, and then another week at the bullfight festival at Santa María del Río and then on to more fights in Monterrey. Sucking the salt and lime off the back of my hand, I drank tequila with an American couple who'd never been south before. They were somewhat provincial, but I'd missed talking freely without worrying about my idioms and references to what only Yanks would know without explanation.

We toured a colonial church where the statues were dressed in wool tunics, purple capes, and jeweled crowns. The woman turned away from the crucifix where Christ's plaster wounds were painted as ripped flesh and bare muscle, and she refused outright to go to the *corrida.*

"The bulls don't stand a chance," she said.

I explained that especially brave bulls were rewarded with their lives. But she said, "How often does that happen? One in every five million?" and went shopping instead.

So the man and I went alone and I explained what he should look for—how close the fighters came to the bulls and how gracefully they dispatched them. I taught him how a good matador plunges the sword in at the moment the animal's front legs are parallel so that the spinal column is left exposed by the scapulas. I was caught up in the excitement of the crowd and saw the fight as the Latins did—a stylized ballet with each man costumed in pink silk and the bulls wearing ribbons like May Day queens.

After the last animal had been dragged to the butcher's wagon, the man and I pressed out with the crowd and went back for a beer at Sanborn's where it was cooler and quieter than the local bars. I chattered about the finesse of each kill, but the man was subdued, I thought, by the heat. Finally he said that he'd never met a woman who was so much like a man.

"Maggie," he said to me, "most American women would have covered their eyes or fainted."

"Not fainted," I said.

"I got to hand it to you. You know how to take it."

When we went back to the hotel, his wife was waiting with her packages in the lobby for us, the ribbons of a *piñata* sticking out of one of the bags.

"The concierge has a message for you," she said, chewing her lip. "A long-distance call."

I was so far in spirit from home that the news of Simon seemed to come from another lifetime. At first I thought the hotel clerk had garbled the message or given me one meant for another *gringa.* For hours after I contacted Neal and knew for sure, I felt I had heard about the death of a child from another family, perhaps the couple I'd just left. Even later in my room, repeating the message over and over, I could not bring myself to understand that my Simon could die.

I'd told Neal that I could not get back for several days and the funeral was best over and done with. But he'd insisted Nora would want me there, so I rode the first train I could get through Nuevo León.

Up until then, I'd always loved the stark landscape outside of Monterrey—the brown treeless mountains with their naked undulations, and the earth dotted with low scrub. I'd seen the land barren and brave there, as if the mountains were so old they had forgotten anything but existence.

But leaving that place I'd once thought beautiful, I sat by the window of the third-class car and saw how blasted and sterile the land. The smell of unwashed peasants and unchanged babies, their goats and chickens, blew with the hot air and dust against my face. My bones dug at the wooden seat, cinders flew, and the wheels clacked.

Simon, Simon, Simon.

A child should not die before his parents, before his mother's mother. Shouldn't die before his own children are born. A terrible disorder was at large in the world, and his death pulled me home.

All during the arduous journey, from cab to bus to train, across the border and finally to LaCote, I tried to fix Simon in my mind, to capture him as he really was before the mourners and bad memory revised him.

He was this: a boy on the brink of manhood, a student, a son, a grandson, a brother. He had hopes of doing well, being in love, becoming a parent, and raising fine horses.

Then I gave up. I had been away so much that I was only guessing and supposing. For all I knew of Simon, there'd been so much I'd not yet learned, and now the chance for that was lost forever.

So I thought of him and my mother, Grace, who'd died the month before he was born, and fantasized them together with Nora, so much alike and collected at one point of time on the farm they all loved. I liked this image of the three of them gathered in an ageless moment, and I protected it from reason, even when Neal insisted on opening the coffin and showing me Simon, wrapped in satin tissue and laid in a box like a new and awful doll.

But nothing seemed quite real to me. I had been away in my heart for too long. I'd come back too suddenly from the desert into the Midwest, vibrant green from too much rain and thick with growing where the river has not yet bled into the land. I was no longer a blue-eyed exotic, but only a woman on the verge of old age come home for a terrible funeral. I could not quite make sense of myself and this place, and was relieved for the time being that others kept their distance.

My daughter swam to consciousness only to sink back down, her hair floating out like eelgrass. Neal busied himself with office work, and Clea drifted on the edge of the household like some transparency. Around the kitchen table, the neighbor women told me how only this morning and at a time like this, Neal was out filing Mrs. Horst's damage claim and inspecting the Meyers' roof banged up by the recent hail. They shook their heads in admiration and sucked the breath across their teeth. Almost as an afterthought, they assured me that Nora would be herself again, like Sis Hollrah who lost her husband on Omaha Beach or the Bryant woman whose three-year-old drowned at the Dardenne picnic.

The weight of their collective assessment swayed me. I had not yet gotten my bearings, and their versions of what was happening spread like oil skim on the surface of water I would look into.

Neal had carried my bags up the steps and stopped in front

of Nora's door, setting the two suitcases carefully on either side of himself and describing what had happened before I'd arrived. The screaming and hysterics. The out-of-control grief. Through the crack, I saw her sleeping curled up with one hand under her cheek.

"Finally, she's quiet," he sighed. "We'd better not disturb her."

I watched his mouth move but didn't hear the words. His features, straight and regular. Good-looking enough as a boy, but better now, the way men get in their forties with just enough heft and jowl. His eyes did not waver from mine except at the moments his voice trailed off and the sentences drifted into nothing.

"She's like a..."

He shook his head.

"We might have to..."

The muscles clenched as he tightened his jaw, and he looked over my shoulder at some point in the air, like Gary Cooper as Sergeant York, or Fredric March walking into the sea.

"Do you think she needs so much medication?" I asked.

"You weren't here to see how she was when she didn't have it," he said.

He was right, and the others were right. I had not been here and even then did not feel quite arrived. All about this death seemed produced by too much tequila or not enough sleep. So later, after I spent a polite amount of time with the women, I went up to Simon's room to lie down, since I did not want to go alone to my own house in town just yet. But I was overtired and could not get beyond a semiwakefulness that was crowded up with images on the surface of my consciousness. I thought of Simon wrapped in a blue bunting when Nora had brought him home from the hospital; of him clutching a fistful of wildflowers he'd picked for my birthday; of Simon and Nora talking by the paddock fence, each with a foot on the lowest railing and their soft laughter rolling across the yard. Simon, more easygoing than Nora, but with the same kind of competency and control.

I could not imagine Nora needing sedation, even for this.

But I remembered how my late husband, Frank, would lie next to me, the buckle of his belt pressing against my hip.

"Don't make an issue of this," he always said during our discussions. "Not when you can't know everything about it."

The dark tuft of hair in the hollow of his underarm would graze my shoulder as he embraced me, his prelude to the rough sex he liked on Sunday afternoons when we were first married.

I wondered ruefully why he never had to know everything, as he insisted I should. Why I was angry at a dead man.

Then Clea came suddenly through the door and just as quickly backed out of the room. I called to her, but she went on. Later I passed her reading on the living-room couch and asked if she wanted to get some air with me. She shook her head no without looking up.

The outside was just as oppressive as the deadness of the house but in a different way. The air was muggy and violent, the sky greenish yellow, and the leaves white and overturned. Both the tall doors and smaller stall windows of the barn were closed, and I wondered where Ozzie had taken the horses. At that hour most of them were usually up at the water trough with always one or two grazing near the barn.

Perhaps he'd taken them to a far pasture. I walked down the deserted lane and looked back toward the house at the women's cars parked with their noses to the fence like some perverse and backward image. The light was eerie and black by then, as if three hours had passed in a second. I pictured Simon driving up and stopping for a minute to say hello. I saw him riding off across the pasture or crossing the barnyard on his way to dinner, always smiling when he saw me. I could not grasp the fact that he was gone forever and felt stupid for my denseness.

Then the first lightning hit, a silver trident, and soon after came the concussion like a cherry bomb thrown down behind me. Then another flash and another. I ran for the house as the fat drops started hitting. The women were running through the downstairs and closing the windows to cracks.

"How can we be having so much rain?" one said as she passed.

"The river's going up again," another added.

They told me how the storms had come all the time I was away, the lightning strikes splitting trees and the rain so hard an inch would fall in a quarter of an hour, this on top of the spring snowmelt from up north. I wondered briefly why the horses would be at the lower pastures if the river was so high, but a gust of wind slammed a door shut hard, the sound magnified by the damp, and I called to the women that I would do the upstairs.

I went from room to room, shutting Simon's window with the thought that I was closing up a mausoleum, and saving Nora's for last. She was just a mound under the sheet pulled partially over her face. But the storm was coming from her side of the house, and the curtains stood out almost horizontal. Rain blew in and was already standing on the sill and leaving dark trails in the wallpaper under the window. Yet the wind was cool and the wet refreshing. I stood for a moment with my forehead against the sash and wished that I could sleep standing there with the rain misting my face and lightning flashing so bright I saw it inside my closed lids.

"Neal says if you stand in an open window, the lightning will hit you."

Her voice came low and thick from the dusky shadows.

"That doesn't make sense," I said.

"But Neal says it's so."

I closed the window down to a crack and sat beside her on the bed.

"How would the lightning know to do that?"

"It just does. It can find you."

"Hungry?" I asked.

"I can't tell yet," she said.

The room was so dark from the storm that I could barely see her except in the light flares, her face so pallid that I hardly recognized her.

"Do you want anything?" I asked.

"Mom?" She reached out and touched my arm. "I wasn't sure that was you or if I was awake yet."

I wanted to say how sorry I was about Simon, but it seemed both too soon after her waking and too long since it had happened. Four days and a country ago. I had been too far away to help.

"I want water," she said. "My tongue is furry."

Then in a terrible way the words she had used as a child made time fold in on itself—she was small and her tongue was furry. Simon not yet born and yet already dead.

I went to get her water from the bathroom tap, the fat porcelain handles familiar and comforting. She tried to drink lying down, but the water ran up her nose and made her choke. I helped sit her on the side of the bed. She was shaky, and I cupped my hand under her chin to catch any spills.

"Do you remember the St. Blaise candles?" she asked, handing the glass back to me. "Every February when the priest held candles to our throats and said a blessing? It was supposed to protect us from choking to death on fish bones or something. But your hand just then, brushing my neck, reminded me. It gave me gooseflesh."

"Gooseflesh?"

"A nice touch, like an angel's." She smiled.

She let her weight sag against me then.

"I can't believe he's gone." She screwed up her eyes and covered her face with her hands, letting herself fall backward on the bed, at first with her feet still flat on the floor and her fist pounding the mattress like a wrestler who's been pinned. Finally she curled against me, and I lay down and held her. Outside the thunder rolled like some living thing across the horizon, and I tracked its low rumble, punctuated by decisive cracks of nearby lightning.

"My baby," I whispered, "nothing worse than this can ever happen to you."

Eventually I think she slept again for a little bit. The rain settled into a steady pour, and I sent Neal and Clea to the visitation without me. I knew what the mourners would say—that Simon was in heaven and God took him because he was so good. I knew I couldn't stand to take their hands and lead them to the casket to pray for his soul.

I also insisted the women had done too much for us and sent them home to their families. They wrote out the directions for the medication and taped the sheet on the bottle lid, but I threw the paper away. Later Nora, sitting up in the ring of light from the bedside lamp, ate some chilled consommé and toast. I had asked her if she wanted her pills, but she said not. I was glad she seemed better, yet watched her as I would some dog who might suddenly snap or bite.

Once she accidently dropped her spoon and, in trying to catch it, sloshed a little of the soup out of the cup she was holding. I started as if she was throwing down her dishes, and at first she couldn't say anything but that I didn't look for a double meaning or hidden reference. Then I felt foolish for treating her like some snake-pit crazy on the basis of Neal's exaggeration. She was simply my Nora getting through the worst time of her life.

She asked if I'd seen the horses. "I haven't heard them for two days," she said. "They're gone, aren't they?"

I hesitated, not knowing myself what had become of them. I just told her I hadn't seen them but also that I hadn't looked.

"Their sounds are gone," she said.

I tried all the excuses I had thought of—that they'd been moved to other pasture or even another farm to simplify life until after the burial. But she said, "He killed her—Neal killed Zad. He says he didn't, but I know he did."

She was even and matter-of-fact. I told her there was no use in getting upset over nothing if just asking Neal would solve the problem. Certainly he'd have a reasonable answer. Then I turned off the light and told her to rest. Later around two, I heard her get up and go to the bathroom. I drifted back to sleep until I heard the shouting downstairs from the sleeping porch where Neal had moved so as not to disturb her. Their voices were muffled by the drone of rain, but not enough to mask Nora's rising shrill.

I went down and stood on the stairs and then at the door to the room. Neal was sitting on the side of the studio couch pulled out into a bed, and when he saw me, he turned his palms to the ceiling. Nora was pulling books from a case and throwing each stack down flat on the floor.

"You tell me," she said, standing in the pile of overturned books. "I have a right to know."

"Her medicine?" Neal said, raising his eyebrows at me. "She obviously tricked you into thinking she took it."

"I don't need it," she said. "I need you to tell me what you've done with them. They were mine and you had no right."

He rubbed his hands over his face as he crossed the room toward the kitchen. She flew after him, trying to grab his wrists and throw herself between him and the phone.

"Tell me," she said again.

"Neal," I began.

"Maggie," he said, shaking his head as he called the doctor's number, "go to Clea for me. See if she's awake and distract her."

Neal pulled Nora's hand away from the phone and put his own over it like a guard. When she tried to pull the receiver from his ear, he pushed his shoulder between them.

"I don't want any more," she kept crying. "Don't do this to me."

"Don't do this to yourself. Don't do this to any of us," he said.

I tried to pull Nora away, but she shook me off, holding her arms bent in front of her and swinging her shoulders until I stepped back. Then she threw herself at Neal, clinging piggyback as if she would ride him and kicking at his legs as he bent over to protect the phone from being grabbed away.

Again Neal begged me to go to Clea, so I went up the stairs to her room. The night-light threw soft white on her face and she seemed to be sleeping, except that her eyes were closed too tightly and her breathing was too regular. I sat in an old rocker and thought how I'd rocked them all to sleep—Nora and Simon and Clea. Sitting in dark rooms and smelling them sweet from their baths and full of milk. Rocking and singing and fiercely praying that they should all live and grow well. How far away that seemed. In another lifetime, in another country.

The next morning we got ready for the burial in silence. Our heels sank into the spongy ground as we walked toward the grave, an undertaker's assistant holding an umbrella over us like glossy crow wings. We sat on metal folding chairs under a garden-party awning, and the wet, overturned earth smelled tangy like a new-plowed field. The priest read Te Deum, "Out of the depths I cry . . . ," and rain beaded on top of the casket.

I tried to think of other things. Of walking in St. Mark's Square with the rumps of the bronze horses turning gold in the late sun, or swimming so far out in the Aegean that Greece became a white slash between sky and sea. Anything to keep me from picturing Simon's body covered over deep in the ground. I kept thinking that he would suffocate or panic in the total dark. I worried if he needed to eat.

All the while Nora squeezed my hand so tightly that I felt each bone. She looked straight ahead and held still as a deer. A crowd of Simon's schoolmates, his girlfriend, neighbors, and people from the town fanned out from the grave. I tried to concentrate on the flat plunk of rain hitting the awning and umbrellas instead of the first clods of heavy earth on the casket lid.

When they lowered the casket, Clea turned to Neal and buried her face against his jacket. He patted her arm and walked back to the car with her held against him. Then it was done, this public part of Simon's leaving, and Nora sagged against me as if all the wires that held her up had suddenly been cut.

She sat politely in the living room and received condolences for an hour before going upstairs to rest. Meanwhile the women set out platters of chicken, ground beef and noodle casseroles, bowls of potato salad, Jell-O molds, cakes, pies, brownies—enough food for two armies, as one of them said. The men iced drinks in a galvanized tub on the front porch and carried in folding chairs loaned from the parish hall. The mourners came directly from the cemetery and gradually the sound of their voices rose from hush to controlled laughter.

I walked among them as they ate the good food, washed down with beer in long-necked brown bottles or soda, colored lime and orange and purple. They told stories while the children ran up and down the stairs. Farmers with tanned faces and white foreheads and women with hair permed too tightly and kids with their good white shirttails loose from play. I saw their relief that death had come no closer than this and felt the house full of life resuming.

I asked one of the men about his horse that was usually boarded with Nora. He told me Neal had arranged other quarters until the family got back to normal and how thankful he was that Neal hadn't left him in the lurch without a place to keep it. Later I asked a woman about her daughter's Appaloosa, and she told me the same thing, marveling that Neal had even paid for the transportation. But no one knew where Zad or any of Nora's other horses had gone, or why Ozzie Kline, the hired man, had disappeared after the burial.

All afternoon Neal visited from group to group, and by the end of the day I could tell no difference between him and the others. How could he have killed this horse that meant so much to Nora, even under these circumstances?

The rain kept on steady, four inches falling before the day was out, and the cars, even those that did not have to be pushed, left muddy ruts all up and down the sides of the lane. A levee broke in Alton, and the river at Portage Des Sioux rose closer to flood stage. Neal and I sat at the kitchen table that night, leftovers in containers stacked high in the refrigerator and covering all the counter space, and listened to the weather report on the radio. The announcer predicted rain the rest of the week, and worse, heavy storms upriver in the Dakotas.

Neal got us more coffee.

"It was a good crowd," he said, pushing the sugar bowl toward me.

"Yes, a good turnout," I said, wondering why he had thought of that.

"Now that it's over, we can go on."

He set his mouth in a grim, straight line and rapped his fist short and quick on the table. I stirred the milk into the coffee, watching the swirls so I wouldn't have to look at him.

"Neal," I said finally, "what did happen to the horses?"

"Why, I had them moved. I thought you knew that." He sat up straight and cocked his head.

"The boarders, yes, but I meant Nora's own."

He narrowed his eyes and ran his tongue over his upper lip.

"They're gone," he said. "We can't have them around here after what happened."

"Gone where?" I asked.

"It doesn't make any difference. They killed my son and I won't have them around my daughter."

I started to argue that certainly other solutions were possible and Nora at least deserved to know the situation, but he cut me off.

"My son has been killed," he said, leaning toward me and speaking with such vehemence that I was afraid. "An eye for an eye. Not even that. Worthless animals for a boy's life. How can you argue that is even close to fair trade?"

Again he struck his fist on the table, and I turned my eyes away. I could not argue with him, would not on the day of Simon's burial. A voice deep inside kept insisting his logic was turned a click out of place. But I could not explain why and the reasons were lost in the endless day where too much had already happened.

I took our two cups, washed them, and turned them over in the drainer. I asked Neal to turn off the light as he was leaving and stood watching the rain collect in the puddles filling up the yard and paddock. All still, except for the steady downpour and water running through the pipes in the walls, the restless air of the house stirred up by Neal's anger, and Nora tossing in her sleep.

Chapter Six

Ozzie Kline

After Simon died, I went away from Nora like I did when we were nineteen and she wouldn't marry me. I headed out to nowhere in particular, just as I had so many times before. To somewhere in the emptiness of Canada where I could find the quiet to think through what had happened and contain it, the way I had my memories of the war.

Two winters before in Pennsylvania, late in '45, it had been a woman who sent me home, even though she would have done anything to make me stay. After we'd finished making love for the second time, I got up and walked around her room, familiar with our clothes hung over the backs of chairs or tossed on the floor. A blizzard had frosted the windows with ice ferns lit from behind by streetlights, like a glass cave where I was shut with a woman whose love made me weighted down and sad.

She asked if I didn't want to come back to bed and get warm. I told her I liked the cold, the way it made me feel the edges of myself. After a while, she said out of nowhere, "When we make love, I get the feeling you're hoping I'll turn into someone else."

Her voice sounded like part of the dark, and I could barely see the faint white of her arm and shoulder resting outside the covers. I was going to try to explain that my want didn't have a shape, no more than the early morning fog in LaCote coming up thick from the river. The beams of my truck lights would disappear into it, and only parts of objects came visible as I neared them. The quarter curve of a tree, the handle of a car door, the edge of a street sign. All shrouded, and everything beyond, even the rest of those objects, invisible.

When she spoke to me, I wanted to go home. That was the only part I knew of all I wanted, and those were the only words I could say. At least in LaCote I could get around without thinking or being introduced to every single person I ran into. Part of the shape I was looking for was there, though I never seemed to know that until I was far enough away to look back.

Besides, I was getting too old to be ramming around, and coming home had a relief about it, even just driving west. The Appalachians and Alleghenies gave me claustrophobia, the way the land seemed to have been crumpled up and thrown down crooked, and I hardly noticed how anxious that made me feel until I got as far as Ohio and the terrain started to flatten. Then, as the sky and land got more open, so did I get unknotted and smoothed.

I started to think of Nora, too, for the first time since I'd gotten discharged from the army in '44, and what it would be like to live near her again. I wondered how her life had turned out and if she was happy, but then I pushed the thoughts away.

Two months after I was back in LaCote, I headed toward Nora's farm to see Neal Mahler about the job he was offering. I hadn't been able to get over thinking I was nineteen again, going to see Nora's father and what a waste of time that'd be, seeing how he disliked me. I started rehearsing an old speech in my head, the one I'd never given Frank Rhymer about how he should let me marry her. Then I smacked the steering wheel. Almost forty years old and I was trying to convince a dead man I was worthy enough for a woman who didn't want me. I didn't need that crap.

Bad enough to be back in LaCote when I couldn't even tell exactly what had pulled me home. Not that it was a bad place, just one I'd tried to get away from. On the banks of the Missouri, thirty miles from St. Louis. The town the settlers had hopes for before they realized they'd picked the wrong river. Most of the early French kept going north and west. Later the Germans moved in, wanting what they had all neat and inside the lines. They willed that way of life to me, but from the time I was nineteen, I tried to be more like the French.

An old pal had recommended I go see Neal Mahler. Actually, what he said was, "Your old girlfriend's looking for a wrangler. You ought to go see her husband about the job." For once, I didn't say no right away to the thought of seeing her, and on my way down to the farm, I wondered if she was another part of the shape I wanted.

When I first met Neal Mahler, he was leaning against a hay bale, drinking coffee and watching Simon through the open door. Mahler was an all right–looking guy, too well dressed for a barn and arrogant to boot. I'd always believed Nora would marry her match, and mostly I was disappointed that she hadn't.

He nodded in his son's direction, his breath and the steam

from his coffee pluming up white and disappearing in the cold February air.

"I can't for the life of me figure out what they see in those animals."

Then he shook my hand too firmly and told me to call him Neal and went on about how Nora had been after him for more than a year to hire an extra hand to help her exercise and train. He kept putting her off, telling her the men were all busy fighting. But the end of the war had ruined that excuse, and she kept getting more boarders.

" 'Don't let the business get bigger than you can handle,' I keep telling her. 'That's the way to deal with this.' But she won't listen, and it's gotten to the point that it interferes with her family." Neal dusted his hand against his thigh. "We're always having it out over this. When I do the books, I make it look like she's lost her shirt so we get a tax break. Then she has a fit, and I can't get her to understand how much better off we are if it looks like she's in the red.

" 'My business makes money,' she keeps telling me. 'Yeah,' I say, 'but who cares if the IRS knows that?'

"Then there's the time and the routine." His voice took on an exaggerated tone. "We can't go on vacation in peace. We can't even go out for the evening if one of the damn things is about to foal or has a cold or whatever it is they get."

He smiled. But I was uneasy that he didn't seem to know her.

Neal Mahler walked over to the barn door and leaned with one hand resting against the frame. "Simon's interested in riding, and since it keeps him off the streets with all those hot-rodders, what the hell."

Simon was in the paddock putting a little roan through her paces. Watching him, I thought of Nora with her same Dresden colors—the ash hair, dark lashes, and blue-green eyes. Not pale and washed out like most blonds, but startling and definite.

He had a nice way with the mare, compact and handsome as her rider. They cantered in an easy rocking lope, their breath rising up and disappearing into the air over the flat pasture beyond. Then I envied this settled life Nora had made for herself, full of horses and children, and wondered again whether I should have come.

Neal Mahler brushed the hay from the back of his pants, and we walked around the barn and grounds, him showing them off like he'd made the land and since paid himself twice for it. He didn't seem to know and I didn't tell him how many times I'd been here when I was a kid, picking up or dropping off horses for Nora's grandmother, Grace, who liked both the way I handled animals and irritated her son-in-law, Frank. So much looked exactly as it had then that the changes—the new flower bed and garage—were jarring and misplaced. But so were my memories. I sensed Ozzie Kline, seventeen, backing up the trailer hitch or leading a mare out of the barn or watching for Nora Rhymer, like the past was a double exposure on unadvanced film.

Then Neal told me the hours and pay, the jobs he expected me to do. He wanted a lot and was stingy to boot, but I liked being back on old Grace's land where Frank Rhymer would never want me. I thought about teaching Simon what I knew about horses that his father didn't, and out of the corner of my eye, I watched for Nora just as I had years ago.

I didn't see her that day, but I lay awake restless that night, remembering our bodies young and Nora lifting her face to kiss me, her cheeks rosy like when the light shines through a horse's ear and you can see the flush of blood inside.

She had been so small I could wrap my arms around her and feel my size against hers. Yet she was strong, and I was never afraid of hurting her. The old and perfect moments had survived intact—Nora Rhymer coming willingly to me whenever I could find the chance to reach for her, and all but once leaving without a word before my hope was ever ruined.

When I came in the barn the next morning, she didn't even look surprised to see me. She stood up from filling a bucket with feed and smiled.

"Hey, Oz," she said. "That little bay in the first stall has gone gimpy. Why don't you rub her legs down and wrap her ankles?"

She acted like maybe I'd just come back from a few days' vacation instead of from twenty years of rambling. I almost didn't recognize her. Not that she'd changed that much when I really looked, only I'd expected a girl and got a woman. She looked heavier, though most of that was the oversized man's jacket she wore, and her hair, tied back, had gone several shades darker, the way blonds do before the gray silvers them up again. Stupid to even look for her to be the same as when I'd last seen her. Even stupider to hope she'd saved her want for me when I'd never quite believed it in the first place.

"I couldn't believe who Neal hired."

She laughed like this was the best joke in the universe.

"How many Ozzie Klines are there?" I sucked in my gut and wished I'd worn a better shirt. Had a better shirt, for that matter, or gotten a job somewhere else, since Nora in the flesh was so much more than I'd imagined her for all these years.

She laughed again. I tried to take the bucket from her, but she jerked it back.

"Who do you think carried all this since the last time you were around?"

I shrugged and took my eyes away from her, her arms drawn in a V to the handle in a way that pushed her breasts together and showed the line between them at the neck of her shirt. She asked how I'd been.

"OK," I said, forgetting all the comebacks I'd rehearsed.

"No, I mean really."

She came up close and I was afraid she would be able to tell if I lied. So I told her again that I'd been OK.

"But what have you been doing?"

Twenty years that fit into a sentence. *About three years after I left, I married. Another three years later, after she died, I worked around, then went to war and worked around again.*

When Nora asked what happened to my wife, I told her a car wreck, but the words were lame. Too simple to explain what had happened to my wife's body, and then again, too dramatic for another moment of my life that I'd traveled away from.

"It's OK," I said. "We were young and it happened a long time ago."

"Age and time don't make a death OK." Nora set down the bucket.

"I didn't mean OK. I just didn't want you to feel bad for me."

"Why shouldn't I?"

She asked like this was a philosophical problem we had to

solve together and moved so the fabric of her jacket grazed my hand. I was overtaken by the urge to touch her face. Just that. To touch her.

Then I stepped back, mumbling like an idiot about not wanting to talk. I changed the subject to the horses, and that was bad enough, that we seemed to know the other's mind as far as animals were concerned. People get close when they both love the same things. Nora and I had these dangerous things in common, in addition to our unfinished past still full of my leftover wanting.

But in the next months I tried to treat her like my employer and nothing more. Being friendly with a married woman, one I'd held and kissed no matter how many years before, seemed adulterous in some way. It wasn't that I had any high regard for Neal Mahler. As far as I could tell he thought the horses were only there for amusement when he didn't need his family for himself. But I still owed the man in terms of staying away from his wife, the way all men should be honor bound with each other.

I tried to be just an old friend to Nora, but the past kept leaking in, in small, strange ways. I'd watch her going about her business and remember—that she'd had a salmon-colored sweater with soft, furry yarn; an engraved locket with letters twisting into each other; a blue coat with buttons that were hard to undo. I walked dragging one foot twenty years behind the other and was afraid of giving myself away by trying to get back to who we'd been that long ago. I'd wake up in the middle of the night and know I'd been dreaming about moving my hand over the rise of her breasts, past her waist to the flare of her hips. I could still feel her tongue pressing long after I was startled out of sleep, and that sense of her lingered.

Staying shy with her was easier than figuring how to act with all that in the back of my mind or in the front of my pants. But sometimes when we were currying down a horse or checking a swollen knee or passing over reins, our hands brushed. Once, trying to bandage a gelding's leg, she and I were crouched down close, our bodies touching the length from shoulders to thighs. We were leaning against each other, trying to get the wrap on, and I had to get up and walk away. When time crossed over like that and the old moments traveled the years and surfaced right under my nose, then it was easier to turn away than to try and face her.

But she was in it, too. At first I thought it was imagination, but the longer I was around, the more time she spent in the barn and the more often she found excuses to talk. We were like two old ladies, commenting on how nice the day or how dreary or how humid.

I'd look up from filing a hoof or cinching a saddle and see her staring at me in a preoccupied kind of way. After a while, she started laying her hand on my arm when she was speaking, just a touch that settled and lingered an instant too long, her fingers brushing mine when she was handing me a bridle or comb, when in normal time they wouldn't have touched at all. She lounged against the side of the horse I was grooming, sometimes hanging on its neck the way she used to with me when she was teasing. We both pretended nothing was going on, and I kept looking at Neal Mahler, expecting him to notice.

But he went on like he didn't even suspect, and I started thinking of reclaiming all that I'd lost or left behind or given up. It would be like this: I would grab her hand as she walked past, or I'd come up behind as she was bending over her accounts and slip my arms around her waist. Then we would start again, and I would make up to her for what she'd gone without all these years.

But my plans stayed inside, though I could almost hear them hammering and banging to get out. She was Neal Mahler's wife, and I was paralyzed by that fact until one November afternoon about nine months after I'd started work. The weather'd been threatening for days, but finally Nora had said the hell with staying in, took off on Zad and gotten miles away. They'd been far out along the river when the temperature dropped so fast you could feel it, the wind picked up, and the rain came in walls. By the time she got back, they were drenched, her teeth chattering and the horse shivering. For the first time, I saw Nora scared.

She wouldn't stop to dry her own clothes. So I threw my jacket over her shoulders and lit the space heater at the mouth of the stall as she rubbed down Zad and piled on blankets. I kept telling her I'd do it all so she could go up to the house and get dry, but she said we both had to work quickly. She heated up the liniment like milk in a baby's bottle and shouted at me to warm the mash, too. Nora ran from one task to another, and when she knelt to rub Zad's leg dry for the third time, I crouched down in back of her and reached around to take the towel from her hand.

"Stop, sweetie. Stop."

Then I lost my balance and fell back with her. As we sat on the floor of the stall, she began crying, first in little hiccups and then in giant sobs. I held her while she cried, my arms around her shoulders and my belly to her back. I didn't want her miserable, yet I wanted to keep this excuse to hold her.

"Shh, it's OK," I whispered, though I didn't know what she was crying about in the first place.

I turned her halfway around so she sat sideways on my lap, her legs over my thigh and elbow wedged under my breast bone. When she stopped snuffling enough, she told me how the rain had come so hard she couldn't see and how Zad had kept slipping on the new mud. Nora thought the horse would fall and break her leg, or they'd get lost out there.

"The hairs were standing up on the back of my neck, and this cold, not from the rain or wind but a deep cold from down inside, was coming from the horse to me."

She didn't know how to explain it, but then she got to thinking about *Black Beauty.* The damnedest thing. How Beauty comes in wet and the young stable boy doesn't know how to take care of him and Beauty almost dies.

"But I know how to take care of Zad," I whispered, tucking Nora's wet hair behind her ear and listening to the congestion building in her breathing.

"That's all I could think of, of getting back here and drying her down. I had to stop the cold, but I didn't know how."

I wasn't sure what to say. Nora was the calmest, sanest woman I knew, even in those spooked places that other people were too scared to admit existed. Grace had treated ghosts and dreams and death like the weather or unruly visitors, and Nora had learned the same ways. I didn't know what had frightened her, but I tried to help her find reasons. Fatigue, the blues, so much on her mind.

"There's just been too much," she said, grabbing at that. "I can't do it all."

"I know."

"I'm so tired of this," she said.

She turned and we looked at each other, not moving except for tiny swayings, small yeses. Then we hung on each other like we were the gravity holding the other to earth. Like teenagers in love, but also desperate and grateful in a way only learned with age.

Nora was so wet that in a matter of minutes I was, too. But we held on to each other, my hand inching up her ribs until she took it and moved it over her breast. For as much as I wanted to make love to her right there, I wanted as much just to hold her tight and close until we'd made up for some of the lonely, hungry time we'd been apart.

When Simon's truck pulled up in the yard, we scrambled to stand. Her cheeks were flushed, and my body swayed with the strangeness of standing alone after her touch. But Nora, her hair half dry and sticking up at all angles, her jeans still plastered to her legs, busied herself picking up wet towels. Simon whistled low when he came in and said, "What the hell happened here?"

Zad didn't so much as sneeze the next week, but Nora came down with a terrible cold. She stayed in bed for a couple of days, and even when she was well enough to come out to the barn, she shuffled around like an invalid, her face peaked and nose red. When I asked if Simon had said anything, she said no, but later she caught me watching her as she curried Zad and stared back accusingly.

Standing there wanting to remake the laws of physics and gravity and love, I remembered the power of Nora Rhymer to make a man believe he could walk on water or air to please her. How she believed in him so completely, how she trusted him to be as strong as he'd told her he was when lying to get her to love him in the first place.

Her terrible innocence that believed what men promised was sucking me in and forcing me to call my own bluff. I wanted to be her man and protect her from all that would hurt her, from fear and death and the strangeness of being human. But I was no more capable at forty than I had been at nineteen to take care of her. Or even save her from a head cold, for that matter.

So I looked to Simon. Nora had told me that as a kid she'd baby-sat for the family down the road and pretended all the children were her own. I did the same with Simon. Whatever help and care I had saved all these years for Nora now went to him, and where I was clumsy and unbalanced with her, I was easy and sure with him.

I passed on all I'd learned from years of hanging around stables and shows and tracks. Taught him the tricks older riders like his grandmother Grace had taught me, the way I would have if he had been my son. Told him the truth about life, not the sweet bullshit we always feed kids like they were stupid and sexless.

I didn't have the frantic pressure that blood fathers have to make their sons as strong but not stronger than them. I wanted Simon to have everything, including what I wished my own father and teachers had given me. Then I wanted Simon to have extra, the way I would give an apple or handful of grain to a favorite colt.

After a while, he came out to the barn to see me every day when he got home from school, or sat the fence while I worked a horse.

"She's got a hesitation between gaits," he'd tell me like I'd quizzed him on it. Or, "The roan may be going lame."

Other times he wanted to talk. How he drove his girl Janie down to the quarry and parked on a ledge overlooking the pit. How they went there often and sometimes lay together on the backseat with the stars visible through the window. Some nights they couldn't help themselves from touching and didn't know how long they'd last without doing what they shouldn't.

"Sometimes I'm over her," Simon said, "and I feel like sky."

He'd get a look then so much the way I remembered Nora at that age pulling back to study me between kisses, a strangely sober and intense expression on her face. He told me how he wanted to marry Janie when they were old enough and how he had even picked out the ring set to start saving for. When he asked if I'd been in love at his age, I told him yes, and though we hadn't stayed together, I'd never gotten over that girl and never loved anyone as well.

Two weeks later he asked me to buy him Trojans. He was afraid the drugstore clerk getting them from the case might figure out which girl they were meant for.

"Nobody will care who I'm buying them for?" I kidded.

"You've got so many women," he grinned back.

I was proud to do for him what he would never ask his father. But underneath this all, or maybe above it, I felt the satisfaction of the line from past to future drawn through me and secured in Simon.

For whatever combination of reasons, I came to love him. When he died, I stood behind Nora over his body, and a panicky helplessness swallowed me up that I couldn't get air inside of. It was just like when I gave orders during the war that I knew would get other men killed.

What had I forgotten to say or teach him? I'd failed even as a pretend father, and his death flowed back to my wife's. I had not told her to be careful as she went out the door or reminded her to steer into a skid. I had not gone along to drive, just as I had not gone riding with Simon to warn him when he was on dangerous ground.

When I saw what Neal Mahler did after Simon died, what he took as his right as husband and father, I knew I had only the choice to leave the farm or kill him. To shoot a horse out of spite is evil. To do it to maim a woman makes it doubly so.

I wouldn't help him sell Simon's and Clea's mounts or deliver the boarders to their new stables, but I kept track of what went where, in case Nora ever needed to know. I buried the horse and took the dog when I left for good to make sure Neal Mahler wouldn't shoot him, too. I couldn't get to Nora, no closer than the sounds of her screams and crying. Could only stand beneath her window or across Simon's open grave, wishing I could help her.

But I found Clea the afternoon after the burial, in the middle of the mourners' cars, parked every which way between the house and the barn and down the lane. Just standing in the drizzle with her arms loose by her sides like she'd been dropped in from another planet. I didn't really know this kid. She rode only once in a while and never had much to say. She seemed more interested in friends than her family and wasn't around much. But she'd come out of the house filled with people eating and talking after her brother's death and stood looking around the way I'd seen shell-shocked GIs trying to get their bearings.

I asked how her mother was, and she just shrugged. Then I was afraid for Nora and what was being done to her.

"Take care of your mother for me," I told Clea.

I held her shoulders and shook her hard. She didn't seem to be listening, and she looked so much like her father, I wanted to slap her.

Then I left, packed up, and took off. Neal Mahler could do with his family what he wished, and I could only watch. I had neither the money nor power nor right to take Nora away, so I took my truck and the dog and headed up north. Except to get where I could think in peace, I didn't have a plan in mind. Didn't seem to need one, since most of my life I hadn't cared where I was going anyway.

Eight hours after the funeral, I was driving up the highway, so fast and so far that I'd moved past the storm that had hung over LaCote that day. The sky spread out pink and yellow in the dying day. I kept driving to it, and it kept changing, the colors going navy and plum and red in long streaks across the horizon so pretty that it made me want to cry. I thought what a terrible loss that Simon Mahler had not lived to see this sky and all the beauty that would come after it. That he had not lived for us to watch him come into his own. That he had not been mine and Nora's.

I had this crazy thought that had been dancing and twitching on the edges of my mind, that the cold she'd felt the day she'd been out with Zad had been the premonition of what would come.

I turned up the radio loud and sang along so I couldn't think too deep. I accelerated, and the hot air blowing rough through the windows kept me moving on a kind of jet stream. This sense of driving fast and far was all that kept me from breaking, this very motion of flying away so that no one I knew could see or find me. I drove until the colored streaks of sky turned to charcoal smears and then to uniform black, the earth and sky one uninterrupted darkness broken only by occasional headlights like animal eyes coming at me.

Summer

From time to time and at a distance
you have to bathe in your own grave.

—Pablo Neruda

Chapter Seven

Maggie Rhymer

THE NIGHT AFTER the burial I went home for the first time, my house musty from being closed up the month before. I paced the rooms, passing the photos of Simon hung here and there or set about on the tables. In third grade or fifth or eighth, in scout uniform or dress suit or jeans. As if along with Simon we had also lost the small army of these boys who had added up to his sum.

I lay awake forever, watching the shadows from passing cars glide across the ceiling and bend down the walls. I kept thinking about how in the past year Simon would drop in to see me on his way home from school. Just to visit, just to talk. As if he'd missed me or wanted to see what I thought about a certain subject. As if he and I were friends. Then I was angry all over again that he'd been taken from me just as I was beginning to know him as the adult he would have become.

I'd only slept a few hours when Neal called early the next morning to ask if I would stay at the farm, just until Nora was feeling better. He sounded so needy, and I was glad of something useful to do. Of an excuse to be close and watch over her.

She ate barely anything, in silence, as if we'd been forbidden to talk, and afterward wandered around or slept fourteen or fifteen hours at a crack, the black wire fan aimed at her body. Every few days she came out of her stupor like waking from a hundred years' sleep and went after Neal with a fury, accusing him of stealing her horses and killing Zad. He walked away like a deaf man, and she followed after, shouting at his back.

I tried to help by explaining how Neal had been so upset that he hadn't known what he was doing.

"Then why isn't he sorry for it now?" she demanded.

I tried to explain how men like to cover up their feelings.

"How can he in this case?"

She turned all kind speculation into worst possibility, and so we retreated to the practical. Nora and I did with Simon's things what my mother Grace had with my brothers' when they died. I was old enough to remember when Charlie went, how she put his picture next to Frankie's on the dresser in her room, along with a top he loved and a small stone he'd given her. The rest of what she saved went in a box kept in the bottom drawer so she wouldn't happen on his things unprepared.

The memories were not so containable. Especially at first, but occasionally even years later, she'd suddenly break into tears as she was setting a dish on the table or opening the door to the hall closet.

"I just caught a glimpse of him," she'd tell me, meaning she'd just had a flash of Frankie or Charlie sprinkling brown sugar on oatmeal or getting mittens out of a drawer. She kept running into the places where she found her clear images of them, and then she'd draw in her breath as if she'd been slapped and stand in their space, hugging herself and crying.

She always told me how Charlie loved to take his toys to play on the window seat in the dining room, his hair dark gold in the afternoon sun, or how Frankie with aid from his dog once dug up an entire bed of Red Emperor tulips. Her face would twist as if a sharp screw was being tightened deep inside her, and then she'd smile cockeyed before wiping her tears and going on.

When I was young, I thought my brothers still lived with us and that only Grace could see them, the way X rays see bones. Like invisible putti hovering just above the door or under the eaves, the boys were present. When Grace made cookies, she'd comment on how they'd loved to snitch bites of the batter and then eat the cookies hot, and she always left two on a plate until they had to be thrown out. When she shopped for Christmas gifts, she pointed out what she thought the boys would have liked at ages eight or twelve or twenty, as if they'd kept getting older inside her.

"Charlie was going to be a great reader," she'd say, fingering a set of classic books for children, or "Frankie was so active," as she tossed a baseball into the air, and I wondered what she had predicted for me.

But I talked to them also, explaining what was going on at the school they'd barely gotten old enough to attend, and when I passed them in age, I thought of myself as their big sister. Sometimes when Grace was out with the horses or in the fields, I got out their boxes and tried to construct them from the things she'd saved—from lace christening bonnets or misshapened pictures or notes done in chunky, awkward letters. Sometimes I laid out the items in the shape of stick figures on the floor, as if I might, if I only knew the trick, animate the collage to see them for a second.

I even first liked Frank Rhymer because he had the same name as my brother, and I told him so when we were introduced. I thought he'd be the way I'd imagined Frankie grown, the way Grace had described him as kind and wise and funny and strong.

With a similarly stupid thought, I supposed when Nora and I packed away Simon's things, she would go on the way Grace had. But as soon as the task was done, Nora lapsed back into her old routine, each attack against Neal leaving her more worn-out than the one before, and by the end of May the whole household was ragged with her moods.

One late May evening, after he'd told Clea to clean up the dinner dishes, Neal asked me to show him what I'd done in the garden. I hadn't had a garden for years, what with my traveling, but for lack of better to do, I'd worked on this one, at first just to get out of the house and then because of the tranquillity it brought me. As we walked down the rows and he admired the green beginnings of the lettuce, he told me finally he thought it best if he and Clea moved to my house in town until Nora was herself again.

"If you'd talk to her, explain what you were thinking about the horses, she'd be better," I said.

"Nothing to explain. Just a reflex like shooting a cottonmouth."

"But tell her what was on your mind."

"The bottom line here is that Clea's upset, and Nora's not capable of caring for a flea."

"But you have to explain Zad."

"There's bigger issues to worry about now."

He worried the river would come up enough to flood the house, though I pointed out it never had, the house being set on the highest point around. At any rate, he argued, the rising water had increased his work to the point he had to be at the office more, and there was no arguing that Clea was upset.

"She goes to school early and stays late, then hides in her room with homework," Neal said. "The kid's becoming a recluse, and that's no life."

I couldn't argue with that, nor could I break through to her, no matter what combination of approaches I'd tried.

"I know you can handle what needs to be done here," he said. "It's only for a little while."

Later on my way to bed, I passed his room where he was almost finished packing. The next morning he moved himself and Clea while Nora watched like a sullen ghost. Three weeks later he asked me to drop by his office and broached the subject of selling the farm altogether and the four of us living in town.

"Don't you agree this has worked out better for all of us?"

"For you, maybe."

"For Clea, too."

"The farm is Nora's," I told him. "She'll never agree."

"It's ours," he said. "My name is on the deed, too."

Then he showed me where Nora and I had been sloppy with the paperwork. We'd given Neal care of most business matters and put loans and second mortgages in his name only.

Too much bother, Nora and I had both thought, especially when Neal liked doing accounts and searching for tax breaks and financial nits. She did only the books for the stable, and I cared only about the amount available for my next trip, which came from Neal like an allowance. Grace had left us the farm, hadn't she? There was never a question it was ours.

"We need a place of our own," she'd told me a million times. "You must keep the land."

Unlike Nora, I hadn't inherited Grace's love of the place. But I depended on it to exist unchanging, to always be the home I could return to. It held the spirits of my parents, brothers, and now Simon; it was where my past could be found and was worth keeping for those reasons only.

So when Nora married and old Grace died a year later, I moved into town. In time, we settled on an arrangement that suited us all. The down payment and monthly payments for my LaCote house came from Neal in trade for part ownership of the farm, and I signed over two-thirds of it to him and Nora. To make up the difference in value, he promised me a yearly stipend from the trust his parents had left him when they died, which I could use for my trips and expenses.

It had seemed a good deal for us all. I never bothered to get his agreement for my allowance in writing or read the contracts concerning the farm and my house that Neal had said were a mere formality. He was my son-in-law. Family. Up until then he had always kept his promises.

But that afternoon Neal spread the papers out over his desk and showed me the pertinent clauses. He, Nora, and I were co-owners of the farm, and as a signer on my mortgage, he was also co-owner of my house.

"If you side with me on selling the farm, I won't give you any trouble about your house or trips."

For a minute I just sat staring at him, the way I would trying to make out the shape of a copperhead concealed in dry, tan leaves.

"You can't do this now," I told him. "Just to mention it will make Nora crazy."

"I can't go back to that place, Maggie."

"Then stay at my house and let Nora stay at the farm until you both feel more up to discussing your plans. This isn't a time to make any sudden changes."

"It's exactly the time," he said.

We argued. I asked about buying him out, just to settle the matter for Nora. He said that the price was beyond my means.

"Especially," he said, "when as a woman you can't get a loan by yourself. And it wouldn't be right for me to help you do something I think detrimental to the rest of us."

He shook his head.

"How you can want to keep that place is beyond me. Not after what happened."

I wanted to tell him that was in part exactly why, but he was too busy telling me that for now he was going to hold my share of his trust stipend in escrow. Then after we agreed to new arrangements, he'd see that I'd always have enough money to travel.

"You can go around the world so many times that you'll get dizzy and fall off."

"But we can't even think of dealing with any of this now, not until Nora is more herself."

"We will have even more to discuss by the end of summer," he said.

Then he told me that a job as division manager was coming up soon that he'd be considered for—would certainly get if he wanted it—in Chicago where he had been born and raised. He'd only come to LaCote for Nora. He'd accommodated her, and now it was his turn to choose the place he wanted. State Farm would transfer him as early as fall, and there were more opportunities for Clea in a big city: museums, schools, concerts—as if St. Louis didn't have those. Nora could start fresh with no gossip about her breakdown. I'd even have a room to stay in when I came to visit, and he begged me to quit being so stubborn and see that this was best for all.

Pacing his office, he kept socking one fist into his palm like a ballplayer testing a mitt, and then he leaned across his desk, knuckles planted and arms braced.

"Just be sensible about this, Maggie."

So much like Frank who, whenever I disagreed, always said, "I don't know you when you're selfish like this, Margaret." He'd shake his head sadly before walking away, as if I were the one thing keeping us from the Garden or the Promised Land.

Like Frank's, Neal's argument fell in my lap like a seamless ball rolled down an enclosed cylinder. The hypothesis began "How could you want anything but the well-being of our family?" And like all women, I answered, "Of course" before I knew exactly what he had decided that entailed. He constructed his points around me, the words *family, together,* and *happy* nailing me in and obscuring the counterpoints.

I didn't know exactly what I should do, except that I needed to buy time for Nora. Neal and I finally agreed that he would use my house for the summer, and that neither of us would discuss any of this with Nora until she was stronger.

"So silly for us to argue, Maggie," he said when I got up to leave, taking both my hands in his. "I feel badly when we disagree."

"It's a big step," I said. "We have to think about the rest."

"But what could you have against it?"

I thought of Nora riding across a morning pasture; of Grace and Simon and my brothers so close I could feel them graze against me as I walked down the hall or out in the yard; of the land unmoving beneath the swirl of life above it. I could not explain to Neal how essential this was to us all, not when it seemed like vapor against the all-too-tangible rows of his figures.

"Nora will adjust in time," he said, "and in the meanwhile, you can help by staying with her."

I stared down at my hands, pulling the loose skin taut over my knuckles. As I went out the door, he called smiling, "After dinner, I'll talk to you then."

I let the screen slam. The sun was so bright the bones around my eyes ached and the heaviness of the heat made me suck in to get a good breath. Main Street looked washed out, like a snapshot from the new colored film that faded quickly, and in my confusion, I turned the wrong way, away from where my car was parked in front of the Rexall. I didn't want Neal to see me walk back in front of his office, so I went on the way I'd started, turning right alongside the jewelry store and heading down to the alley where the KATY railroad tracks, running parallel to the river, had been submerged by the flood.

I planned to turn right twice again and come back on Main where I could claim my car unobserved. I threaded the narrow space between the river and the outbuildings of the lumberyard and grain elevator that bordered the alley. The path was striped with scum, the mud drying ripe and sticking in hunks to my shoes. The river lapped over the rails and hit high on the bridge pilings. I stopped for a minute and shaded my eyes as if looking from the shore of a great lake. As if after Simon's death not a single familiar thing was recognizable.

I was angry at him then, as if he had chosen to die. Then

angry at myself, both for blaming Simon and for letting Neal Mahler confuse me into considering that if he was pleased, the rest of us would be also.

I picked my way down the alley. Pink hollyhocks pressed against a feed shed, and a mangy orange tom stopped suddenly when he saw me coming. As I edged around a puddle left standing in a low depression, water seeped in my shoes and wet my stockings like clammy skin. Neal's argument ran through my mind like a math problem I didn't know the formula for.

I leaned against the door of an old shed. The level river covered the high bank, scrub bushes, and garbage that had been visible before. I couldn't remember any more than a general impression of it all, couldn't swear to any part of it exactly as I stood between the rough wood of the shed and the gray river.

"You can't do this to Nora, you just can't."

But in the deserted alley I still couldn't explain why, no more than Nora could prove that the river would not come up the last rise to her house. Then the shed door, one hung with wheels on a metal trolley, slid back, and I yelped in surprise. An old bum poked his head out. Dirt filled the creases of his skin like veins in marble; his hair was ropy and his pants shiny with body grease. He stepped out between me and the path down the alley, the hand over his fly bouncing his genitals into position.

"You were talking out loud to yourself, woman," the bum said, grinning with uneven teeth.

He smelled strongly of liquor, urine, and, strangely enough, the Mexana Powder that I'd used on Nora, then Clea and Simon, for prickly heat when they were babies.

"Got any extra money for me?" He reached out as if he might pluck my sleeve, and I turned my shoulder away.

"You can give me a little, can't you?" he asked.

I laughed, a short, nervous yelp. He leaned forward unsteadily and spat.

"How about that money?" he asked again. "I know you got it."

I rummaged in my purse, quickly hiding a five in a side pocket and dumping a change purse full of coins into his hands. He stood there counting it.

"Thought the water might come up in my place, but it stopped just in time, so far. See?" He tapped the toe of his shoe on the high-water mark only inches from the shed. "Pretty damp in there, though, and the river stinks bad."

Inadvertently I breathed in air ripe with mildew and rot.

"Saw two dead pigs and a mule go by," he said. "Even a couple of coffins the river dug up. Pretty interesting flood, and it's not half over yet."

Abruptly he stepped back enough to let me pass.

I hurried to my car and locked the door, not opening the window until I was four blocks away. Then the breeze dried the sweat from my face, turned beet red in just that little time, and I drove out through Blanchette Park and around Elm Point Road and through the streets of tiny new bungalows being built, just trying to order my thoughts while reason slid away. I couldn't shake the sensation of the bum reaching for me or my shame for not pushing past him. Couldn't forgive myself for not knowing how to manage or intimidate or simply say, "No."

I drove to my house and let myself in with the key I hadn't used in a month. I walked through the downstairs rooms, my own things unfamiliar after my absence, and made the circle lap four quick times. Wondering if in time I'd lose this place because of Neal. Swinging my arms and stomping my feet to work off my fury from realizing that when in LaCote I reverted to my old ways of approved behavior there. That I deferred and obeyed like a well-trained dog.

Round-eyed and flushed, Clea leaned over the banister and pushed back her hair.

"Grandma?" She sat down on the top step and peered through the railing. "I thought you were Dad."

Her beauty startled me. Creamy like pink-white petals. Not since before Mexico had I just looked at her.

"Your father said you'd gone on a picnic."

"Cramps," she said. "I'm lying down with the hot-water bottle." She pointed toward her room. "I'll go get dressed."

She pulled at her rumpled blouse, the shirttail out of her shorts. Her bare legs, long and slim, skipped up two steps at a time.

"Be down soon," she sang.

Then the door of her room closed on the sound of footsteps and the bed creaking, both at once. I went quietly up, stopping with my hand on the newel. Rustlings and whispers were barely audible, and the silences between like the house holding its breath under the rattle of the attic fan.

She opened the door, and now in a white sleeveless blouse and full skirt scattered with yellow flowers, came chattering toward me, telling me rapidly about her summer and offering iced tea or iced coffee in the kitchen, trailing the carrot of herself away from the suspect door.

As I stepped into the upstairs hall and toward her room, I could almost hear her catch her breath. I stood for a moment at the closed door as if I could see through it. Could, in a way, see him crouching behind it, the young man lean like a colt.

I imagined them lying on her bed and holding each other. I thought of Grace, leaning over the kitchen sink and cleaning the earth off newly pulled carrots one night while I was getting ready to go out with Frank.

"The Koran," she had said, without looking up, "says you'll be held responsible for those permitted pleasures in which you did not partake." In the twilight kitchen she held up and inspected a fat carrot, its ferny top waving.

"How do you know what the Koran says?" I asked.

"Because I read most of it once, while I was pregnant with you."

I assured her Frank insisted on waiting for our wedding night.

"All men have their faults," my mother said.

I wondered, now that I was more than old enough, what pleasures Grace had permitted herself. Had the hired men adored her because of what she'd given or forever withheld? I thought of pleasures I had finally permitted myself, long after Frank had died. But how much of pleasure should Clea know at age fifteen?

I told her I had come to get a book I wanted out of her father's room. I said "her father's" instead of "my." Her face relaxed as I came back down the hall carrying the excuse of the novel, and I felt a twist of regret over Clea's childhood, running like water through my fingers.

"I need to talk to you," I told her, "about where we all will live."

"Oh?" she said.

"What do you want?"

"It might be nice to stay in town this fall." She held her eyes wide.

I pictured her twinning with the hidden boy after school each day, safe in her bedroom since Neal never left the office a second earlier than five.

"I meant to Chicago," I said.

"To Chicago? No, I wouldn't want to go there."

"It's where your father wants to move."

"You're wrong. He just wants to be in town for a while."

"No, to Chicago. This fall and for good."

She chewed her bottom lip.

"Your mother and I miss seeing you," I said.

"Oh," she said, her voice trailing off, "with work and friends. I didn't want to disturb you."

"Be very careful with that boy upstairs," I said, holding her chin pinched between my fingers. "As your great-grandmother once told me, don't take on what you can't handle or care for."

Stubborn and unblinking, she looked up at me.

"Do you understand me, Clea? There are some things you're not ready for. At first it's all so innocent, but then it becomes difficult knowing when to stop."

She lowered her eyes and nodded. After I left, she watched me through the sheer curtains covering the long oval window of the door, I'm sure not moving until my car was out of sight. I kept thinking of her so young for all this, until I thought of myself at the same age, of how much I thought I knew and how much I wanted a boy to want me. I remembered my desire at that age, which alternately shrouded me in exquisite anguish or broke open into crystal joy. I wanted those pleasures for her, but I just as badly wanted her safe.

When I stopped to pick up groceries at the IGA, the parking lot with cars nosed against the brick wall depressed me and the thought of having to buy food for Nora and myself used up my last store of energy. A woman passed with a baby in her cart, a fat-cheeked girl who showed teeth like pearl nubs swimming in drool, who made and unmade fists by way of waving. A child like Clea, left too much alone, might produce. Or one like Simon might have had, bright and friendly like himself.

Too many thoughts running through my mind. I stood aimlessly by the produce, running my hands over curves of lettuce and not remembering why I'd come to the store. A mirror ran the length of the counter, reflecting the piles of fresh vegetables and my hand reaching in to lift their separate shapes. I cupped my hand over the red, ripe tomatoes, and as I leaned over to select one from the back of the pile, I glanced up in the mirror at the wide pores of my nose and doughy skin. When had I gotten so old? I was passing out of life before my very eyes.

I thought of Nora holding Clea when she was born. I felt the weight of Nora in my arms, and myself in turn held by Grace, and she by her mother. I felt the contradiction of wishing Clea innocent and regretting that Simon hadn't left something living of himself for us to keep. A boy-child who would come to visit and talk with me the way Simon had.

After I got home and put away the groceries, I stood on the porch as Nora slept upstairs. Trying to see the land as Grace would have, as a place of her own that now we must keep for Nora. The sun, angry and red like Mars in close-in orbit, belonged only to that day, but the yard cinched by pickets and the drive, falling away to the highway and fields, and the bluffs overlooking the river couldn't have changed much since Grace stood here.

I tried to stand in an exact place I remembered her, arms

folded and feet planted apart, as if imitating her precise stance would give me entry into her mind and I might discover how she would have handled what was happening now.

What came to me was the strange combinations in Grace. How she'd taken over the farm and her family and even Nora when it became clear they were alike. How she'd left me alone to become my own self, so different from her. She knew, somehow, what to take over and what to let go.

That distinction had always been a fearful mystery to me. But I could learn, as she must have learned. As the evening sky turned the color of a bruise, I was both delighted at this possibility and afraid of its power. I balanced on the balls of my feet and bounced slightly like a boxer. Thinking of Neal Mahler not as someone I must please but defend against.

Chapter Eight

Neal Mahler

THE MINUTE I WALKED into Maggie's house, I felt relief from so much of what had been bothering me. The house itself wasn't much, one of those middle-sized, red brick Victorians with a white spindled porch and a stained-glass window on the landing. The plumbing needed to be replaced with new copper, the faucet washers changed, and broken sash cords repaired—the kind of things a single woman couldn't do herself, even a woman who was home more than Margaret Rhymer liked to be.

But for the summer, at least, it was comfortable enough with big oaks to keep it cool and a nice yard to sit in. I was close enough to walk to the office, if I wanted, and Clea's school was just five blocks, should we stay into the fall. But I was already thinking that by then we would all be in Chicago.

First though, I had to deal with the flood. It was bad enough in May, but by the middle of July the river still hadn't crested, and none of us had any idea how widespread the damage was going to be. The farmers were showing up begging to be paid for a soybean crop that was never planted and corn three months from harvest. I told them I couldn't guess how much might survive the water, but they gave me their sob stories about how they needed the cash to make payments on their combines and compensate hired hands and see about grocery and doctor bills. They said the banks wouldn't give advances on crops that might be ruined and that I was their last chance. I told them my heart went out to them, but my hands were tied by State Farm and the Missouri River. I told them I'd take care of them at the appropriate moment, but this was just one of those times when most people were going to be unlucky.

The rest I wasn't so sympathetic about, the ones I had tried to talk into flood insurance. They had enough excuses when I was giving them the sales pitch. Their daddies never had such a thing, or the river never came up on their property, at least not enough to do much damage. They didn't have the money right that moment or they promised to see about it just as soon as they got through repairing the barn or storing the silage. I reminded them what a mess all those previous floods were and how we were due for a real big one.

When the water first started rising, they came around asking if I still had that policy I'd talked about. I told them they couldn't buy accident insurance after the accident or fire protection while their houses were burning. Same way I couldn't sell them flood insurance while we could step out of my office door and practically watch the river coming up the side street. Even I had already moved out of a house that had never gotten it before because I was worried about my family. Some of them argued they should still have a chance, but most of them understood what they'd done wrong. They knew insurance was a kind of game and they'd rolled craps.

Sometimes I thought about how that worked. How if you bought a life insurance policy and died the minute after you paid the first premium, why, then you'd won and beaten the company, moneywise, at least. When my kids each went into eighth grade I'd gotten them insurance policies they could borrow against when they went to college. Now I saw that as bad luck and cashed in Clea's. I felt better then, putting the checks from both in the bank and being done with them.

That same night I was hanging up my suit in Maggie's closet, her dresses pushed to both ends of the rod and my shirts and suits wedged in the middle. She had so much crap piled in there. Shoe boxes stacked on the shelf with hat boxes, and scarves and belts hanging down like snakes from trees. It looked like the whole mess was about to come down on my head, just like Nora's closet. So I thought I'd do her a favor and clean it up a bit. I was going to put some of it in neat piles on the floor, but that had more boxes than the shelf. They were mostly odd sized and when I tried to pull one out, it stuck and the lid broke. The box was old and soft, I'm sure that's how it happened, and the old photos skated out over one another.

I was going to scoop them up and throw them back. It was late, only the bedside lamp was lit, and I didn't like all those little figures and faces looking up at me. Nora as a kid—on her horses, and with her dad before he died, and dressed up for dates with corsages pinned to her shoulder. Then Nora and myself, our arms around each other and standing in front of Grace's house the day we got engaged. Nora sitting on my lap inside the Meramec Caverns, and us holding Simon so small he looked like an overgrown cocoon wrapped in his receiving blanket.

How young we looked. How happy. I couldn't really remember how that had been or understand how I had once looked at her and believed she would love me for our whole life together.

I held a photo of her and her father under the lamp to see the details more clearly. She was mounted on his Tennessee walking horse, the one he showed all over the state to win those ribbons getting dusty and brittle in the tack room of the barn. Frank Rhymer held his fedora to his chest and leaned forward a little, his crop behind the horse's knees, stiff and braced, as if they were both getting ready to take a bow. The horse's neck and tail were up in an arch, the way show horses were taught to stand, and its coat was glossy enough to see my face in. Nora was wearing a long black riding habit and a top hat with a veil draped under her chin. Probably fifteen, about Clea's age. She looked like a young widow from the olden days.

I couldn't for the life of me remember that horse's name. It was nervous and high-strung and once tried to kick me as I was walking in back of it. Just shot out that leg and would have shattered my kneecap if I hadn't jumped. Nora's father wanted her to be excited about showing with him, though old Grandma Grace had gotten to her first and brainwashed her into thinking show horses were mistreated. Still, Frank figured if he made Nora ride for him once in a while that she'd get to like it.

"When I see you in that winner's circle," he kept telling her, "I'm so proud."

He died, of course, when she was nineteen, shortly after she and I met each other, and Margaret Rhymer sold that horse almost before they got Frank in the ground. I always figured it was to pay for funeral expenses, but years after we were married, Nora got to talking about it one night, at the start of the war when she and I weren't getting along. She'd been jittery all month, worried that I'd get drafted and then killed. Acting like the Axis Powers were arming just to invade LaCote and murder her two babies. I kept telling her there was nothing to be upset about, just relax unless there was a real emergency. She wanted me to promise not to enlist. She said that's what she was most afraid of, being left to take care of the kids and everything alone with all that dying going on.

I told her she was just being silly and morbid, and that she'd never gotten over her own father dying so young. I knew she and her mother had had a hard time of it for a while. Frank Rhymer hadn't left any insurance but sure enough plenty of bills. Even before the depression, they'd almost lost the farm and were down to two horses for a while, until I married her and helped them out. But as much as I kept telling Nora that nothing like that would ever happen again, she kept acting like the Japs were on their way and if I left her, then she'd be dead or poor for sure.

"Be brave," I told her. "Make your father proud."

She got quiet for a while, looking out the window like she was expecting to see him through the glass. I thought we were done with the argument and sat down at the desk to pay some bills. She went upstairs and I heard the bathwater running. When she came back down, she sat on the couch across the room from me and just started talking like we were in the middle of a conversation.

She said at first she tried so hard to please her father. He wanted her to be his rider in the adult competitions and trained her with his horse every day but Sunday. She rode in circles for hours, trying to get the gaits perfect, and did everything he said until her back and legs and arms ached from holding them in the exact place he wanted. But nothing was ever right. One day, about a year before he died, Frank Rhymer told her a half-wit could follow directions better. He was so angry his head shook with the effort of controlling himself. Then he turned and left her sitting on his horse in the middle of the paddock.

She said that moment was what changed everything between them. I didn't know what was so terrible about what he'd done, but Nora seemed to think that was the straw that broke the camel's back. She decided to prove him right and from then on always made sure she didn't win a good ribbon. Maybe a white or a green, but never red, blue, or purple. She'd dig her heel or pull the reins a bit so that horse'd step out of his stance or toss his head as the judges were coming up. Anything to look bad and get her father's goat about not winning. After he died, she and her mother sold that horse, getting rid of what Frank most would have wanted to keep, and I knew they did it for spite.

The night Nora told me that was the first time I began to see her right. She was sitting tucked up against the corner of the living-room couch, her bare toes sticking out from under her robe she'd put on just after her bath. All the time she was talking, she kept curling her toes and rubbing her foot like she'd sprained it or something. That she'd gone against her father shocked me. I couldn't believe a woman could have an anger like that or a girl be so mean. Not when her own father was offering to let her help with what meant the most to him.

And the whole time she was talking, I had the feeling that

she was threatening me in some way. Her voice was so low and shaky. She kept glancing up at me every once in a while to see how I was taking it. She didn't come right out, but I could tell she meant me to understand that she'd have no problem doing the same to any man.

I didn't say anything when she got done, except that she'd been selfish for hurting her father the way she had. She tilted her head and narrowed her eyes like she was watching me sprout another nose.

"But what about what he did to us?" she asked.

"What *did* he do?" I said. "Worked his whole life to provide a good life for you."

"That wasn't it," she said.

"What part don't I have right?" I said. "I seem to remember you as a little princess. You went to that private school we've got Clea in and had your own horse and just about anything else within reason a girl could want. Where did he fail you? Just tell me."

She looked for a minute like she was going to cry, and I thought I'd convinced her. But Nora, as always, wanted the last word, even if it didn't make any sense.

"It wasn't for us he did those things."

"Don't be ridiculous," I told her.

"He thought he was the only one who counted."

I shook my head and left the room then. She called after me.

"We weren't real to him."

Standing in the dark hallway, I was so angry that I thought I'd have to hit her if I didn't get her out of my sight. She seemed to blame me for what she thought her father had done.

But I had promised the priest to stay with this woman forever, not to mention those two kids who had to be taken care of. What choice did I have but to stay?

So I got my hat and coat and went out, slamming the door behind so she'd know. I drove the fifteen miles into town, to Earl's, a bar in LaCote. I rarely went there, but it was too cold that night to stay out and I wanted other people around. The bar had a counter of glass blocks with blue lights behind them, and a big Wurlitzer jukebox lit up red and green against the opposite wall. The place was smoky and hazy and comfortable after the cold, though practically anywhere would have been better than at home.

I sat at the end of the bar and ordered a Griesedieck Brothers. Looking at my hands through the brown bottle, at the way my fingers seemed not to be mine or even fingers at all behind the glass, I was thinking of Nora curled up on the couch and rubbing her feet like some invalid.

At a table behind me a group of men talked about the battle going on at Wake and who in town had either signed up to go or been drafted. After watching the men in the mirror, a baby-faced, pudgy guy at the center of the bar suddenly swiveled around on his stool.

"I'm going next week," he told them, picking the label off his beer. "Signed up, passed my physical, and I'm on my way."

He lifted his bottle like a toast in their direction.

An older guy pointed at the bartender. "Get this man a drink on me."

"He's already drinking on the house, Bill," the barman said.

"Then give him some to take home on me. Whatever he wants if he's going to fight those damned Japs."

"Might end up in Europe," the new soldier said.

"That's OK, too. Fight those damned Huns. Fight any damned person who wants to come over here and change our damned way of life."

"Then why aren't you going, Billy?" one of his friends asked him. The others at the table guffawed and hooted.

"Asthma." He pounded the flat of his hand against his chest. "They won't take me, not at thirty-five." Then he laughed. "And Doris. She won't let me. Says if I want to fight I can stay right here and go at it with her."

"To Doris," the new soldier said, raising his beer again.

"To asthma," said Bill.

They all raised their drinks to the new soldier, and it was like he was already a hero. The worst feeling came over me, as though the walls were closing in and I was running out of breath. I could picture Nora sitting at home, her head back and lips pursed, sucking up the air until she held it all inside her with none left over for me. I thought about having to stay here and put up with her, knowing she didn't love me the way she should, and the kids so active, and the same old work every day with nobody else knowing what I was going through to take care of them.

I had a couple of more beers before driving home, all the while thinking of our house as a box where I was shut up with her. I stood at the doorway of our room, the light from the hall laying a wide triangle of white on the floor, and watched her sleep like nothing happened. I wanted her then, though I can't explain why seeing her made me hard. I shut the kids' doors first, then my own before getting undressed. I ran my hand over my chest and belly, all the way to the end of my cock standing straight out. Under the covers I lay close against her back and started rubbing my hands over her, up under her nightgown that I pulled high under her arms. I spread my fingers wide over her stomach and shoved her tighter against me. She kept acting like she was asleep, though I knew she couldn't be, so I rolled her over, straddled her hips, and fondled her breasts, turning the nipples like little radio dials.

She twisted her head away and moaned. When she tried to brush my hands down, she couldn't use any force since she was still pretending to be asleep. If she really didn't want me, she could have grabbed my wrists and held them. She could have gotten out of bed and moved to another room or her mother's house. But she didn't, and I figured that meant she'd let me. I liked being over her, the way she seemed so small and flat against the mattress and me with my legs apart over her.

She opened her eyes then for a second and pressed her fists against my hands on her breasts. Her whole body went rigid and her eyes squeezed closed again. But I figured she owed this to me, after how she'd been acting. I wanted her to feel me like her husband.

She lay like a limp fish and wouldn't react to anything I did to her, so I pushed harder and at first waited after each thrust to see what she would do.

"You can't fool me," I told her. "You're awake, aren't you?"

But she wouldn't move or look at me. I kept pushing harder and faster. I couldn't stop it then. I gripped her shoulders and braced my arms against her. I pushed and finally came, but still she acted like she was dead, even when I fell on top of her and lay there breathing hard. I wanted her to stroke the hair back from my forehead or put her arm around me, but she wouldn't move or act like I was there, this woman I was stuck with for the rest of my life. I pulled her closer, but she wouldn't open her eyes. After I rolled off her and turned my back, I could hear her crying into her pillow.

The next day I went to McDonnell's and got a job making fighter planes. I was two months past my thirty-sixth birthday. I told Nora she'd have to keep the insurance business going, not that I expected her to sell any new policies, but she'd have to learn how to maintain the ones I had so there'd be something left of my agency when the war was over. I warned her that she had to put this first, not her "hobby" horses or even the house, because we all had to do our part. She did all right, like all the women left on their own during the war. She even enlarged our client base, which just proved she was a smart woman who could do what she had to.

I worked double shifts, and the only thing she ever said to me was that I'd only taken that job to get away from her. After a time I stopped listening. Who needs a broken record anyhow?

Hell, people I barely knew stopped me on the street to say how they admired what I'd done, even though my own wife never had a good thing to say about it. But I was glad. The change had been good for me in that I wasn't bothered by Nora so much and felt then I could last it out with her.

Moving into Maggie's house gave me that same kind of new start, away from the old like the war had. I didn't know why Nora would want to stay at the farm. I couldn't ever come in the front door again without picturing Simon clattering down the steps or sit at a meal without him smiling from across the table. I couldn't pass his room, even with the door shut, and not think about the times I'd walked down that hall and glanced in to see him reading or studying or just looking out the window into the branches of the mulberry. I thought about all the times I'd walked by and didn't stop to ask him how he was doing or what was on his mind or even straighten his covers or put my hand on his head while he was sleeping.

I couldn't go back to that place that was so full of Simon. I wanted that land gone from my life so I didn't ever have to think of it again. Even giving in to Maggie's request to defer the sale made me edgy, though I realized Nora wasn't up to making rational decisions yet.

Her doctor said women sometimes got like her when they'd had too big a shock. That they often needed help getting back to normal. He suggested we take her to the state hospital in St. Louis for rest. Just being away from the place where the accident happened would benefit her, he said. Not to mention she'd have nothing to worry her head over and be where nurses could see to her medication.

He also recommended a therapy that had been used on women for depression and out-of-control behavior. That was what he called how Nora was, and he said the treatment worked. I wasn't sure, when he explained it, how causing her to have seizures would help. But he said she wouldn't feel a thing and that the treatment would jar her back to where we wanted her.

He showed me articles out of his medical journals and sold me on it the way I'd sell him insurance. It would be worth it if Nora would get well and we could start over in a place with no memories. It would all be for her own good, and she'd get used to a new place eventually. After all, she belonged with her family. None of us could have argued with that, could we?

Chapter Nine

Clea Mahler

THE RIVER SQUEEZED the ground into islands. The wet-footed corn had already turned brown, and the crops smelled slimy like water left in vases with rotted flowers. My father drove me out past Orchard Farm to see what the flood had done so far; even low spots on the far roads were submerged, and our tires churned up the muddy water like an eggbeater. Then we walked down to the riverbank in back of his office, and before he sent me home, he told me again how lucky we were to be in town.

Walking the steep streets from the river to my grandmother's house got me out of breath and made my legs ache. I turned to look back at the river, usually neat in its channel, spreading gray-white and smooth over everything. Trees that bordered the other side, which was low and flat, stood almost covered in water that carried away other trees and logs like it was alive.

My father called living at Maggie's "our little vacation"

before we all started over. "Like drawing a line in the dirt and stepping across," he said.

I wanted to do that. One night before we moved to town, he had called me in to dinner, just him and me. He'd told Maggie she needed the night off and sent her to the movies. I wasn't much hungry and pushed my food into a little square with the backside of my fork.

"Eat the meat," he said. "I didn't give you much."

I took a bite and ran my tongue over the greasy film it left on my teeth.

"Isn't she coming down to eat with us?" I asked, meaning my mother. Before all this, the only time she hadn't sat down to dinner was when she'd had strep throat and stayed in her room with a rubber ice bag like a huge beige slug around her neck.

My father, chewing, broke a roll into halves and shook his head no. When he finished, he pushed his plate away and leaned with both elbows on the table.

"I need you to answer some questions, Clea," he said. "The coroner has to write a report because this was an accidental death, and I told him I would rather talk to you privately than bring you into his office."

The fan on the floor swiveled and I counted five times the air hit my legs and went away again.

"Just tell me what happened," he said.

I shifted, my legs sticking to the chair.

"About Simon?"

"Who else?"

"He was behind me, with his leg thrown over the pommel."

"Why?"

"We were just talking."

Simon asking me if I'd noticed anything different between my mother and Ozzie Kline.

"I wasn't watching him every second."

Only when I turned around suddenly when he'd asked that and just as quickly turned back so he wouldn't see my face.

"I heard it more than anything."

The hoof hitting the stone and ringing hollow.

"I looked over my shoulder and saw her knees bend and nose come forward..." I shrugged and my voice trailed off.

But before that I'd heard Zad whinnying and Simon calling to her.

"She threw him then?"

"She fell."

I couldn't be sure if I remembered any of it or made it up later. None of it made a difference now anyway.

"She could have bucked him off and you wouldn't have known."

"She fell."

"But you wouldn't know for sure." He lay his arms out on the table like a wide net and drummed his index fingers in time with his words.

"I saw out of the corner of my eye."

Saw the rock the size and shape of a box turtle, that he'd hit his head on, but that was all.

I started to cry then, to tell him she never bucked, that she came when called and stood as still as earth to be saddled and responded to the slightest pressure of Simon's knee or movement of his hands. I didn't want to know that she had killed him or to make my father more angry at my mother for this. I didn't like to think that if I'd done what my mother had wanted and learned to ride like my brother, I might be the one dead.

Most of all I wanted to never think about any of this ever again. My father patted me on my arm and said we were done. I was glad, as if I could leave the whole issue at the farm for the summer.

The end of May we moved to Maggie's. Often women from my father's parish cooked us casseroles and dropped them by for dinner. Other nights he and I went out to eat at the Duquette Café. People stopping by our table asked about my mother like she was sick in the next room. He always told them we were getting on as well as could be expected and by next year at this time would be back to normal.

A couple of weeks later when school was over, he told me the period of mourning was done and I could go out with my girlfriends if I wanted. We told our parents that we were going to play tennis at the park, but instead hung around the refreshment stand and ball-field bleachers to talk to guys. Three of them from the public high took us driving out in the country where the air was cooler, and everything, including parents, was left behind. A couple in front, two in the backseat, the boys deciding the pairs. Mine had brown eyes and a long scar along his jawbone, and I felt strange, being around people again and especially him.

I stuck my hand out the window to ride the wind, bumping along on it like a tree down the river, and my hair flew back, wild and cool. The boys teased us about being little nuns from the convent school, but I could tell they liked us, the way they draped their arms over the backs of our seats or leaned across us to look out the windows as if they'd never been down these roads before. Out in the farmland, cows stood in dusky pasture. I leaned my head back against Tommy's arm, and it seemed that the car was going the same speed as the earth turning and the hearts of the cattle beating.

He and I were talking in a bubble away from the other four, and we seemed alone in the car like on a small and separate planet orbiting the country night. I leaned closer and his hand dropped over my shoulder. We touched all the way down, my hip and thigh against his as if I was meant to fit the space under his arm. My cheeks were achy, and the space inside my ribs tender. He lifted his hand to my face and kissed me. I knew I was supposed to refuse and act insulted, but we both seemed wound up and ready to spring while at the same time we floated out like warm water.

Then the aloneness of the past six weeks was replaced by his arms holding me tight and his solid chest and his wet, sweet mouth.

When we pulled up in front of Maggie's house two hours late, my father was waiting on the porch, the tip of his cigarette glowing. Tommy offered to walk me up, but I told him it was better if he didn't. He helped me out, squeezed my fingers, and told me he'd call. Then the kids drove off, the red taillights sad and disappearing.

My father held open the screen and watched me come up the walk. I thought I might tell him that the car broke down. But that seemed such an obvious lie. We did not come in because it had felt so good to be out.

My father just looked disgusted, but I was thankful for his silence. The house was dark except for the streetlights through the windows, and I went upstairs with the stair rail sliding under my hand and the sounds of my father locking up behind me. I got undressed in the darkness and odd-angled shadows, still feeling Tommy's hand on me. I moved very softly so as not to jar it away, not even covering myself with a sheet so that the air against my skin would remind me of touches. I lay awake a very long time feeling the vibration of the car and the secret private magic of the ride, and it felt as if the walls were falling away open to the sky, filled with stars and possibilities.

I thought of Simon at Homecoming with his arm around his girlfriend Janie or leaning against the gym wall holding her hand. Simon and his easy slouchy walk, the way he hooked his thumb in the pocket of his Levi's and watched her as if he couldn't get over how amazing she was. I thought of her at his funeral, crying so hard she couldn't stand up straight. Then missing him pressed its corners against me—the way he squeezed my shoulder softly whenever he passed by or teased me out of bad moods.

He had this way of putting down whatever he was working on when I came in his room or the barn. He'd come over and sit close, our knees touching, and watch me the whole time we talked. I didn't think anyone would ever listen again as carefully or right away know exactly what I meant.

Remembering the quiet way his eyes got spooked me, like Simon wanted to know all that had happened since he died and talk it over. I made Tommy's face drift up close like before he first kissed me and was off again, turning over every moment of him, and so awake that the church bells rang three o'clock before I slept.

The next morning I was dead unconscious when Father woke me. He told me that with the flood keeping him so busy, he needed me to help out at the office a few days a week and that I could start that morning. Then he told me to dress up like I would for church so I'd look decent.

He didn't get out any dishes or cereal for me when he got out his own, and he put the cornflakes back in the cupboard though I was standing next to him waiting for them. When we were just about to go out the door, he stopped to turn the lock and said, "Don't ever disappoint me again the way you did last night."

"No, sir," I mumbled.

"You're not old enough to be running around like that."

"No, sir."

"Who was that boy?" he said.

"Tom Steiner," I told him.

"The one who got drunk with his brother and smashed up a car last year? Went through the windshield, if I remember the insurance report correctly. He's no good, you know that, don't you?"

I nodded so slightly that it could've hardly been taken for an answer. We rode in silence to his office. The river was up to the alley behind the stores on Main Street. Men were setting up wooden horses with detour signs, and the owner of the grain elevator was clearing out his storage building nearest the water, the sacks of feed laid like bodies on his handcart.

"Better start bagging around your office," he called to my father. "It's coming up higher than we've ever seen."

My father waved and laughed. "River wouldn't dare enter an *in*-surance office." Then he left me in the car while he went down to chat with the workers blocking off the street. He gestured, and they gathered in a little circle around him. I got out and leaned against the fender to catch the breeze. When my father walked back past me, I followed behind and waited as he unlocked the office door.

"Here." He tossed his keys on his desk and opened a file

drawer stuffed tight with folders. "Go through all these and color code them for type of policy, and while you're doing that, make a list of those who have flood coverage."

He handed me a tobacco can full of colored bits of paper and a sheet with the code. Green for life, black for burial, red for home owners, blue for auto, and so on through purple and yellow and orange and white and magenta. He cleared off a table and set a bottle of mucilage next to a foot-high stack of folders.

"When you finish the first drawer," he said, "just keep going in order. The whole file is full."

He pulled open three more drawers stuffed to bursting. Enough files to cover the whole county. The first dozen took all morning. I had to search to find the policy names on the sheets in each folder and keep looking at the color chart. The bits of paper got stuck to the glue I spilled on my fingers, and I stacked the folders backward as I finished and ruined the alphabetical order. My back hurt from sitting so long bent over, and my stomach growled for lunch. But the more I worked, the more my father seemed to forget how displeased he was with me.

It wasn't so much anything he did or said, but something more, as if his anger had actually churned up the air between us. I worked harder and felt the currents settle as the muscles of his face relaxed. I felt myself turn back into a shape that pleased him, as if last night had made me look different and each folder that I finished made me look a little more like myself. I thought up tricks to remember the colors without looking and found a rhythm to moving the papers and mentally calling out the names. I put the finished folders facedown so they stayed in the correct order.

Finally he said, "Aren't you hungry?" He raised his eyes to the wall clock which said one-thirty. "We forgot all about lunch."

My head ached and eyes burned.

"Come on," he said, "we'll go to the drugstore to eat."

I sat next to him at the counter and we both ordered burgers, fries, and shakes. The soda fountain was at the back of the store, and the smell of the frying meat mixed with the cool, antiseptic perfume coming from the front counters. The waitress slid the thin beater into the chrome container and switched on the pale green shake machine. She set glasses of water in front of us.

"This your girl, Neal?" she asked, though she'd waited on me before, whenever Simon brought me in for a cherry Coke.

"This is Clea. She's working for me this summer."

"That's real good to help your daddy," she said.

I nodded as my father said hello to a man on his left. In the mirror over the fountain, I watched the three of us like strangers across the room. I did not know what I was doing here in the middle of the week all dressed up.

My father said again, "This is my daughter, Clea, who's helping me out at the office this summer."

The man asked how I liked my work. My father said I was doing a good job for him, and I was relieved of anything more than floating mindless in the shadowy mirror while they talked.

"Nice to have such good-looking help," the man winked. My father glanced at me approvingly.

Then they went back to their own talk, and I stared at myself more. The lighting made my skin sallow and eyes dark like a raccoon's. My ponytail was leaking messy strands, and the dust from the folders had left a smudge on my blouse. I didn't feel pretty or competent, but the man's words and my father's pleasure in them had made me consider the possibility.

When I went back to the office, I lined up my pencil neatly by the pad and the colored bits in rows across the back of the table. My father told me that he had to meet with a client and for me to answer the phone while he was gone. I moved from my table to his big oak desk and swiveled around in the chair. I arranged the papers and pens, Simon's and my bronzed baby shoes, and the brass nameplate that read NEAL MAHLER: STATE FARM AGENT. I answered the phone "Clea Mahler here" and waved at a couple of girls walking by wearing short shorts and halter tops. They gawked at me sitting at the big desk, jotting down the message. I arranged the drape of my skirt over my knees and felt older, though they were both in Simon's year at school.

I called Janie for the first time since the accident, but the cleaning lady said her parents had sent her to Minnesota to spend the summer with her cousins. I didn't know what to say. I'd only wanted to tell her about Tommy, and now that seemed a really stupid idea. So I went back to the files. Now that I had a system, the work and time went quickly. I thought about what I'd say to him the next time we talked, and this with the work filled my mind too full to think about Simon or my mother. The piles shrank and I filled with satisfaction when the *A*'s were done. When my father returned, he looked over my work and nodded.

"Isn't this better, Clea?" he asked.

That evening after we finished the latest tuna casserole the women had brought, he asked me to clean up the kitchen while he went out to finish signing up a policy. It was a nice night, the red-and-white checkered curtains billowing out and fireflies just starting to blink on the lawn. Wiping down the counters when the phone rang, I got hot and guilty before I even picked up the receiver.

Tommy asked if I could talk, his voice lazy and deep, the way boys sound when they're sure you'll say yes. But I knew he was forbidden even without asking and told him I wasn't allowed to see him again.

"It's not you," I said. "My father won't let me."

"You sure?"

"I'm positive."

The floor seemed to be falling away beneath my feet as soon as I said that out loud. But I felt holy and good like I'd given up candy for Lent or resolved not to be lazy.

"If that's the way you want it," he said.

Lighter and cleaner and safe, I listened to his breathing.

"We can figure a way to see each other," he said finally.

"I don't know," I told him. "I've got to help him at the office now."

"Tell him you're out with your girlfriends again, or that you don't feel good and have to stay home while he's at work. He's going to give you some days off, right?"

After we hung up, I sat in the living room with the lights out and the summer dusk making everything shadowy and soft. I pretended Tommy and I were riding in that car out into the country dark, just the two of us doing what we would if we never had to go home. It would be easier without him, I knew. Simpler to do what my father wanted. But I thought I would break with the hurt of not seeing Tom ever again.

Sometimes I woke up in the middle of the night and forgot I had moved to my grandmother's and what the room looked like there. I thought I'd been kidnapped or lost, or maybe even that I'd woken up in someone else's life. After a while I sat up and looked around and it came to me where I was. But I stayed uneasy, as if I'd moved here because my mother had died along with Simon.

I missed them both and all the horses. I missed the dog following me around, even his smell, and the barn cats rubbing up against my legs to be petted. I thought about our old summers, how we slept until we woke and sometimes stayed in bed reading until we got hungry for lunch or Mother brought us sandwiches and peaches in our rooms. How we lounged on the porch hammocks or went out riding to sit under the trees by the river and had whole days to be in our own time until Father came home. That place was so far away that it didn't seem to have ever existed. So long ago that the only way back was to dream myself there.

Chapter Ten

Ozzie Kline

I LEFT LACOTE LOOKING for space to sort out the feelings that had gotten so tangled up while I was home, all those old memories that I mistook for love and then mixed with sympathy when Simon died. By the time Nora was five hundred miles behind me, I figured it wasn't so much her I'd gone back for, more than a year before, but for a place where I belonged.

On my way to Canada I started looking for land to buy. A farm where I could raise my own horses. I stopped in small towns and got real-estate agents to take me out to places for sale. I checked the local ads and called farmers on my own to see how much they wanted. Passing land that caught my eye, with houses and barns sitting neat in a cluster, I imagined what it would be like to walk out on my own porch on a summer's morning to watch colts chasing each other in the fields.

But none of the farms seemed just right, and I got overwhelmed with the pointlessness of not knowing exactly what I was looking for. Sometimes I drove past where I was headed because I wasn't ready to stop. I'd plan to be a certain place for a fair or horse show, but the idea of dealing with all those strangers seemed a poor trade for my solitude, and I'd go on for an hour or day more before circling back. When the job was over, I was more than ready to get off by myself again, driving the truck the same speed as my mood and letting my mind drift, out where no one could get to me.

I went northeast at first, the winter wheat still green and the bean fields fallow. The farther I went, the later the crop cycle; so the wheat when I arrived at the second place to work was at the same stage it had been when I'd gotten to the first place, and the third was the same as the beginning of the second, and so on until I started to believe that time was always being yanked back to its starting point and I was forever caught in this motion.

After looping in and out of Canada I gave up the idea of a place for myself. I turned south and made time collapse quickly forward by covering in a week the full turn from newly bearded fields to dead ripe gold to shorn stubble. Somewhere in Kansas, on a direct latitudinal line with LaCote, I stopped outside some hick town dwarfed by the bins of the grain elevator out on the plains. Then I got blind drunk paralyzed with a fifth of Jack Daniels to resist the urge to get in the truck and drive straight across Missouri. Due east and back to Nora.

I lay on the bed at the motel, staring at ceiling cracks, and thought what good would I be to her? Couldn't even make myself hold still long enough to get straight how I felt. Couldn't offer her any security, not money or land or even a house, not like her husband. Couldn't even give her support while she got over Simon because I couldn't get over Simon.

I didn't know why. I'd seen boys die before and not as

cleanly as him. Seen arms, legs, and faces blown away, a head lying on the ground staring up at me, and once the hips and legs of a boy sitting against a tree, the rest of him cut off at the waist. Went around after battles, picking up pieces of boys and trying to figure which piece of what boy I'd found. Found other boys whole and empty of blood. Found strangers and friends every way imaginable and then some.

I got used to it in a way, there was so much. I learned to shut off thinking that a body had ever been a boy with a name or family or girl waiting at home. The other soldiers and I gave each other nicknames which erased ourselves from before the war. I was Wizard of Oz-zie, sprung with the rest like dragon teeth into warriors, with no need to worry about the loss of one tooth, more or less.

I liked that I could forget I'd been Ozzie Kline. I didn't have much that was worth remembering up until that time. Just that I'd been in love with Nora Rhymer and she in love with me. That I'd never stopped loving her or let myself love any other woman the way I did her. That nothing came of nothing.

I was thirty-four when I shipped over, old enough that I never would've seen combat unless I finagled my way like I did into a unit bound for the front. Hell, the country had to fight, no question. But more than that, I wanted to say I'd done one substantial thing in my life, and I didn't seem to know how to do that on my own. I had thought once that loving Nora would be that thing, but I couldn't pull it off when I was with her, and it turned out, I couldn't even do it from a distance after Simon died.

But I was a damn good soldier. Told what to do every damn minute of every damn day, I was trained as a machine—to load my rifle and attack on command, to shoot or bayonet or slit the throat of any Nazi coming at me. I learned the reflexes of a junkyard dog and never had to think much. Just watched who survived and who didn't, then imitated what the survivors did. Weird stuff, like not fastening the strap on my helmet so if a concussion knocked me flying, my head didn't ram around inside like a bell's clapper. Like figuring which weapons were the best, the German as well as the Allied, and keeping extras with me even if they were contraband.

I never thought twice about running out under fire to haul in a wounded buddy or charge with my ass exposed if that helped gain our advantage. I once spotted a machine gunner in a nest below a foxhole that would give me a good angle at a shot. I ran like hell, zigzagging like it was some crazy game of dodge ball, and threw myself into cover. Then I aimed at his cheekbone and split his head like a melon. They wanted to give me a medal for that, but I wouldn't let them. Too many punks got medals for nothing, and besides, I didn't see what I did as dangerous at the time. Just a strategy problem like in chess that I had to solve quickly. Just a game move with real men on the board.

But when I thought back on it, driving past the wheat and through the flat, even land, I knew there was more. War was easy in a way. Feelings came in three main flavors—fear, relief, and boredom—and most others were drowned in adrenaline or stored away. Even with all the variations on killing a man, the idea of making him dead was uncomplicated.

Not like the objective of loving a woman when sometimes she didn't know for sure how she wanted to be loved, or wouldn't tell me when she did.

A freedom had come in how I lived far away from my life before the war and was cut off by death from a sense of future.

The immediate moments and constant chances to do what could be called noble and gallant suited me. Besides, I had nothing to lose to death; it didn't scare me the way it should have.

Yet on some nights, when the mortars were being lobbed over my head like sinister comets, I'd settle into a shallow hole for sleep and think about Nora more than I had for years. I'd imagine that she wrote daily and sent pictures of herself for me to carry. I pretended that she worried about me coming home safe and promised to be there always for me to come to. Then I'd remember tracing the bones of her face with my finger and running my tongue over the arc of her teeth and cupping her breasts so my hands were full of Nora. When her essence came over me like that, I would have given up Europe in a minute to have another chance to claim her.

I also knew that if she'd been waiting, I would have wanted to protect her from being left alone without me to care for her. I would have risked less for the sake of the war if I'd heard her crying in letters for me to come back in one piece. Hell, I might not have gone in the first place.

But I didn't even have a snapshot of her, and I couldn't remember, exactly, the face of the girl who I'd made love to half a life before. When she came to me during nights on the battleground, I'd distinctly see the rosy flush across her cheeks or a tendril of blond hair loose against her temple. But I could not put the pieces together to see Nora whole, nor even hold each separate piece still for long.

Then in a way, I was glad to be without her. The war had a comforting if terrible simplicity, not like with her where I couldn't make sense of my own feelings, let alone how they fit with hers, nor cope with her absence like a hole in my gut. I stopped myself from thinking, especially about us together. Instead I concentrated on protecting my buddies, and that comradery seemed the only good in a world where men across its wide surface were trying to blow each other into kingdom come.

The Ozzie who yearned for Nora ceased to exist, except in stray moments when Wizard forgot to keep him at bay. Then Wizard got wounded and discharged early in '44, and I rammed around for a couple years, not exactly sure what to call myself. I was really OK, but nerves had been damaged when the bullet shattered bone, for a while making my hand so weak I couldn't hold a weapon or pull a trigger. I had trouble being a nobody again and had dreams a lot, about dead men that I believed I could have saved if only I'd been a little smarter or quicker or stronger.

After those I didn't like to be around people for a few days. I couldn't stand the annoyance of petty jobs or putting myself at the mercy of idiots. I pumped gas or clerked or sold shoes. But some bitch would complain that I'd missed washing a bug off her windshield, or some bastard draft dodger fussed because his feet were too big for the wing tips he'd ordered. Then I'd want to tell them they didn't know what was important in life, not this little crap, but men dying and losing limbs and going out of their minds.

I also had the strange feeling that I didn't have any shape of my own, no bones to give resistance. Some days I'd think of writing Nora about what I'd done when I was over there. I bought a tablet of paper and a decent pen and would go as far as to sit in front of a clean page and put the date in my best writing. I wanted to tell her all the terrible moments, and the funny ones, too, and explain how sometimes I'd saved a man before I'd even had time to think what I was doing. I wanted her to know the nights so lonely that I kept myself awake after the others just to cry and the moments so terrifying that I wet myself or threw up.

I was proud of what I'd done there, and I wanted her to know that side of me. Not the inadequate boy her father had looked down on. The one she'd abandoned. But then I'd get ashamed of wanting so badly to write a woman who'd deserted me for better things when we were nineteen. In that mood I'd just lie in bed for hours, my hands folded behind my head. Sometimes I'd doze off, and the faces of the dead got so mixed up with flashes of her that it seemed like she'd been with me.

Then I became so angry with her—for having wanted money and status and approval more than she had wanted me—that I wished she really had been with me in mud so thick it almost sucked us under and that she had touched the awful pieces it had held—the hands and lengths of intestine and bits of brain. Look, Nora, I wanted to tell her, look where I went because of you, into the dirt and shit and sick-sweet rot of death. Let us dream this over together while I hold you, so you can carry it with you as clearly and forever as I.

For a while I couldn't concentrate on anything else, and then Nora became like a kind of death I wanted to get away from.

Eventually I made myself work ten to sixteen hours a day, two jobs if I had to, in order to wear myself out. I did construction during the day, building first Quonset hut housing and then bungalows for returning vets. Nights I was a janitor at a school or watchman at a hospital. Anything to keep busy, especially where I didn't have to talk much to people. I didn't want to be around horses then, either, since it was like I'd brought back some fierceness that would spook or corrupt them.

I worked constantly until the dreams came less often, and I found a way of carrying myself that told others I didn't want to talk much or be around them. I stopped thinking of Nora so often and wanting to punish her for what she'd done to me. Eventually I craved to be settled, so December of '45 I left the woman in Pennsylvania I'd been seeing, packed up my gear, and drove to LaCote.

Once I was back, though, I understood why I'd kept away. I'd been gone long enough that most everything had changed. A couple of friends had been killed in the war; another had moved to Houston to build liberty ships and stayed. Stores had changed hands or gone under, new streetlights had been installed, and construction started on a huge pool at the park. The most familiar places were those still full of Nora, places where I'd held her or made love or just been with her.

I wanted to see her and wanted just as much to not. I'd go to the grain dealer's where she might be getting feed and be like a kid excited over picking up his girl. I'd sit on a pile of sacks talking with the guys working there, and pretty soon I'd be in a panic to leave because I was afraid she'd walk in and I wouldn't know how to act. I was sure she'd be able to tell I was only there to run into her. Just to see if she was well and exactly how she looked. Just to tell her I missed her as I would my heart.

Even when Jack Rothermich recommended me out of the blue to Neal Mahler for that job, I wasn't sure if I should take it. But being back with horses sounded good, especially when it gave me a reason to be around Nora at the same time. I wouldn't be Oz who'd once loved her, but only the hired hand who discussed feed orders and training schedules and ways to keep the animals healthy. A man with all the right in the world to watch her ride, like when we were sixteen and I had watched her work her horses like she knew their minds.

By the end of that first March I was back, Nora came out to the barn every day after she got the kids off to school and talked while she worked, telling me about this horse or that, its quirks and needs, as she ran her hands over them. The two ponies and six horses boarded there, the two belonging to her kids, and then finally Zad, practically dancing with joy when Nora came into her stall.

I could hardly take my eyes off of them, both so pretty and in love with each other. She combed out Zad's mane and braided it up in twenty pigtails tied with red ribbon, all the while glancing at me and smiling to check if I was as pleased about this horse as she. I grinned back, happy to know how funny and bright and whole she was.

I thought I would get over that initial euphoria. But even after I was there a month, I couldn't help myself from making excuses to follow her around or talk about nothing just to keep her in front of me. It was like we were both kids again, though I'd seen her only once in those twenty missing years, down on Main Street before the war, shopping with Clea and Simon. She'd walked by at first, not recognizing me. I stopped and called after her, but it took a minute before it registered who I was. Then she asked how I'd been and pulled her kids back against her legs. Neal Mahler's kids.

"I haven't been around much," I said. "Once in a while I'll pass through for a few days, like now."

"I've always been here," she said. "Right where you left me."

Then she laughed and said she had to get going.

I'd almost wished later that I'd never seen her. She was beautiful at thirty, that pretty-girl look given weight and substance with age, and motherhood adding a self-assurance that intimidated me. But what hurt was the way that she treated me. Not a hug or even a touch on the arm. No indication of what we once had been to each other. Of what she still was to me.

I left town again a few days after that, to wrangle horses in the Arizona desert, which suited my mood better, and after Pearl Harbor, on to the war, which seemed more fitting still.

When I finally came home, Nora seemed the only constant that had survived the breaks and jerks my life had taken. I loved to watch her and Simon with Zad, all so headstrong and beautiful. They made over Zad and curried her until she shone, and hovered about if the vet was there. She, in turn, followed them like a kid and shoved her nose against their butts if they didn't pay her attention.

I started offering suggestions, at first little things like a better way to file Zad's hooves or a different way to shoe her, and then later, improvements for her training. Nora had always trusted me, about horses at least, and usually tried what I told her. Simon would watch us while we talked, and once said, "You're the only person she listens to."

Nora and I talked over ideas the way we had as kids. Not regular conversations, but more like tossing around thoughts with her in my own head, like two voices in one mind.

When she got that terrible cold in November, she came out to the barn with great dark circles under her eyes and her skin as pale as a salmon's before it dies. I wanted to put my hand on her shoulder for a moment to steady her; I wanted to pick her up and carry her to a bed of hay for her to rest on until she was fully well. But even those thoughts of comfort made me more guilty about our brief loss of control the day before.

"You don't look so good," I told her instead.

"I didn't want to leave all this for you." She turned her palms up and shrugged.

"I'm used to taking care of business by myself, you know."

She gave me a funny look then, like I'd said something to hurt her, and went back up to the house.

Now, Zad hated bits. I'd known people who with horses like that would've tried a snaffle just to give them more of what they hated and to show them who was boss. But Nora used a hackamore and sometimes not even that. She'd get on Zad bareback, grab a handful of mane, and take off across the pasture at full tilt like they were both suddenly possessed.

Riding Zad for the first time, I could tell right off how smart and precocious she was, hardly needing the hackamore to guide her. But then, when she had proved she could do all I asked, she broke gait and danced sideways, throwing her head back and turning in a circle, stiffening her front legs and kicking out quickly with her rear. For a moment she caught me off balance, the change was so sudden, and I didn't react the way I would've with any other mount. Zad was Nora's, and I did not want to kick or tug or dominate in any way that might hurt her.

In the second I let her have her way, she bolted forward and threw me. My foot caught in the stirrup and she dragged me after her across the pasture. My head slapped against the ground, and I started having flashbacks from the war, of bombs sending sprays of dirt and bodies flying.

I yelled "Whoa," but she rolled her eyes back and kept

going. Nora had taught her crazy commands that she and Simon decided on as a game, Arabian words that sounded like nonsense to me. While my back was being dragged raw, the translation wouldn't come. I started yelling every combination of sounds I could think of that sounded Arab until I accidentally got it right. She stopped immediately and looked back at me, her gray eyes curious like she was wondering what the hell I was doing on the ground.

Mad that some headstrong animal who couldn't even understand English had beat me, I walked her to the barn and got a bridle with a bit. She fought me, but I backed her against a stall, got it in, and rode her out, holding the reins hard so she would know I had her number. She never bucked or bolted with me again, and I never told Simon or Nora that she'd thrown me or that I'd abused her. I didn't want to lose the bond I had, this feeling of family for the first time in my life.

But with the deaths of Simon and Zad, I lost it anyway. I watched helpless as Neal Mahler beat Nora down just as surely as a bad rider will take a crop to a horse until welts rise and blood wells up. Then somehow this seemed another kind of war, but one too subtle and confusing to know how to fight. She was his wife. But I wanted his place with her, and that covetousness made suspect everything I did for her or against him.

The evening of Simon's death, I went up to the house, but Neal Mahler blocked the doorway like he would stop me from entering, by force if necessary. When I asked how Nora was doing, he said she was out of control and had to be heavily sedated. I doubted that, I wanted to argue. But after all, he'd been with her and spoken to the doctors. Swayed by the memory of how I'd brought Zad under control when I thought she needed it, I gave him the benefit of the doubt.

I should have figured that he would destroy the horse. A life for a life. But I dismissed the thought until I heard the shot and came running out of the barn. Her eyes rolled back, her legs twitched, and the ground under her turned black. Seeing her ruined was almost worse than watching a man die, since there was no war or politics or anything but Neal Mahler's meanness that had caused this sacrifice of a creature so fine.

He turned as I came out and raised the gun barrel slightly. Just that triggered the adrenaline, the old thoughtless instinct to kill, and I started toward him with a pitchfork in my hands. There seemed nothing more right and natural in that moment than running him through and leaving his body pinned next to hers.

"Damned horse killed my son," he said.

I hesitated enough to think—how I'd killed some Nazis with more force and satisfaction than called for, just to get back for the death of a buddy. But this wasn't a war and this man was not the enemy. He lowered the shotgun and nodded toward the pitchfork.

"What'd you think? That the Germans were coming after you?"

What had I thought? That I'd kill Neal Mahler and that would set everything right again?

"I heard you veterans sometimes get crazy when you hear loud noises," he said, nodding.

Then he told me to drag Zad's corpse down to the river and let it rot. He said he hoped the crows ate out her eyes and the river carried the rest away for the fishes.

I lowered the pitchfork and wondered how much of my anger against him came from wanting his wife.

When I hooked the tractor chains around Zad, she was still warm and the quarter-sized holes behind her eye looked too small and neat to have taken all her life from her. I felt shamed obeying Neal Mahler like that, for backing down because I didn't want Nora to see what he'd done. I ran my hands over the horse's coat, and as I touched her, Simon's death, which had been too immense until that moment to comprehend, came crashing around me.

I towed her down the bluff, sorry all the while that I had no other way but to drag her roughly. I buried her with a defiance that was small consolation for all the other ways Neal Mahler had it over me.

The ground was soft and easy to dig out after all the rain and the river coming up, and I dug as deep as I could. But when I rolled her in, the broken side of her face turned up to me, the raw exit wound so much more truthful of his act than the small neat places the bullets had entered. Then I cried over her like I never had over Simon or the boys killed beside me. Not that I mourned her more, but it seemed safer to cry over a damned horse instead of those I might never stop crying for.

I beat the ground over her with the flat of the shovel. Then I walked to the riverbank and threw the shovel turning like a whirligig far over the swollen water. I was disgusted with Neal Mahler and what Nora let him do to her. With the fact that I knew how to be a soldier in battle but not a man in the regular world.

When Mahler told me to hitch up the trailer and take the boarders to their new stables and Nora's other horses to the auction barn, I told him to take care of it his damn self. I just wanted to get away from that place which reminded me how I had had no power to protect the two people I loved. At the last minute before driving off after the funeral, I whistled to Simon's dog, Bandit, to jump in the truck because I didn't want any living thing left in Neal Mahler's path, not if I could help it.

Sometimes when I was getting off to sleep and the dog would sneak beside me in the bed, I'd think what a sorry ass I was, wanting a woman and ending up with a dog. But I liked him against me, with his own warmth and movement and heartbeat. A living creature who counted on me.

I wondered if any of the excuses I'd given myself for leaving were true. They sounded good, all that crap about it not being my business what a man did with his wife and not being able to help her anyway. But especially on days when I'd been driving too long in circles around the place I was supposed to be, or on nights where I was glad of even the dog's company, I thought of what I should have done instead. Taken Nora's hands in mine and told her how I loved her.

But I could not fathom the next step. My desire which consumed me even at a distance seemed too great to ever bear at close and constant quarters. How would I live with and take care of her? How would I let her love me? I trembled with the idea of love that seemed the same as being ripped open and hollowed out, my guts unwound and left exposed for flies and crows and Nora to rearrange however she chose.

I kept driving. Far from Nora who would find me out. Far from Simon's death which seemed also the death of the boy I'd been, the one almost brave enough to at least think about claiming Nora as his own.

She was better off without me. I knew that. She'd be fine by herself, just as she had been all the years I was without her.

CHAPTER ELEVEN

Nora Mahler

FOR TWO MONTHS AFTER Simon died, I wouldn't leave the farm. I just wanted to stay quiet in the center of the land where my family had lived for seventy years, as if I couldn't yet bear to leave the last place Simon had been until I healed a little more.

With my children and the horses gone, I had no work. We used only the pastureland, renting out the crop fields to neighbors. But my grandmother Grace had run a full-fledged operation. She bred and trained horses, managed the finances, and planted the land. She got out in the fields with her skirts tucked up and worked along with the three hired hands, who at her funeral stood grizzled and old by her grave and wept like babies.

When Grace was widowed, she'd had three children under age five. She might have gone on having a baby every year or so until she reached menopause or exhaustion. She might have died in childbed as many women did. But a blood vessel in her husband's brain exploded before these possibilities could. A year after that, Frankie, her oldest, lived through the first strike of diphtheria and survived into the pneumonic stage. Everyone, including the doctor and Grace's family in Boston, was afraid of contagion. For ten days she stayed alone on the farm nursing Frankie and hoping her other two babies remained immune.

Her mother and cousins and aunts wrote, saying how they wished they could be with her during this terrible time. But their doctors had advised against it because of age or fragile health or commitments to their own families. Grace kept their letters with the later notes of condolence tied with a black ribbon and never had anything to do with her family again. She buried Frankie alongside her husband in a little cemetery down toward the river and went on.

When her second son, Charlie, was six and playing in a wooded area near the barn, he was accidentally shot by deer hunters who had ignored Grace's NO TRESPASSING signs. They later told the sheriff they hadn't thought she'd really meant for them to stay off her land. That was considered apology enough and the end of the matter, except for Grace who thereafter carried a rifle while she walked the perimeter of her farm. Twice others came on the property, and she aimed close enough to remove any doubts that she was serious about those signs. On Charlie's tombstone she had carved a fawn.

The last child, my mother, Margaret, called Maggie, grew up and married a man she believed would protect her as fiercely as Grace did, and maybe better because he was a man. But he could not stop the deaths of all the tiny embryos and almost-big-enough fetuses that they had created between them, not any more than Grace had been able to keep Frankie or Charlie alive. But finally I was born in an upstairs room of the farmhouse, on the mattress marked with old brown spots of blood.

By the time I knew Grace, she was like a great old cow, her hair braided up in loops. In her last years she walked with a cane for her arthritis and, when not with the horses, kept mostly to the sleeping porch, which she had claimed for herself. When she and my father met on the stairs or in the hall, they squared off like two rams ready to fight. My father always gave her right-of-way, I'm sure because she was an old woman and he wanted to be known as polite. But he always hesitated a second too long as if he could not quite bring himself to let her pass.

Grace's directions for her funeral were simple. No wake, plain box, much liquor. The house was full after her burial, and neighbors one by one stepped forward to tell what they remembered. The first testimonials were polite tributes to her good deeds, skill at raising horses, and accurate marksmanship. By the third fifth of Wild Turkey the stories were more about her quick wit and acid tongue and no-nonsense nature. People were laughing so loud that Simon inside me kicked and turned the whole afternoon.

I thought of Grace and Simon often while I was in the mental hospital the summer after his death. "St. Louis," Neal always called it, as if I'd gone to the Chase Park Plaza for high tea and not to Arsenal Street, that big wedge of building with barred windows and locked doors. Where the inmates drifted in their own separateness as if each saw the ward as a different kind of jungle or desert, existing in a time before the other drifters had been born. When I arrived, a few stared after me, a strange intruder in their private landscapes. I was pushed past in a wheelchair like a tourist overcome by her exotic surroundings.

At first I had no expectations. Neal and the doctor had sat on either side of my bed at home, Neal holding my hand while they told me about the arrangements. My mother leaned against the window frame and looked out over the yard. All I could see were a few squares of gray sky and the ends of the mulberry branches bouncing in the wind of a coming rain. The men had made time at Arsenal sound like a vacation or long lovely nap. They told me everything would be taken care of and I would come home a new woman. I didn't know what to say except that I was all right. After all, it was too soon to feel good.

But they said I'd been under too much stress and the plans had all been made. "A rest can't hurt you," Neal told me.

My mother didn't say anything. She didn't even look up as she packed a few of my things in a small case to take, so I thought she agreed and maybe even had helped them plan.

It all went so fast, like a precision fire drill that had been practiced to evacuate the victim quickly. We were across the bridge and miles down the Rock Road before I began sorting through what had happened at the house. It had been almost like those tableaux we used to present for the nuns at Christmas, the curtain rising on Mary holding a doll Jesus, the expression and draperies arranged just so. Almost like the earnest faces on a *Saturday Evening Post* cover, the kindly doctor making a call. He and Neal had convinced me I simply needed a rest from the upset of Simon's death.

But those other upsets—Zad and the drugs and Neal's coldness—came sifting back to me during the ride. The familiar road was hazy with heat and practically empty as if the humidity had made the air too dense for anyone to move about.

A muggy breeze whipped my hair into snaky tendrils, the hot air blowing dirt around the car. We passed lots strung with flags and the Steak n Shake where people ate from silver trays attached to auto windows. Neal sat unmoving, his profile like a head on a coin and his knuckles like lines of neat mountains on the curve of the steering wheel.

When had I said yes to this journey?

"Pull over," I told him.

"Why? Are you sick? If you're sick, hold it until you get out of the car." He swerved into a parking lot and leaned across me to open the door.

I watched his hand turn the silver handle and stared at the hairs on the back of his arm. I read VENT printed on two latches sticking out like fingers from under the dash. I counted the buttons on the radio. All things seemed distinct and disconnected, especially myself from Neal.

"Are you going to throw up or not?" he asked.

"I want to go home."

"You're not sick?" he said.

"No, I'm not sick."

"You said you were sick."

"No, you said. I just want to go home."

"You already said you're going to the other place. They're expecting you."

"I don't think I said, exactly."

"Well," Neal said, "you implied it. What would we tell them if we didn't arrive?"

I stared out the front window at a woman struggling to carry a huge basket of dirty clothes into a Laundromat. As she shouted to her two kids to stay with her, they ran into the parking lot, and a car screeched to a halt. She dropped the basket, spilling sheets and underwear to the ground, then ran grabbing and swinging at her sons.

"I told you never to run away from me," she shouted as the kids howled and tucked in their rears.

"Well," Neal said, "if you're not sick, we better get going."

He glanced over at me, his hand resting on the gearshift. I had another of those moments where I could swear I had never really seen him before. Then he reached across the back of the seat to squeeze my shoulder.

"Don't be like this, Nora," he said. "You've had a bad time of it, but when you get back, we can start over just like it was in the beginning."

His hand still touched my shoulder. I wanted him to be right.

"I mean well," he said softly. "You know that."

I don't know what made me believe him then. Habit, I suppose. Desire that it might be so, or the relief of his approval. Maybe only gratitude that he cared. I didn't say, "All right, go on," but simply closed the door and leaned against it, staring out at the woman kneeling on the sidewalk and stuffing her laundry back in the basket as Neal pulled past.

When he left me at Arsenal, I still had not thought clearly about what might be coming. His words had left me with the vague idea that I was going to a spa or special kind of hotel where I'd be helped through my recovery, or at least left alone to rest. But the attendants took my clothes and all my belongings, and when I asked about this, they told me it was the rules. I was still too polite to argue as they wheeled me past the double lockup and the women lost in their visions, one reaching up under her dress to touch herself.

I lay down on my bed when they told me to, all the while

thinking that I did not belong here. I lay flat with my hands over my chest while they took my temperature and medical history, and even the next morning when they came in to tie me, did not do more than pull my hands away.

"You behave," the largest orderly said, squeezing my wrist hard.

I twisted my hand up between her index finger and thumb, breaking her grip for a moment, and kicked my legs so the other attendant could not get hold of my feet. I kept telling them that I shouldn't be here and they had no right to do this.

"Stop it now or else," I told them.

Then one of the practical nurses came in, said "Oh lordy," and threw herself flat on top of me. She was big, maybe two hundred pounds, and had that sickly sweet smell that fat people have in the heat. With all her weight on my diaphragm I couldn't breathe or kick or yank my hands free. Movement became heavy and slow as it does in a dream.

"Now you just be still," she said. "We have to take you for treatment, and it won't do if your hands and feet are flying around."

She lay there like a white mountain over me, her arms wide to help hold my arm and leg, and sweat formed on the hot places between us where we touched. She was too massive to be quite human, wrestling me like a calf to hog-tie. She lay there while the others finished and stayed just in case while they gave me the injections.

"Give her extra so we won't have any more trouble," she told them.

"I don't want any," I told them.

"Double dose to keep you quiet," she said.

Then they left me alone in the ward with the pale sick

walls and shiny black grating crossing in diamond shapes across the windows. I was heavy with the drugs swimming hot through my veins. So weighty I let my head fall to one side so my vision filled with rows of beds with mounds of patients thrown down like scoops of mashed potatoes. On the other side (my head so heavy and detached it was like being inside a rolled medicine ball) a woman stood with her back in a corner, her gray hair wild and spiky. She kept talking low to herself and backing up more into the corner as if she wanted to climb through the line where the green walls met. Through the windowed door to the hallway, a face drifted beyond the black diamonds, its eyes like hollow disks of metal shining.

That was all I saw before I spread out like thick oil, and an orange tree hung with red monkeys came floating by. I kept spreading until I lay flat and broad like the land. Corn grew on the high ground of my breasts and beans from my fingers. Squash leaves curled around my toes, the roots webbing down like veins and arteries.

Simon fed off berries picked from my belly. The juice stained his lips black and ran down his chin in red streaks. He put his arm around Clea and placed one berry on her tongue like a Communion wafer. I wanted to shout, "Be careful, it might be poisoned." But the drugs kept me from making a sound, no matter how I fought to warn the children. Then Grace appeared and began feeding first Simon, then Clea. I felt her voice inside me, like a soft chirring.

"What's wrong, Nora? The children must eat. They can't live if they don't eat."

Then the attendants came again. As I was being wheeled to the end of the hall, the ceiling lights passing over me like channel markers, I was sure Simon and Clea and Grace had been there with more substance than any of the white mounds in the beds or the gray woman in the corner. I wanted to tell the attendants that it was all right now—better—I could go home, not that I ever needed to be here in the first place. Almost funny, how I was wound like a half-wrapped mummy, bound in the sheets with long strips around my wrists and ankles and wheeled on this cart when I could walk.

"You can let me go now," I told them.

They didn't say anything. They parted my hair, wiped bare scalp with alcohol, shockingly cool, and taped metal wires to my head. I kept asking what they were doing, and the nurse said, "It's all right. This will make you better."

When she tried to jam the thick rubber between my teeth, I thrashed back and forth, but they pried my mouth open and forced it in.

"Don't fight us, honey," the nurse said. "This is for your own good."

When I woke, I felt scooped out like they had taken melon ballers and trowels and serving spoons to scrape me empty, and I panicked at not knowing where I was. I could not feel Grace or Clea or Simon near. Could not remember them. Could not even feel myself.

For the next few days, I lay very still as if I were caught at the instant I had been exploded, just before all the pieces of myself flew off at random. I slept dreamless and, even when awake, felt flat and endless. Food had no taste or texture, all the world slept in a still hump, and I was terrified at finding myself unknowing as a baby.

Logic told me that nothing, as this was pure nothing, should not hurt as it did. But this emptiness and its seeming permanence was like finding myself in a place where life had been suspended and creation could not take place.

What started to come back first was the faraway time. Just random fragments. Grace teaching me when I was seven how to peel an apple without breaking the long curl of skin and laughing in delight when I succeeded. A fish in a coloring book that I'd done in pink with a black outline around each scale. My mare turning to watch me every summer morning when I was twelve, as I saddled her to ride down to the lower pastures so quiet and clean in the early fog that I felt like Sacajawea.

Then thoughts of Ozzie and the three years we had been with each other as kids. His upper lip curving in a beautiful rise. His face brightening as he walked toward me. His touch like first spring air on my bare legs.

For whole evenings and entire afternoons we could stay as quiet as I was now, only we had been completely content in our stillness. Even when we kissed and touched in ways that made us so frantic with desire that we could barely stay in our clothes, our peace with each other remained in the center of all that lovely turmoil.

How easy with him to be thoughtlessly myself and cherished for that. Never editing what I would tell him, never hiding any feeling. Our moments came back separate and distinct in themselves, unfolding into the space left by the treatment. The memories bright, shining and whole, smoothed perfect by time. Like someone else's life that I was borrowing to fill up my present nothingness. I stayed lost and happy in its company.

When Maggie came to visit in the dayroom, I didn't know her for the first few seconds. She bent over me and held my face in her hands until I focused.

"It's your mother," she said.

"Of course," I told her as if I'd just remembered the forgotten answer on a history quiz.

Then she wheeled away, and a voice came from the hallway that sounded just like Grace.

"I don't give a tinker's damn," it said, and I pictured Grace stamping her foot. But Grace was dead, and I couldn't make any more sense of it than that.

I could do nothing more than a rabbit that freezes at the sound of steps or a mouse when it hears a cat. I had figured that much out at least, that when I was quiet they left me alone. I forced down the tapioca and Jell-O cubes. I rolled to one side and then the other when the fat nurse changed my sheets. I even managed to smile stupidly when she praised me for being a good girl. To please her was easy, so much easier than fighting. It felt good and familiar, even though it was fake.

They released me from the hospital a few days later. I supposed because I had been so obedient. Maggie came to sign my papers and drive me quietly home. I liked that. I didn't feel like talking. The animals, except for the barn cats, were gone. Neal was with Clea in town. Thistle and Queen Anne's lace dotted the fields, the whole farm stilled except for the buzz of summer insects. When Maggie came to check on me in my room, I closed my eyes and feigned sleep. I told her I didn't feel like coming down for meals quite yet, or going for walks since it was so hot. She told me to take my time.

"It's no good for walking out there anyway," she said. "The river's so high that the moccasins are coming up along with the water. We're fifteen feet over flood stage with no sign of cresting."

I asked to see Clea, but Neal had left word that the doctor advised us to wait a few weeks. I asked why Neal hadn't come to visit, and Maggie said he didn't want to upset me. I said that was ridiculous.

"It's all been ridiculous," she said as she rearranged the water glass and pitcher on my bedside table.

"When I came to visit, I expected to see you pampered and resting, not shell-shocked. When I asked what they'd done to you, they all said you were out of your mind and it's what they had to do. But while I was waiting to talk to your doctor, a nurse pulled me aside and told me she thought the treatment much too severe.

"She said you'd just had the first of a series that would take months. That you'd be more docile than a lamb when they were done. 'And more mindless,' she said. I asked her why they would do such a thing if it wasn't necessary. 'To stop her from making fusses,' she told me.

"I drove straight to Neal's office and asked him if he knew what the treatments would do to you. He said they were to make you feel better, that the nurse didn't know what she was talking about. I told him if he saw you after just one of those things, then he could never allow another."

She smiled slightly as she adjusted the window shades to exactly the same position.

"I was scared, Nora, arguing with him like that. For forty minutes we went on. But it was as if I saw you standing in front of a speeding car and ran to grab you without thinking."

"He just didn't understand," I told her. "Doctors never tell you what they're going to do."

"He showed me a magazine the doctor had given him.

About how the shock can help major depression. But it also said how the patients can have loss of memory and not know who they are."

"Neal was just trying to help. He didn't know."

"He should be able to tell the difference between depression and grieving," she said. "In his own wife, at least."

She folded my robe over the back of the chair and patted down the creases.

"You rest now," she said, and left the room.

But the next few weeks I lay in bed, feeling battered and sad and sometimes furious. I turned over all the bits and pieces I could remember since I'd straightened up out of the garden and saw Clea riding across the pasture like the devil was on her tail. I cried because I would never again touch or speak with Simon, and I felt his absence as a constant, physical ache. I was angry that I could not punish the force that had caused his death, could not get my hands around its neck and make it spit back my child before I choked it.

But I also got tired of lying in bed and sick of the same room. I drifted around the downstairs in my housecoat and got sick of that, too. I finally went out to see how far the flood had come after the last rains and walked the pastures, carrying a stick in case of moccasins that might come at me in the fields with their white mouths open. I could not bring myself to go back down the trail where we had carried Simon, but I went to another spot nearby that overlooked the bottoms land. The river stretched out so wide that the treetops had become little bushes.

Neal was always arrogant about the river. I'd told him you couldn't control it, but he'd always said that if the Corps of Engineers just put in a few more levees, a dam here or there, then floods would be stopped forever like they were in the Tennessee Valley. Every year since we were married he'd said that, except the five flood years when he could only talk about insurance and the fools who wouldn't get it.

I stood on the edge of the bluff where I could see water to the horizon. Not a quick strike like a tornado or an ice storm, but patient, relentless, and firm in how it reclaimed what had been taken from it, in how it had settled and stayed.

Maggie and I went out each morning and scouted for cottonmouths in the flower beds and in the weeds around the fence posts and in the high pasture grass. Unlike the other snakes who had moved to high ground with the flood, they were poisonous and aggressive and needed to be removed. We wore boots, thick gloves, and carried a large covered basket. I draped the snakes I found through the teeth of a long rake, though they often slipped off before I could drop them in the basket. She pinned hers with a hoe, then grabbed them at the base of their skulls.

"Grace taught me how to do this," she said. "We never killed our snakes."

"Ozzie was so quick he didn't even need the hoe. Just grabbed them. Simon, too."

"I remember," she said, not looking up from the snake she held.

Then she and I hauled the basket to the johnboat tethered halfway up the steps that led from the backyard down to where the riverbank used to be. I rowed out a bit, and she upended the basket off the bow, pushing the snakes with a paddle out into the current that would send them downstream.

"I suppose we could just cut off their heads," she said, "but Grace always said even snakes have their purpose in this world."

I watched them swim off, black S's. Then she and I went back to eat lunch on the porch where it was shady and cooler. We stared out at the pattern of leaf dapples across the grass and the swinging bars of sun moved by branches in the breeze. We set out what was left of the horse feed for the fleeing deer and dog food for the foxes. We napped, we read, we barely spoke. After we'd cleaned up the dinner dishes, we sat again on the porch and rocked and stared at fireflies until we were ready for bed.

The water got so high that the road went under. Neighbors to the east of us came in their johnboats, dragging them up on the high ground of our yard. Then one of the men, usually Jim Richardson, took all our grocery and pharmacy orders and drove the tractor a mile through the two-foot-deep water to where the road reemerged again. More neighbors there picked him up and took him into town to shop, then returned him to relay the supplies back to those of us who had suddenly become islanders.

At first their presence was abrasive, but after a few days I began to look forward to their coming. While we waited, the men talked to me about how the silt brought by the flood would make the land more fertile, though they'd have to work like the devil to harrow out the new weeds. The women, released from daily routine, visited on the porch while Maggie and I served lemonade, and no one mentioned Simon.

Daily I phoned Clea, who was full of chatter about her job. I talked to Neal as often, but he said even if the water went down and the road cleared, the farm was too dangerous for her. She might be bitten by a snake or might get depressed by the memories. I was not quite up to arguing with him and let it be, though I could see the confrontation coming as if it were number three or four on a list of things I must do in order, once I decided to start.

In mid-August as the water began to recede, I got out Simon's things that Maggie had helped me pack earlier in the summer. His letter jacket and photographs, a striped rock, an old dog collar—things of no value except that they were Simon's. I opened a journal he'd kept sporadically since grade school. But the sight of his handwriting—the line "*Mom and I went down to the river this afternoon to talk*" and the fact that I didn't remember that particular day or what we'd said—made me shaky and queasy. I closed the book, and not knowing what I had expected to learn from his belongings, I packed them all away again.

The next week Maggie and I painted over the beige walls of his room with blue and did the woodwork in white enamel. She made new curtains from flowered feed sacks and got out one of Grace's quilts for the bed. We put the furniture back in a different arrangement and hung different pictures on the wall. She said she liked the room but didn't move from the sleeping porch where Grace used to stay.

Two days after we finished, I opened the barn doors and stall windows. I walked around the tack room, fingering bits and stirrups and cinches, knocking cobwebs on my way. For a long time, I sat on a bale of hay and stared past the dimness of the barn to the bright pasture beyond where the noon sun made the grass look green-white.

I knew it made no sense, but I had almost expected Ozzie to be there. At least to feel his old presence, the way I had at the hospital, and the old comfort I hadn't even realized came with him being near. I thought of him in the past year—leading a horse into the paddock or working over a hoof. Just being around to talk to and keep me company.

I remembered him with Simon, their heads bent over Zad as they groomed her, or Ozzie in the ring calling suggestions to Simon as they trained, or the two of them riding off across the pasture. Then the images broke loose into Simon and Zad falling, as if I had watched from a mile's distance and in that imagined moment was forever too far away to stop their falling.

I thought how Grace and Maggie had both gone on after the deaths of their children, and I felt like a baby. To move in any way seemed the last thing I wanted, though I knew it was what I must do. I wanted Clea. I wanted to go on, I thought.

But when I called Neal to ask him and Clea to move back with me, he said he had good news, that he'd taken a promotion in Chicago and was moving soon. I didn't know what to say at first, but then it came to me.

"No, you can't," I told him.

"That's not the issue," he said.

"We have to talk about this."

"I've already accepted."

I didn't want to, but I started to cry, and my fragile peace broke away. I told him I'd stay on the farm no matter what, but he said that was an issue we'd have to discuss. Then he explained that he'd had the joint checking account closed.

"The banker asked if you were incompetent," he said. "What could I tell him, except that at the time you were."

"Then tell him different, change it back."

"You don't want to be bothered with all this now, do you, Nora? Wait a bit and I'll give you money in the meantime."

"I'm fine, I'm ready now."

But I wasn't sure, especially since the banker had agreed with Neal and the doctor that I wasn't as well as I seemed to myself.

I could hear Neal stirring on the other end of the line, his chair scraping against the floor.

"You have to move eventually," he said.

"What?" I said.

"Now, since we're making changes, I've talked to a realtor and he thinks we can get a good price for the farm."

"But you haven't talked to me," I told him.

"I have to go where the work is. You want to eat, don't you?"

"We've always eaten, damn it, and you have work here. Those are not the parts that are different."

I stopped shouting and broke into tears again. I couldn't help it. He let me cry until I wore myself down to small sobs.

"I'm worried about you, Nora," he said. "How easily you get upset. It makes me think I was wrong to let Maggie talk me out of going through with your treatment."

I didn't answer.

"If this goes on," he said, "we'll have to reconsider what would be best for you."

"Bastard," I said.

I slammed down the receiver and stood shaking over the phone. Maggie came in from hanging up wash. Slightly damp and smelling clean like wet laundry, she put her arms around me. I rested my head on her shoulder as I had not done since I was a little girl, and I let her hold me just above the panic of these next things coming.

I wanted Oz to talk this over with, but I didn't know where he'd gone. I wanted to tell him I was tired of being a stranger and an enemy. That much I knew. Worn out with it, as if for the first time I'd noticed how much effort it had taken all these years to keep out of Neal Mahler's way and how dangerous it was to stay near him.

The next morning, before ten, a woman came to the door. She was dressed in a short-sleeved navy suit with a cluster of plaster cherries pinned to the lapel, and she held out her business card to me before I could ask who she was.

"Your husband asked me to come by to look at the property so we could agree on an asking price."

I just kept staring at her and then down to the card which read "Mid-West Realty."

"If it's too much trouble for you to show me around," she said, "I can just go through the house and around the grounds by myself. It won't take long."

"No," I said finally.

"I can come back, if it's a bad time."

"No."

She looked flustered but didn't move until I stepped out on the porch. I didn't even realize what I was doing, coming at her, only that she took a step back for every one I took forward.

"Get out," I told her. "You don't belong here. I don't want you on my land."

I chased her halfway across the yard. After she drove off, I stood and watched the dust from her car drift up and over the pasture, the white billow finally disappearing into the still, hot air.

I felt sick to my stomach, not only because of what Neal was up to, but because of how I'd reacted without thinking.

Like some madwoman who had lived too long and unhappily by herself.

I wanted to do over the encounter with the realtor. To politely explain the situation between Neal and myself. To walk her quietly to her car. To convince her that I was not crazy for wanting to keep what I loved.

Anything, so Neal could not use this against me.

Fall

Now it dawns on me that I have been
not just one man but several
And that I have died so many times
with no notion of how I was reborn.

—Pablo Neruda

from "Return to a City" by Pablo Neruda

Chapter Twelve

Ozzie Kline

ALL CHEAP MOTELS were the same, and that sameness erased time for a while after I left LaCote. I always dated time from polestars, from things so out of the ordinary that I remembered them clearly. Before or after Simon died, for instance. Before or after I saw Nora like a refugee. But the nondescript rooms flattened time to one long gray string reeling out until I usually couldn't remember what day or week it was, and memory got drowned in the monotony.

But during all that driving, thoughts started ricocheting around, and images of Nora riding Zad or Simon lying dead snuck in anyhow. I wanted to push them away, not to mention that I got sick of being by myself. At the little restaurants in the towns I passed through, I began striking up conversations to counteract the fact that my only companion was a dog.

Getting people going was hard, though, and that brought me back again to thoughts of Nora. A few days after I'd started work at Mahlers' the year before, she'd come in the barn, leaving the stall door open like she was expecting the butler to come along behind and close it. She used to have that way of walking when she was a girl, exaggerated by the fact she usually wore riding boots. I liked seeing it again after all these years, the way she swung her hips and stepped hard and seemed to know exactly where she was going.

Anyhow, she picked up the brush and began running it across Zad's side, at first leaving slight furrows straight across from withers to croup, then swooping up and down so they rose and dipped like the jet stream on a weather map. She stood back, admiring the faint design like it was finger painting, and I started laughing at her.

"What's so funny?" she said like she didn't already know.

"You might as well hang that horse on an easel."

"Don't have to. She stands up by herself."

Nora ran her hands over Zad's side and smoothed out the ridges. Ran her hand all the way along Zad's back to her tail, following the contours like a wind over slopes and rises.

"You used to draw." She stood leaning against the horse. "Before we really knew each other."

Then she grinned and cocked her head like that was all she needed to say. But I hadn't thought of drawing in ages.

"That right?" I said, lame as usual.

"C'mon, Oz. Once when I first knew you, you showed me a sketch you'd done of a satyr in thick, shiny crayon. I couldn't believe it."

"Couldn't believe I'd know what a satyr was?"

She waved her hand like she was erasing that part of the conversation. "I told you how good you were."

"I'd just copied it straight from a fountain at the St. Louis

Art Museum. I was never good at drawing the way I was with horses."

"But it was so good, and that was the first time we talked about anything other than riding."

"Then it served its purpose."

I winked like a sleazy pick-up artist.

"That's hard, you know, knowing the first thing to say." She twisted a strand of Zad's mane absently around her finger. "When I was pregnant, people—strangers—came up to me on the street or in stores all the time. They would ask how I was feeling or how long I had to go or if I wanted a girl or a boy. They could look at me and see right off the most important thing in my life then, and that made it easy for them to know where to start."

Then Nora looked up like she was waiting for me to say one of those first new things to her. When I was on the road, the memory of that tripped a wire that opened old places in me, and I'd catch myself sketching for the first time in years. Usually just pieces. It always started like that. The foreleg and hoof of an Arabian, the rump and tail. Then Zad's face, big-eyed like a pretty baby. Then a baby, perhaps Simon, and Nora pregnant.

I'd been away and could only guess what shape she'd been then. Young and slender, but big in the belly. Wearing a loose blouse like an artist's smock, and flats so she wouldn't fall or throw her back out. I tried to picture her to draw, but she kept turning into a mare walking toward me, her belly round and distended, with the same bulk and sway as a donkey loaded with baskets for pack work.

I still wanted this Nora. Wanted to crawl back through

time so that I could lay my hands on her belly, if she let me, and feel the baby kick inside. So that I could warn her that unless she made changes, this child would not live as long as we wanted him to.

I kept trying to draw her. Then I'd get a little crazy with regret and have to go out before the motel walls started closing in or the place where I was camping got filled with too much of nothing. At the diners I sketched the waitresses or other customers on napkins, then handed them the portraits. Sometimes they just looked confused and walked away. But mostly they liked it, especially if I flattered them a bit. Then they'd start talking, usually about their families, and I'd tell them back about mine.

I never said my grandparents only tolerated each other and the house we lived in smelled of onions and mold. That my mother ignored all the many things she couldn't deal with, including her husband. That my father beat me until I was seventeen and I moved out. Instead I made them into anybody I was in the mood for, usually heroic little people that in no time became more clear and familiar than the people I'd actually lived with.

Then one night, walking home alone from a diner and goosed by too much caffeine, I stopped in a park and sat on a bench. I knew I had to get back to take out the dog, but I couldn't face the room. I was middle-aged and feeling sorry for myself. Out of sorts and out of time.

The moonlight made the park, the bushes, my shoes even, silver and beautiful, the exact opposite of my dingy, ugly mood. I sat there on that bench and thought of my father. Not the way I'd just invented him for the truck driver I'd been drinking coffee with, but as my father really had been before he died of cancer. Skinny like an old doll without stuffing, his lap flat and arms limp by his sides. I raised my hand the way I remembered him trying to and wondered what it would be like to have the power go out of every muscle until I couldn't even raise my chest to breathe the air right under my nose.

Back at the room, the dog threw himself belly up at my feet. I rubbed my fingers deep into his coat and thought how the ghost of Nora's touch might still be there. Such a sorry bastard I was. I picked up an old tennis ball and whistled to him. We went over to an empty lot across the street, and I threw the ball as hard as I could, yelling at Bandit to go get it. He went tearing off, only slowing when he got to the patch of shadow where the ball had bounced and disappeared. I didn't know where it'd gone, the edges of the silver field a deep black only an owl could see through. But the dog smelled around and eventually came trotting back, dropping the ball at my feet. I threw it again, half curious if he could keep retrieving in the dark. After twenty minutes he lay down a few feet away with the ball between his paws, a dog on strike with his tongue hanging out in a slobbery pant.

I lay back next to him in the grass to stare up at the sky. So late and quiet I seemed the last man on earth, or maybe Adam before the others, the earth solid under my back, like I'd been in motion so long I'd forgotten anything could be that still.

Once when Nora and I were seventeen, we had lain on the football field like this. At the sock hop I'd taken her by the hand to slow dance, the dance only an excuse to hold her. But too many people were around, and I kept leading her past them, looking for a little space, and ended up out of the gym instead. She didn't ask where we were going, down the tiled corridor, past kids hanging out in the parking lot or leaning against cars along the street. I didn't find a place for us until we got to the stadium and stood in the middle of that big field.

Hours earlier half of LaCote had been screaming in the stands. But now it was quiet and more deserted than the side streets that the cops patrolled to catch kids parking, and dark, though not so we couldn't see each other. We lay down on the fifty-yard line, right at the center point, and she settled against me. It seemed like we'd left the town far away, and we laughed about how if all of LaCote went looking for us at that moment, the last place they would think of was where we were.

We might have talked for a while, but if we did, I can't recall what about—only that she and I were in the same happy, defiant mood we always got in when there was nothing put between us. We lay as solid against each other as the ground under us. Just Nora and me completely.

Hardly ever do two lovers meet with their whole selves, just that alone. Like the two of them were made in the moment before and are so innocent they don't know there is a moment after or anything else in creation. I don't know how to say it. How only once in a while it's like being wide awake and both of you at once. Like feeling the blood moving through her veins and yours.

In all my life, it's been like that only with Nora, most specially on that night when we were seventeen. All contradictions dissolved for as long as she was turned to me and I could touch her hair and lips and breasts. The two of us perfectly grounded, but also risen so high that all else fell away like black space.

Maybe that was the problem with her. Moments too good to be hoped for. Accidents. Flukes. Magic. Nothing I was in charge of or could have reproduced on a regular basis. We could have gone against her father, but I never believed I would have lived up to what Frank Rhymer demanded, or she, through him, had come to expect. Not even to what I wanted to give because I loved her and she deserved it.

I never got over her, and no other woman had ever been enough. But on that summer night, lying under the moon with the dog's breathing keeping time, I kept trying to convince myself that it had been better to let go of everything between Nora and me—though at the same time I could hardly get my breath, what with the weight of her memory.

After that night, I stopped drawing. I kept thinking I would stay in one place and work, and that this would feel good, the way my last stay in LaCote had until the end. But I always felt like an outsider, and in landlocked towns I couldn't find their centers or get my bearings. I missed how LaCote came up neatly from the Missouri River, with the streets laid out squarely from its unmistakable starting point. I missed how I could stand on the banks and, without moving from my place, feel that I was part of it and all the other rivers connected to it and the lands they touched, all the way to the ocean and beyond.

When I got so lonely I could barely stand it, I looked for a woman to be with. A waitress on the graveyard shift, a horse owner in fancy jodhpurs, a little barfly who didn't want to be by herself. I moved my mouth over their faces and necks, smelling the perfume on their skin—the lilies of the valley and carnations and Chanel—and their dinners and drinks on their breath. I held them, hoping each would weight down my restlessness, at least for the night.

After Nora always sticking out in my life, poking up in

ways I didn't know how to do anything about, I wished for each woman to stay as undistinguishable as the rooms and clearings I slept in. But as I touched and listened, watched their eyes and gestures as they talked and talked, they each became more distinct. The likeness that I'd hoped for was only in that they were all cowed and fearful in some deep part, like horses who'd been broken with force instead of gentled.

I didn't know what a man hit a woman with to break her. But I told the women to listen to me, not whoever had convinced them that they were less than good enough. I'd touch them like I would a foal's nose for the first time, letting them get used to me and praising each part of them as I moved over their bodies.

Then they, too, touched themselves like they had never before felt themselves as lovely. But like with the towns, I never felt at home with them. I always eventually wanted to get away from what in the end made me feel worse than being by myself. I told them stories to ease the hurt of my sudden going, ones that would give them a sweet ache to cherish like a gold locket left behind.

I said I was seriously ill and they'd given me the love to get me through. Or that I longed to stay with them, but my wife was crazy or wouldn't be divorced. Anything that let them think they'd been so special that I wouldn't be able to forget them, that I would have stayed if I could.

They seemed to want that affirmation of their worth and didn't mind me gone before that might be taken back. They cried when I left. But tears to enjoy, I always told myself, the way they'd cry at a movie.

I'd started with the idea of having a woman so unlike Nora that I'd forget her. But they all became her, and what I told them was what I prayed for her to hear. That she was beautiful and strong, that she couldn't be beaten, not by Simon's death or Zad's loss or Neal's meanness.

I told them with the conviction I wanted her to take to herself. I prodded and insisted the way I would have with a horse who was down with the colic. *"Stay there and you'll die, damn it. Get up and walk the kinks out or you'll kill yourself."* I kept saying what Nora needed to hear.

Coming to them and leaving became the small seasons of my life, the cycle always coming back to Nora until one night I was with a girl not much older than Simon. I'd met her at a horse show and shoed her hunter, showed her how to apply handfuls of mud to keep his feet from cracking. Afterward, she hung around, asking questions about hooves. She hugged a post at the mouth of the barn, her leg moving up and down like a cat rubbing against a wall until I could hardly concentrate on the nail I was driving. When I finished the last two horses waiting, she offered to show me the best place to eat. After we stayed talking at the café for three hours, one thing came clear, that the only way this woman was less than me was in her age.

I told her about Nora then, and the girl laughed.

"So why don't you take what you want?"

"I'd have to pay for what I took," I said.

"What could cost more than not having her?" the girl asked.

Then she drove us out past town to a dirt road and the top of a hill that looked out over farmland. The town's lights made the horizon brighter, and I sat staring like a tourist. She pointed out the direction of her house. She slid across the seat to clarify the location, and as she lifted her arm, her breast pressed against me and she slipped into my arms like water.

I'd planned to leave her alone because of her age, but she flowed around me. She took my face in her hands, smiled, and kissed me hard. Something about the parked car brought back times with Nora. Something about the youngness and openness of the girl and that feeling of nothing worth nothing except that we were connected.

I came up for air and asked her, "What about your boyfriend?"

"What about your woman?"

"She's not mine."

"Oh yes, she is," the girl said. "Don't you listen to your own self when you talk?"

I tried to make out her eyes in their mask of shadow but could only see her crooked grin.

"In honor of her," she said. "I want to know a little of how you love her."

We made love, our arms tangled and shoulders wedged against the steering wheel, our clothes pulled half off and wound around our legs like hobbles. She arched against me and dug her fingers into my arms. She cried out, singing her pleasure and power as Nora had once known how to do. Then I drained out of myself, bracing one arm so I wouldn't crush her, and afterward rested my forehead against hers to get my moorings.

I wanted to be with Nora. That was suddenly clear. Wanted her talk and companionship. Wanted her closeness and touch. Wanted the kind of life she led and work she did, all as natural and right to me as it was to her. Wanted, at very least, to see if she was all right and if there was any small thing I could do to help her.

The next day I started working my way home. Not that I

had a plan of what I would do once I got there or went straight back right away. But I started circling the way a dog swings in arcs tracking a scent, the way he covers the ground, missing nothing and making note of what cannot be seen. Following his senses home.

Chapter Thirteen

Maggie Rhymer

THAT FALL NEAL WROTE Nora every week from Evanston. About his apartment on Ridge Avenue in the same neighborhood where he'd grown up. All his family was gone now, but he knew the butcher and one of the bank clerks for sure and said hello as if he'd never left. He could walk to the post office, drugstore, cleaner's, grocery, restaurants, and movie. He was only two blocks from the "el" station that took him to his office in downtown Chicago and Clea to the private Catholic girls' school just outside the Loop.

"Everything's right here," he wrote. "You'll love it."

Once he described the breeze off the lake blowing down State Street, and how the sophisticated ladies had to clutch at their skirts and hats all at once with their little gloved hands. How he liked to lunch at Field's Walnut Room and watch the single shoppers set their purses and parcels on the empty chair across from them and then order peach salads and cream cheese on brown bread. How some of their hats had veils that covered the upper part of their faces with delicate threading.

"I want to buy you one of those hats," he wrote Nora. "I can picture you sitting at a table in millinery, and the salesgirl bringing you a hundred before you find the one you like. Then us walking down Michigan Avenue, you carrying the round box and wearing that hat and a smart suit beside me."

He promised if she'd come to live with him that he'd take her to the Palmer House for a second honeymoon and they'd shop in the hotel stores and sit in the lobby with angels on the ceiling, and it would be better than it ever had been between them.

Sometimes on the last page he even tried to woo her into making love. "You can close your eyes and not even move. I won't mind, if you'll just let me."

Nora stood in the kitchen and read the letters when they came. She furrowed her brow and shook her head as if she'd gotten a proposal from a Tibetan who'd asked her to join his harem or become a nun. She shrugged and tossed the pages on the table.

"I don't know what he's talking about," she said.

Then she'd go out to the barn as if she'd expected that horses had been returned there in the night. She'd shuffle the tack and sweep out the stalls and rake the paddock. I told her she had to call her old customers or advertise her return to business, but she made excuses—she said they would be out or she'd disturb their dinner or it would be too late to call. What she didn't ever say was that she was afraid they'd refuse her because Neal or the gossip had convinced them that she was too unstable to ever care for their animals again. Then she'd have to admit that for no reason she'd given up Clea for the eight months of this school year.

That was the agreement, the best I could get without starting a fight Nora wasn't ready for. When she came in shaking and crying after the realtor's visit, all the progress she'd made since Simon's death seemingly wiped away, I held her and told her we would work it out. Then I got in the car and drove to Neal's office.

He looked up from his work and smiled smugly as if he already knew why I was there. But just that gave me a sudden freedom from believing that his intentions were well-meant and should be given my consideration.

"What are you doing to Nora?" I asked.

"Nothing *to* her," he said.

"You're going to kill her."

"No, Maggie. I just want her with me."

"Then move back. You're the one who left."

We argued for an hour then, going over the same territory we had before, with its seemingly impenetrable Maginot Line: Nora wanted the farm, Neal wanted to sell it. But I never got the feeling he and I were having a true discussion, since he kept trying to cajole me like a stubborn child.

When the phone rang and he stopped to talk to a client, I sat back in my chair, exhausted. I swore at myself for letting this man have control over part of everything my daughter and I owned. But before hanging up, Neal told the client he would drop by later with the policy to sign, and just that simple direction pushed a thought clear in my mind. What if Nora and I wouldn't sign the deeds? What if we refused to do anything?

Years ago an agent from one of the big grain companies

had tried to cheat Grace. They'd signed a contract for her to deliver a certain amount of wheat for a certain price. The next day the market went down, and the agent came to the farm to convince her that she should agree to less money per bushel if she didn't want to jeopardize the entire sale. But she held the contract under his nose, pointed out that she knew how to read, even if she was only a woman, and said she would notify his supervisors if he ever tried to pull a trick like that again.

When I suggested to Neal that he couldn't do anything—not get the money from either of the LaCote properties or buy the co-op in Evanston—until Nora or I consented to sign one deed or the other, his eyes narrowed and his arrogant congeniality fell away. Then I was doubly angry: that he had assumed she and I were both so stupid as not to have realized our power of ownership, and that, in fact, we had been.

"If she makes any more scenes like the one with the realtor," he said, "it won't be too difficult to convince the world that she should be at Arsenal and I should have power of attorney."

I sat there stunned, not quite believing what he had said.

"How did you expect her to react under the circumstances?" I asked.

He turned his palms to the ceiling and shrugged.

"Then," I said, "you'll have to have me committed, too, and I can't think on what grounds, except that I won't give in to you."

"What are you talking about?"

"Simply, that you need my signature to sell the farm, and I'm not signing until if and when the three of us come to a mutual decision about that."

To buy time, I offered him a compromise. Not one I

wanted, but the lesser of two evils. I would help him sell my house on two conditions: First, that my share of the proceeds would entitle me to half-ownership of his Evanston apartment, at least until we settled the other issues. Second, that he would leave Nora alone until she was strong enough to deal with all this.

Neal tried to talk me out of this idea, but I dug in like Grace, who did not give up anything rightfully her own without a fair trade. Finally, he agreed to leave Nora in peace at the farm if he could take Clea with him to Chicago. But he was angry at losing this skirmish with me.

"I don't know why Nora would want to sweat it out in Missouri when she could be with me on the lake, but if she needs to get eaten by mosquitoes and die from the humidity, well, that's her problem."

That afternoon I called three lawyers before I found one who'd see me. The first said he was Catholic and didn't deal in domestic cases. The second was an acquaintance of Neal's and claimed conflict of interest. The third arranged an appointment and took notes while I talked. I knew him slightly, the way people in LaCote know everyone else. His family owned the funeral parlor where Simon's wake took place, and his wife had been a few years behind me in school. When he gripped my hand and told me how sorry he was, I wasn't surprised he was aware of our situation.

I told him Nora wasn't quite back to her old self since the accident, and that's why I wanted to get the information for her, so she would know her options. He said that was understandable, what with Simon and the horse and all.

"But Neal left her. Isn't that abandonment?" I asked.

"He took a promotion and invited her to come; he sends her money and supports his child," the lawyer answered. "It's more likely she would be seen as the one who's deserted her family."

"Then can she sue for custody?"

"Since they're still married, a judge will rule that the father has a perfect right to take his kid with him, especially since she's well cared for.

"But if your daughter filed for divorce, then the custody agreement would be part of the divorce decree, which almost always favors the mother."

Driving back to the farm, I wondered why it had taken us so long to come to the idea of divorce. Perhaps some remnant of Frank and Neal's Catholicism that had rubbed off on Nora and myself, or maybe the rarity of broken marriages in LaCote. I didn't know. Nora looked surprised when I asked her about it.

"I can't get divorced," she said. "It's not right."

"It's not right what he's been doing."

But she explained that he was upset, just as she was, and this wasn't a time for them to make up their minds about anything serious. Then she went out the door and across the pasture.

When I ran into people I knew, I pretended I was in a hurry and couldn't stop to talk. I didn't want to discuss why Neal had told everyone the worst he could have about Nora: that he loved her deeply but she cared too much about herself to go with him.

I didn't even want to talk to them about other things—harmless topics like the weather or the mayor—because I knew all the while they'd be thinking about Nora and how she would not give up her way of life for her own child. How, other than a slut, that was the worst way for a woman to be.

Not that she and I were very close to those around us. Neighbors rarely dropped by, nor did we need them to. Grace with her eastern ways and education had always been an outsider, made more so by her terrible strength and efficiency. More than once she told me how people said after Frankie's and Charlie's funerals that they were glad to have seen her cry and know that she was human.

"I couldn't understand," she said, dropping her fist against her thigh, "how they were consoled by my sorrow."

But she taught us her ways of self-sufficiency, and so Nora and I were usually left to ourselves. I tried to get her to come shopping with me or go to St. Louis for a museum or a play. I even called Ozzie Kline to see if he was back and would bring Bandit to us. But his number had been disconnected so long ago that it had already been given to another person who didn't know what I was talking about.

"I'm not making any moves for the time being," Nora said, as if someone might steal her land if she were to leave it. "But Clea is better off now away from the memories."

I didn't agree, but it was her decision. She sat like a spider in the center, the invisible spokes of web spinning out from her belly. Yet no living thing moved them, and they trembled only from the wind crossing on its way to other places.

After Neal and Clea moved to Evanston around Labor Day, he made excuses about her needing to get settled there before she came home. The longer Clea was away, the surlier Nora became. She wrote her every day, though there wasn't much to tell. Mostly Nora suggested that they could "do things" together when Clea got home. But other than reading and going to the movies, there was never much the two ever had in common outside of their daily lives, crossing at meals and other brief moments when they told each other their small news of the day. With that gone, Nora seemed unable to imagine what would take its place.

Other than with the letters, Nora was engaged only by inspecting the farm. We continued our snake patrols, leaving the black, king, garter, corn, and blue racers where they landed after the flood, but throwing the poisonous moccasins back in the river as it receded to its regular channel.

The land reappeared in stages, marked with lines of debris like dirt rings on a bathtub. The trees that stood too deeply submerged were leafless as if already dormant, even though the sumac on higher ground had just begun to turn scarlet.

"They've drowned," Nora said as we made our way down the bluffs on foot, sliding on the mud slicks and picking our way over driftwood. "Their roots were covered with so much water for so long that they suffocated."

The trees huddled around us like unseasonable ghosts. Nora said, "I told him the water wouldn't touch the house." Then she complained that we had no horses to ride out on. I told her the mud and snakes would make it too dangerous, but she said, "It's his fault."

"We'll save enough to get more animals soon," I said, though Neal didn't give us enough to make it through a month without a deficit.

More and more I let her go alone; she seemed to prefer it, and I was glad to be out from under the weight of her unhappiness. From an upstairs window I watched her trudge across the pasture, shutting gates as if it still mattered. She wore boots, carried a shovel, and was gone for hours, sometimes taking sandwiches and a small Thermos tucked in the bib of her overalls and other days coming back to the house to eat with me on the porch. She brought bones with her and lined them on the railing next to a few late tomatoes ripening and a Mason jar of final zinnias.

With the garden hose, she rinsed the mud off dark hooves and rings of spine, soaked them in chlorine bleach, and dried them in the sun. The flood, she told me, had dug up some of the shallow horse graves in the bottoms land. She brought one piece of each, reburying the rest.

"I can't put them out of sight again," she said, slipping a vertebra on her thumb and turning it like a ring, "not just yet."

At first when I saw her washing and arranging them, I feared what I'd done by going against the shock treatments. But the more she gathered and sorted, the more she became revived and purposeful, going off each day to reorder what the flood had disturbed. She came back hungry and tan, and in the evenings, she worked over the bones, talking under her breath and catching me up in trying to decide their ownership.

She told me where she found them, partially uncovered by the flood or washed loose. "Which one?" she asked, holding out a flat rib, gray and worn, or a femur with the honeycombing of the growth plate exposed. "It's old," she said, "one of Grace's horses."

In the twilight smelling of late grasses and old dust, I tried to name for her all that I remembered. I thought I had forgotten them, but Nora wanted to know what each horse before her time looked like, what kind of personality, what quirks. And since for the first time since Simon's death she seemed interested in anything, I tried hard for what I thought was no longer there.

The horses returned to me slowly. I began telling her the easy ones—Missy, the Shetland I had learned to ride on, and Lady, the little sorrel mare who was mine alone. I even began to regret that I had ever stopped riding. The more Nora pushed me to describe them, the more clearly I remembered, though sometimes their images hung suspended and I could not place them in a context of time. But I told her as much as I remembered and remembered more than I thought I knew.

We looked for Grace's ledgers and notes, packed away in the basement. It took two days to find them, stuck at the bottom of a box pushed far back in the crawl space. The names of horses. Barney, Champ, Cid, Maeve. Gus, Tess, Beauty, Joe. Grace had sketched each one, side profile of full figure and close-up portrait head on. Fine crosshatching and strong lines. Stars, blazes, and solids. Stockings, dapples, and pinto spots. The personality of each clear in their faces, in eyes made to look as intelligent as humans'. She'd also kept records of their breeding and training. Of how they died, even those she put down herself. She wrote about them as a mother who keeps a journal of her children, though I never found that Grace ever kept such a book for me. Yet now that was minor, my mother's slight. Her past filled up the vacuum of late summer and kept Nora busy.

Nora lined up rings of spine bone and tried to guess by density and weight which of the horses they might have belonged to. She told me a corner of Zad's grave had been uncovered, revealing a square of matted, muddy hide.

"I had to cover it over again and pack down the earth with the back of the shovel."

She said this matter-of-factly. The next morning she took all the bones back to where she had gotten them and put Grace's ledgers on the bookshelf in the study. Nora still would not call her old clients, and I still could not get hold of Ozzie Kline or find anyone who'd seen him. But after my arguing with Neal for hours, Clea wrote that she was coming home for a long weekend around the first of October, and Nora and I went to the depot to meet her an hour earlier than her train was scheduled to arrive.

She was dressed in a wool suit, burnt orange like fall leaves, smart calfskin pumps, white gloves, and a pillbox with a small black veil. Her skirt was pencil slim and the luggage new. The porter lifted down a two-suiter to the platform, and she carried a small overnight case herself. Behind the station the water tank was painted with LACOTE in high white letters, but Clea seemed to have stepped from a place we could not get to and brought the breeze of it with her. She kissed the air by our ears and looked out beyond, arranging her feet just so, like a model, while waiting for the porter to get her third bag.

"You didn't have to bring so much," Nora said. "Most of your clothes are still in your closet."

"I have new," Clea said. "Dad and I went shopping."

Indeed. The luggage was full of pleated wool plaid and round felt skirts, sweaters for each with a cardigan the exact color of every pullover, and corduroy jumpers matched with their own blouses, most still with Marshall Field or Carson Pirie Scott tags, enough clothes for weeks. We had a polite dinner. She wiped her mouth, and the pink lipstick, carefully applied, came off on the napkin. She ate with one hand held in her lap and the studied grace of someone who was attending more to her table manners than to the food.

Nothing had happened at the farm except the cataloging of bones, and we didn't mention that. When we asked Clea about school, she went off on tangents filled with Chicago references she didn't stop to explain. Most often she mentioned a Frankie.

"Is he your boyfriend?" Nora asked finally.

"Frankie's a *girl,*" Clea told us. "Short for Frances. Anyone would know that."

"Anyone who's met her," I said.

Clea rolled her eyes. I wanted to slap her into sense, or at least civility. But I was afraid she would balk at visiting again, and Nora seemed easier with her there.

"I'm going out." She rose to clear the table. "Some friends are picking me up for the LaCote High game."

"Which friends?" Nora asked.

"You don't know them."

Nora leaned a little forward as if she was about to say more, but then she lowered her eyes and shrugged. Like me, I thought. Not yet ready to confront Clea and risk driving her away.

The lights of a car swung past the kitchen window. The horn sounded. If we scolded her for running out like this, would she stay with Neal for spite?

"Don't wait up," Clea said, heading down the hall and grabbing her jacket from the hook by the door.

Of course I did, and I heard Nora moving around in her room. Past midnight the car pulled up. Clea and the boy were no more than the shadows around them, and occasionally an elbow or arm or curve of back came visible in the light from the porch that reached just beyond the edge of the car's dash.

I thought about a winter's night with a boy whose name I

didn't remember, the two of us standing out behind our school after a dance. The heat between us had distracted me from my toes going numb with cold, and later I'd sat on the side of my bed and chafed the circulation back, feeling more than anything my sweetly bruised and tingling lips.

I flexed my toes, their rustiness now coming from age. In her last years Grace used to complain how her bones creaked, and I'd been irritated by how her body absorbed her. But now I understood. I reached my ear to shoulder, then chin to chest to feel the line of vertebrae down the ridgepole of my back. For the first time in my life I wondered about Grace in the moment she died and if she had been in that second conscious of this string of bones running the length of her.

I shook myself out of the mood. Time to reclaim Clea, but before I could go down and knock on the car windows steamed by breath, the boy opened the car door and pulled her out after him, swung her around, and kissed her as he set her down. They came toward the house, their arms around each other, and stopped halfway up the walk and by the steps to kiss again. There was a long pause before I heard the door unlock and swing open, and another pause before he strode back to the car. I tried to gauge by his gait what kind of boy he was. He walked easy and sure, comfortable in his body.

He picked her up the next morning at ten, and Nora made her bring him inside to meet us. Tommy Steiner wore tight jeans and a navy letter jacket with butter-colored sleeves. A blond, brown-eyed boy who had reassured himself that he was handsome and then gone on without another thought. He looked directly at us when he shook our hands, but couldn't keep himself from glancing at Clea as if she might disappear.

I told Clea she had to be back at six for dinner, but she

and Tommy went out again that evening and to mass the next morning. Nora did not seem to mind if Clea went out, just so long as she was with us instead of in Chicago. Whenever she and Tommy left, Nora stood at the front window until his car disappeared down the lane.

"I'm glad she's happy," she said.

I was glad the longer Clea was here, the less she seemed the haughty spoiled brat we had collected from the train.

Tom went with us to the station on Sunday afternoon, and Clea almost cried when she said good-bye to him. Two days later I ran into him buying gum at the newsstand, and a day later at the gas station, though I never remembered seeing him around town before. He waved at me, a quick flash of hand and nod of head. I went over to talk, and he seemed glad to see me, stuck as we both were with each other as substitutes for Clea.

He drove a gray '32 De Soto with running boards and seats like couches. Wide and roomy inside like a little cottage. He said he bought it from an old guy who couldn't see anymore to drive, and it was good, except it needed a new ignition. I admired the car to keep Tom Steiner talking so that I could hear and see him as Clea did and know firsthand what she would not tell me by proxy. He leaned against the fat curve of fender and hooked his thumbs in the waistband of his jeans. While the attendants filled our tanks with gas and washed the windshields, I asked Tommy what else he did and he told me about football.

I did not care about football, but he was the left guard and the team was undefeated. His eyes lit up and he held his hands cradled as if the ball would drop there to tuck against him and be carried forward. I liked his sweet affection for the game and the dimple that came when he smiled. I thought he was like Simon might have been, this boy that Clea loved, and I enticed him like a spy.

He asked me if there was a chance Clea's dad would move back to LaCote, and I told him no. I hadn't thought of it so finally before, but somehow then I was sure. Then he asked if Clea's mom would go there to be with him, and I told him no again.

"But Clea will come to visit," I said.

"Some consolation," he told me. "Her old man moved to Chicago just to get her away from me. He'll figure how to keep her there."

"Oh, I don't think so," I began, immediately sorry how like a parent I sounded.

"You should hear how he puts me down," the boy said, and I thought of my husband, Frank, years ago ranting about Ozzie Kline.

On the drive home I passed between fields of corn being harvested, the stalks thin and dry like tall old yogis lying down before the combine. I was amazed at how quickly and definitively it had become autumn, how easily I knew that Neal and Nora would stay separate and make Clea a migrant daughter. I missed Grace; I mourned Simon. I regretted how my own life had been rearranged.

But when I turned into our drive, I stopped for a moment that overwhelmed all else. The roof triangles rose cleanly against the dense cerulean sky that came only in October, and late tan grasses glowed. The sun lit banks of leaves like red Chinese lanterns, and a flock of birds flew over, their shadows streaming across the road before me. They landed chattering and filled the bushes with ruckus like children pushing and shoving for room. Far out in the silent sky, a wedge of ducks followed the river south, and if I held my breath, I could hear their honking and almost the beating of their wings. Then the world broke my heart with its creatures so lovely and strong and fleeting, and I was greedy in that instant to stay on the earth forever.

When I pulled up to the house, I saw from behind the barn the beat-up tailgate of Ozzie Kline's red pickup, dented, crooked, the paint oxidized soft pink in places and slashed through with dull silver gashes. When I turned off the engine and listened with the window down, his voice and Nora's were just audible.

I found them sitting across from each other on hay bales outside the barn, Ozzie sucking on a piece of tasseled grass and Nora taking long drags from her cigarette. I had not seen him since the funeral, almost six months before. He looked up and lifted his chin in greeting. Time folded over on itself, and I thought for a moment I'd dreamed his absence, or somehow just seen his ghost in Tommy Steiner.

"Hello, Maggie," he said.

"I've been trying to call you," I told him.

"Been out," he said.

Up north into Canada, sleeping on an air mattress under a tent rigged over the bed of his truck and getting at least part of his food from what he could catch or hunt. The weather cool, the mosquitoes big as bombers. He liked being alone and away.

"Needed to get out of here."

I sat up on one of the bales, left over from spring and smelling rot-musty, wet and cool. He told stories about working his way back south, wrangling and blacksmithing at the horse shows and running carnie rides at the fairs that stretched like stepping stones to here. He told us about the drunks who worked the game booths, cheating people they didn't like the looks of, which was almost everyone. About 4-H kids who broke down as their prize-winning stock was led off to market. About the fat lady freak, all 350 pounds of her, who wanted him for a lover and cried when he wouldn't.

"Then who did you save from crying?" Nora teased.

"Too many to talk about," he said.

I wanted to ask what had happened to Bandit but was afraid he'd died or gotten lost.

"C'mon," Nora said, reaching out to kick the toe of his boot with hers. "Whose hearts did you break?"

"My lips are sealed," he smiled.

I asked him to stay for dinner, and they stopped by the garden to pick a few squash. Then Ozzie's head came up suddenly. He stood looking off to the bluff and whistled low.

I didn't recognize the dog at first. Border collies have thick enough fur that when shaved, they look scrawny and silly like poodles. Bandit came running full tilt like some huge naked rabbit bolting out of cover. I called out to him, and he slowed his pace, turning to look at me. But when Ozzie called him again, he was off without another thought, leaping the garden fence and banging his skinny tail fiercely against Oz's legs.

When I caught up with them, Oz held Bandit still for me to pet. Under the new fuzz, pinkish skin showed.

"Skunk," Oz told me. "Pissed off a skunk and came back smelling worse than you could ever imagine. I thought of just dropping him off at an animal shelter and being done with it. But that seemed like the worst betrayal, so I got him shaved.

"At first he looked like a Marine recruit. Now the fur's grown back some, and he's had so many baths that he's never smelled so good, though I can't say the same for my truck. Every night after I park it, I set an open bottle of Air-Wick on the floor with that green thing pulled up as far as it goes. But the minute I take it out again, the smell starts to take over."

Nora was laughing like she'd never heard anything so funny.

"Serves you right for taking in an animal like that," she said.

"Serves me right?" he said. "It's your dog, woman. I was just baby-sitting to save it."

Nora knelt down and ran her hands over Bandit as if she were trying to guess his weight or read his mind.

"Why would Neal do that?" she said. "I never could figure what he had against her."

"Just finding the whipping boys," Oz said. "That's all."

"Well," I said. "We better get going on dinner or it'll be midnight before we eat."

I started back to the house, just enough ahead of them that I couldn't understand exactly what they were saying. But I liked the sound of their voices filling up the late afternoon and running like water over the silence that had been there. We fixed dinner and afterward sat around the table, the dirty dishes pushed back out of our way.

"I found a filly you'd like," Oz said finally.

"Can't afford her," Nora said.

The light in the room was yellow and sad.

"The woman who owns her was an old friend of Grace's. I talked her into trading the filly for her foals when she has them."

Nora played with a fork.

"She's gray, like Zad. I can take you over to see her when you get the chance."

I held my breath and waited for Nora to break down, to cry or walk out in anger. But she just shifted in her seat and set her jaw tight, and I breathed out, feeling as if we had survived some kind of test we didn't know we could get by.

When Oz got ready to leave, Nora stood on the porch talking, and the cool night air streamed in the open door. He leaned against the post. Nora hugged herself and rubbed her arms to warm them and laughed at some joke he made as she turned to come in.

I lay in bed and couldn't sleep. The clock struck one and two. As I stared into the dark, it turned and rolled like black water until I imagined the shapes of horses swimming toward me. Ozzie was somehow different, as if he knew how to fill at least part of the enormous and barren space Nora and I had been living in.

Nora, too. More girlish and relaxed than I'd seen her. More attentive and alert. Much like Clea when she'd been around her boy. All different, as if people and life were returning here after the still, wet summer.

The next afternoon I called Tommy Steiner and asked him if he would like to see Clea the weekend after next and come to dinner while she was here and every other weekend when she came to visit. Then I called Clea in Chicago, at an hour when I was sure Neal was at the office, and told her I'd bumped into Tom at the filling station.

"Tell your father that if you don't come home more often, your mother might get upset again without you. Then he'll have to start over with her from square one."

I could only hear her breathing over the line.

"You like Tommy?"

"He reminds me of a boy your mother was in love with when she was just a little older than you."

She gave a little snort.

"But, Clea, remember what I told you this summer about being careful."

She didn't answer.

"Do you know what I'm talking about?"

When she didn't answer again, I told her what I suspected neither of her parents had thought to say the past summer about sex and love, now that it was time for her to know such things. I spoke too quickly, glad of the anonymity the phone gave us, and referred to what she'd seen of horse breeding to escape the technical descriptions.

"Do you hear me?" I asked.

"Yes," she said.

I listened to her breathing and the sound of distance carried on the phone wires.

"He'll be glad to see you," I said finally. "We all will."

Then she laughed in a way that I took as a mixture of joy that she would see him and relief that I was finished with her instruction.

After we hung up, I sat for a while twisting the phone cord. I was caught between gratitude that she had found comfort with Tommy Steiner and indecision over whether I should buy condoms for them, just in case. But for the first time since Simon had died, I saw the shape of what was coming, was aware of small joys filling what had been emptied.

Chapter Fourteen

Ozzie Kline

I THOUGHT I HAD IT straight about going back to Nora, but headed to LaCote, I'd found a million reasons why that was a dumb idea. The familiar ones I could admit, that she wasn't my problem and I couldn't do anything anyway. The dark ones I hated even catching a glimpse of. The ones that said I was of myself not good enough and she had been mistaken about loving me in the first place.

All during the drive across Missouri, I kept thinking how I was afraid of that as much as I was of her. Every time my old man got on me about never amounting to anything, he'd beat the shit out of me for good measure, just in case I'd missed his point. The worst was when I was fifteen, a couple of years before I left home. At two A.M. I'd rolled his car to the bottom of the street and taken off to run the dirt roads outside of town. When Dad got up to take a leak, he noticed the car gone. By the time the cops brought me in, he'd had a few shots of Jack and was waiting on the porch in his underwear.

Then he broke my nose, two ribs, and my collar bone. I was almost as tall by then, but he outweighed me and didn't care what damage he did. Later I discovered that power of not caring in my own fights, of having no rules about what I did to others. But when I was fifteen and getting pounded, I was sure he was going to kill me, and I finally crawled under the kitchen table like a dog so he couldn't get a good swing.

He kept shouting how he had to be on me all the time to keep my miserable self out of trouble, the same way he'd been yelling and walloping me since I could remember. When I was younger and my mother still alive, she used to sit there and stare out over us just like she couldn't see or hear my old man going at me right in front of her.

I never did much in school, either, because I'd been told I was just average, and by the time Frank Rhymer started telling Nora how worthless I was, I was pretty well convinced myself. Except for what I'd learned about horses along the way, I didn't know much of anything worth knowing.

But Nora Rhymer, who'd had her pick of any boy, fell in love with me. She left the house with girlfriends to throw her father off and chanced having anyone around town mention to him that they'd seen her with me. She craved for us to touch and in time let me make love to her—in my dad's car parked in the boonies or in her room when her family was out or at the river cabin when she could sneak down in the middle of the night. She let me be the first and trusted me to take care of her, even with the risk of getting pregnant. She did all that easily and gladly, and I seemed to make her happy, just me alone. That was the miracle.

I didn't have money to take her places the way other guys could, but she never seemed to care. Some nights she and I would do no more than hold each other, dozing in each other's arms. To make sure I got her home on time I'd bring an alarm clock in case we fell too sound asleep. Other times we talked, or sometimes just kissed like we couldn't get over being able to touch. I loved it when she threw back her head and laughed or smiled because something I'd done or just my being pleased her. There was no place inside me I didn't let her touch, nothing of me that I wouldn't let her have. I was ready to give over my life for our life together, and I believed for long moments that I could do anything with her beside me.

When she started college and I couldn't afford to go, something between us shifted, like she'd taken off to where she knew I couldn't follow. Yet when Frank Rhymer died suddenly after her freshman year, I was allowed to come to the house then, and Nora wanted me to hold her for as long as Grace would let me stay each evening. At the burial I sat on a folding chair under the open tent with the family and walked back to the hearse with Nora against me. Her heels kept sinking into the ground, and she cried so hard her tears wet my shirt. I just kept telling her everything would be all right.

I thought his death would be our solution, and I trembled at the thought of having Nora as my own. I bought a set of rings and for once felt I had done something important and good for my life and hers.

But before I could even show her the rings, Nora turned skittery, refused to be touched, made excuses why she had to be with her college friends instead of me. After putting me off for weeks, she asked me to drop by. It was late September when the dark seemed closer around and leaves rattled hollow on the trees. The yellow porch light was on and the light in the kitchen down the hall. She kept herself in a dark pocket behind the screen that she held shut and told me she didn't want to see me again.

"Why?" I asked, barely able to talk.

"I found the guy I think I'll marry," she said.

"I thought that was me."

"That's been over for a long time," she said. "You should've known."

I shrugged.

"Well, you should've," she said. "If you weren't too stupid and weak to face up to it all."

She started to turn away then said, "Well. Don't you have anything to say?"

But I didn't have the words and couldn't have spoken them if I had.

During the next few weeks I must have driven back and forth in front of her property a thousand times. I rehearsed how I would go up to her door and how relieved I would be to see her. I'd tell her that I wanted her back, and we'd be just like before. But I didn't have the balls to do that or the hope that she'd accept. I'd asked around and heard Neal Mahler was the kind who'd provide for her well. I figured she'd be better off.

In a way, I'd always expected her to leave, always suspected my old man had been right in the first place. So I looked up the wild boys I'd been with before I started going with Nora and stayed semidrunk so I didn't have to think what she'd finally noticed that made her stop loving me.

I couldn't take the chance of running into her, didn't want to be within a thousand miles. A month after she ditched me, I decided to head out west to drive trucks for the wheat harvest. Two nights before I left, I got drunk again. I sat on the KATY tracks down behind Main Street. Drinking straight out of a bottle of Jack and watching the car lights moving across the bridge, all the while praying I would pass out right there.

I wanted back any moment I'd had with Nora Rhymer to erase it from my life. I wanted to be ignorant of love and as completely numb as that ignorance would make me. But she sat like a white coal in place of my heart. I hated her for giving me hope before snatching back what she'd made me believe was mine, and I wanted to hurt her in some terrible way.

But I also wanted to hold and forgive her, and if she'd come driving around the corner and gotten out of her daddy's old car to stand in front of me on that riverbank, I couldn't have done anything but hope she would let me take her in my arms.

I knew that wasn't about to happen. I took the ring box out of my breast pocket. Snapped the button that flipped open the lid. Stared at the diamonds shining like the car lights in the river water. The stones were small and cheap, nothing Nora would be proud to wear, and I was embarrassed at ever thinking that she would. Even the best I could afford was not nearly enough for her.

I stood up, cocked my arm, and sent the box flying out over the river. I waited for the faint splash, and then I sat down again on the rail and cried until I was worn-out.

The next day as I was saying good-bye to friends, I ran into Grace at the feedstore. She wore old muddy boots, and her gray braids were wound around on either side of her head like ram's horns. I nodded and hoped that would be it, but she came up and blocked my way in the aisle.

I liked Grace. She'd sometimes let us know in advance when Frank and Maggie would be out, guaranteeing to keep them there until after a certain hour. She'd always treated me like her equal with the horses. Now standing before her, I was full of crazy regret because it seemed I was losing Grace and all she'd been to me as part of what I'd lost with Nora.

She tilted her head and squinted, her blue eyes pale and filmy, the way old people's get.

"Well," she said, "you're both miserable, but you have the good sense to know it."

I grinned crooked, the joke like salt. Grace stepped up so others passing wouldn't hear.

"What are you going to do about it?"

"I'm leaving tomorrow," I told her. "Going west."

"Any place special?"

"No, just someplace different."

"Were you coming to tell us good-bye?"

"Hadn't decided."

She cocked her head and studied me like I was a horse with a bad gait she was trying to remedy.

"You know," she said, "I'll miss you, and I'll bet Nora will, too. Eventually."

I wouldn't take her seriously except in closely guarded moments. Even then it didn't matter. Nora had made her decision, and I couldn't help it that she wouldn't have me. But sometimes after an ambush or battle, Grace's words came back to me. I'd be proud of myself, though I knew also in some way I'd used my bravery as an excuse for my lack of courage in love. Coming back to LaCote the October after Simon died, I'd wanted to be at least strong and good enough for Nora to love, even if I could never have her in the way I'd dreamed.

I'd put off going to her place for two days. Then I got angry for backing away again. I had to bring Bandit, I told myself, so it didn't look funny, me dropping by out of the blue. When I pulled up next to the barn and opened the door, Bandit jumped over my lap and flew out, stopping to sniff quickly at Nora in the paddock, and then swinging back and forth across the yard, his tail banging and nose to the ground.

"He's looking for Simon," she said, and Bandit stopped at the sound of the name and pricked his ears.

"No," I said, trying to keep her from bad subjects. "Dogs don't have that long a memory."

"Watch," she said. She crouched down and started a low singsong. "Hey, boy, hey, Bandit. How you doing? Come see Nora, come on. Come see Oz, right here." She patted the ground beside her. The dog kept on sniffing each fence post until she called, "Where's Simon? Find Simon for us."

Bandit froze at attention again, his eyes darting to catch a glimpse of movement, of maybe Simon hiding like a rabbit in the grass. I swallowed hard and wondered how Nora could stand to call Simon's name.

Her hair was a little dirty and tied back with an old blue ribbon, her face tired like those women who'd lugged their families through the dust bowl. But as she watched the dog, her eyes brightened with interest that made me glad.

"What the hell happened to him?" she laughed. "He looks like he got caught in a combine."

"Skunk," I told her. "Had to shave him."

"Serves him right for going where he shouldn't."

I followed her over to sit on bales stacked low near the door of the barn. She kept her eyes on the dog while she asked me where I'd been. Not like Nora to look away while she was listening, or sit with her hands laced together on her lap—usually she played with a piece of grass or length of rein, twisted her rings or a lock of hair, waved her hands around like some crazy Italian while she talked. Something about her now seemed far away like driftwood out on the water, but at the same time, heavy like a lead shaft that would go right under.

When I asked how she had been, she shrugged.

"Neal's gone, you know. He expects me to come with him."

Then she explained the past months, her voice flat and her words simple.

"A man's got to go where the work is," I said finally.

She looked at me head-on in a way that reminded me of Grace going after someone who'd mistreated a horse.

"He had work here," Nora said. "And a family."

I turned my palms up. I'd only wanted to defend him to make it easier for her to go along, and I only wanted her to go along to save her more struggle. But she was no longer so intimidating with her careful life ruined.

I didn't like to admit that vengeful thought, but inside my head I kept singing *Neal Mahler is gone,* like some stupid proof that she'd been mistaken in sending me away when we were nineteen, like a brainless hope we could now start over and fix what we'd done badly.

When Maggie came home and asked me to dinner, Nora and I went to pick squash and walked down the rows of withering vines while we talked about everything and nothing, the way we had as kids.

"Half the vegetables drowned this season," she said, indicating where each variety had been planted. "The plants got soggy and rotted with all the rain and standing water."

She loaded another squash into my arms, brushing the dirt off and apologizing for what fell against my shirt.

"It's old," I told her, not minding anything she did to it, though it was my best.

Then we started back to the house, the yellowish light and brown smell of dry grasses around us. Nora was a few paces ahead of me as I juggled the squash and remembered her same walk as I followed her out of a dance half a lifetime ago. She stopped and looked off over the tree line while I caught up.

"You know," she said, her back to me, "fall's always sad, but this year I can hardly stand it with Clea gone."

Then she said something I couldn't understand.

"What?" I asked, coming up close.

"I said," her voice hard and angry, "he would have been a senior."

She took off again, walking so fast I knew she didn't want me to catch up. I came in the back and dropped the squash in the kitchen sink. Maggie ran water over them, and the dirt streamed off. Upstairs, Nora slammed a door.

"Is she OK?" I asked.

Maggie raised her eyebrows and gave the carrot she was peeling a vicious swipe.

"I don't mean OK," I said. "You know."

"She doesn't trust anyone or anything. She's not even sure the earth will hold still under her feet."

Maggie leaned toward the window and peered out.

"Go close up the barn for me, will you? It's supposed to rain by morning."

I swung shut the door on that empty space, so strange with no horses, not their movement nor smell nor sound. Even worse. The paddocks empty, the land churned up by flood, and two women alone. In the early dusk I looked out over the pasture where the grasses had grown too high and felt an eeriness.

But the changes gave me an excuse to be around Nora without coming too close. The next day I got a job at the Cahokia racetrack as a farrier because I knew Nora couldn't pay me and I might have to even help her out once in a while. I dropped by her place almost every afternoon when I was done and took care of all the heavy work that had gone to pot since Simon's death. The flood had ripped up the bottoms land, leaving a lot of debris in the lower pastures that I cleared out with the tractor and a hitch. After that I started mending the fences that were knocked down or plain washed away. I liked that arrangement for starters, just seeing Nora every day and doing what I could to help.

CHAPTER FIFTEEN

Clea Mahler

WHILE MY PARENTS were separated, I took the train so often that the conductors at the La Salle Station knew me by name. They had me call them Joseph and Ezekiel and Fern and teased me about going to see my boyfriend. Their eyes lit up when they saw me coming down the platform, and they always took my suitcase and gave me a hand up the metal steps.

Easier to be with them than my father who got more distracted the longer my mother stayed stubborn. He and I went to dinner every night at the Orrington, and he bought me whatever clothes I wanted. But I got bored with dressing for dinners that took half the evening and hearing about what he did at the office. With being grown-up one night and the next having to have the old deaf lady down the hall stay with me if he was going to be late.

I started pretending the apartment was Tom's and mine. My chores were easy when I imagined him sitting on the couch and admiring how I took care of the place. I even talked out loud to him and ran my hand over my pillow like it was his chest. But all that got old, too, and then I got restless.

My father liked having me live with him. He bragged to the friends he brought home after work that he was my only parent, and he liked seeing their shock when he told them Nora couldn't take care of me. But he got tired of actually being with me.

Sure, after he heard that Ozzie Kline was back, he went with me to LaCote every chance. Even after all the arguing over having Thanksgiving in Chicago, he later suddenly decided we would go "home" then, too, for my mother's sake. But every time, he sat with his briefcase open on his lap and read papers, so after the train left the station I went to sit in the last seat with the conductors to talk.

The first time we both showed up at the farm, he was smiling and carrying our luggage across the yard. When my mother opened the front door, he called out, "Where do you want me to put my bags, Nora?"

She stepped out on the porch looking like she was going to cry and waited with her hands on her hips until he got to the bottom of the steps.

"You want to stay here?" she asked. "After all your talk about why none of us should, why the hell would you do that?"

He got this surprised look on his face, something I hardly ever see my father do, and just stood there for a minute. Then he took his bag back to the car.

"I'll be around," he told her before he got in. "You remember that."

Afterward, he started telling his friends in Chicago how she blocked the doorway and wouldn't even let him in the house. And since he wouldn't force himself in where he wasn't wanted, he had to get a motel room instead.

The trips after that were all the same. He had one of the insurance agents drop off a car for us at the depot and, going down the highway to the farm, would start swiveling his head at all the oncoming traffic to see if my mother was passing. Before he set my suitcase by the door he started looking around for her. If she wasn't there, he asked Maggie if she'd fix him coffee, then made up things he had to talk to my mother about. If she was out in the barn, my father sent me to get her. If she was down walking by the river, sometimes he waited two hours or more for her to get back.

He always told my mother how good she looked and how well she was doing. But then he got every conversation around to her moving to Chicago. She folded her arms over her chest and said, "Neal, we've been over this a million times," and then he stormed out, yelling back over his shoulder, "I don't know why you have to be like this, Nora."

When he came to pick me up late on Sunday afternoons he still looked injured. He stared at my mother the way boys do when you won't let them kiss you, but she acted like she didn't notice him following her every move. Then I wished I could spend my life riding between Evanston and LaCote, never having to get off in either one of these damned places. That would have made both of them happy in a spiteful sort of way, to never have me spend a minute more with one over the other.

But at least Maggie was on my side, and Tommy was there. I didn't know who else I could have talked to. My father wouldn't tolerate even a casual mention of Simon, and I had to be careful. Sometimes I started talking about something that had happened to me when I was a kid but then remembered Simon and had to break off.

"What was that?" my father asked.

"Nothing," I told him.

But my mother followed me around and stared. She watched me eat and read and brush my hair and tie my shoes and do my homework. When I asked her what she was doing, she said, "Just looking."

"You've seen me before," I said.

"I want to remember exactly," she said.

Then I got the creepy thought that she was saving up these memories in case I died young like Simon.

Sometimes she brought up his name in a scared, quick way that made me nervous. When she asked if I missed him, I said, "Sure, why wouldn't I?" If she started talking about something he did as a kid—even something funny like when he used to kidnap my toys and send me ransom notes—I just wanted us to talk about nothing in particular the way we used to. Not like then when I didn't know how to answer her without crying.

But Tommy always came by, and we usually drove to St. Louis where we could be alone. We went to the movies or out to eat. Once in a while we walked through the zoo, empty of people after October, or to the art museum where we could hold hands in peace. Sometimes we spread a blanket on the ground near one of the lagoons and lay there and kissed, just our body heat keeping the cold away.

Tom kept me from feeling like I was going to dissolve, and I was afraid to even think of giving that up. But I couldn't explain to my father. When letters came before I got a chance to pick up the mail, my father never missed a chance to say, "You're not still interested in that kid, are you?" or "I know you're too smart to get involved with someone like him."

So we escaped to Art Hill to make out under the statue of St. Louis with his sword raised, Tom's leg over mine and my hand on his chest. I could kiss him in public, kisses full of tongue, and walk with his arm around me. Not like in LaCote with everyone so busybody that I didn't want even statues to see.

In St. Louis I didn't feel Simon around, either, not like in LaCote and especially in my mother's house. I didn't think his ghost would appear or I'd hear his voice or anything stupid like that. I didn't worry that he'd hurt me. But I felt like some part of him might have been left behind where he lived, and I didn't want him to see me with Tommy any more than I wanted my parents to know.

Simon had been my own personal army, and I had been famous because of him. Groups of boys had parted in front of me and girls made over me to get in good. But when Tom pulled me close, then I wished to be only myself, not Simon's sister or Neal Mahler's daughter, just me alone with Tommy, going where we wanted.

My mother kept asking about him. She sat across the kitchen table and leaned forward slightly when waiting for my answer. I told her all I thought a mother should know. That he was a senior and played football and didn't know if he'd have enough money for college. That he was nice.

"What does that mean?" she asked.

"Nice means nice," I said.

I wanted to ask her back about Ozzie Kline. When he first came, he stayed out in the barn and paddocks, and though I looked for what Simon might have seen, I didn't notice anything strange. But by my next trip home, he was letting himself in the house without knocking, and fixing himself coffee or lunch like he lived there, and spending the evenings sitting with my mother and Maggie. By early November he'd moved his things to the river cabin. Even when he and Nora were playing cards or mah-jongg, she had to show him if the card or tile she'd picked was good or not. He kidded her and called her "Poker Face," and they always had something going between them.

But he always went back to the cabin to sleep. When I came in late or got up in the night for a glass of water, I went by her room with the door ajar and poked my head in to check. If she was still awake, I said good night like that was what I'd come for. Sometimes when Tommy dropped me off, Mother and Oz were sitting up talking with just the light from the lamp between them. They always asked me if I wanted to sit with them, but I felt like an intruder.

Going up the stairs, I tried to overhear, but they took a while to get back into the conversation. Usually they talked about me a little. How well I looked or wasn't it nice to have me home. But once, halfway up, I crouched down until they got past the chitchat. Then Mother said, "I hope she's not getting in trouble," and Ozzie Kline told her, "No more than we did at the same age."

Then she laughed.

"Oh, that's a great consolation. We were just lucky, you know."

"No, not luck," Oz said. "I was so careful with you."

Then they both got quiet for a while, and when they started talking again, they spoke so low that I couldn't understand.

That night I lay awake for a long time. The tree branches slapped against the house, and the wind made their shadows jump and twitch on the walls, the way they do in November. I pulled the extra blanket up and shivered, not so much from the chill in the room but from what was going on between my mother and him.

I tried to imagine them like Tommy and me but couldn't. The next morning as Oz made breakfast, I tried to picture him as my stepfather. Humming under his breath, he took the coffeepot off the stove and burned his fingers as he tried to fish out the basket. His boots were scuffed and muddy, his flannel shirt worn at the elbows, and his hair too long around his ears. I tried to see what my mother saw in him and wondered why she couldn't do better or why she needed him at all.

When he offered to cook me eggs along with his, I told him no and went to get the cereal. I ate, staring at his back at the stove, and was embarrassed that he cooked like a woman.

Then my mother came in, her cheeks red and all about her smelling of cold. She threw her plaid jacket over the back of a chair and trailed her hand over my shoulder as she passed. She and Ozzie leaned their elbows on the edge of the sink and stood looking out the window, talking with their butts stuck out. Not anything important, just about the two horses they were boarding.

He served her eggs and sat down to eat with her. He sat in my father's place and she sat in Simon's next to him. Then my cereal tasted like paper and the room was too hot. Everything was changed, and the empty spaces filled in new ways made it seem they had forgotten Simon's death and my father altogether.

I put my bowl in the sink and turned on the water until the milk and flakes ran over the side like a fountain.

"Not hungry?" my mother said.

"No."

"You're supposed to tell her about the starving children in Armenia," Ozzie said. "What kind of mother are you?"

My mother rolled her eyes and laughed.

"Then she's supposed to tell me to wrap up her cereal and mail it to them."

I hated her dumb comment and took my coat off the peg by the back door.

"I'm going walking," I told them.

I started down the lane toward the highway and kept going because I didn't know where else I should go. The wind was bouncing the bare tree branches around and rattling the dead grasses. My eyes got so cold I could feel their roundness, and I kept thinking that maybe my mother and Ozzie were just good friends. But I didn't want to go back to the house any more than I wanted to go down the lane. I didn't want to be anywhere except with Tommy, and we were too young to have a place of our own.

Then I wanted to grow up fast to have that power of grown-ups to go where they wanted and do as they liked. But I could not imagine how many years before that happened, how long I would be left alone and gray as sky. I wanted Tommy to hold me then, to take this away even for a short time. I would have given anything for that—the bright, hot feeling that came with him and shut out everything else.

Chapter Sixteen

Neal Mahler

Since Maggie had gotten so stubborn, I tried to convince Nora that if she moved, all her problems about money would disappear. Any day she wanted, she could take a cab down with Clea and shop the Loop until she couldn't carry home all the packages without help. And she could decorate this apartment. I would have liked that, in fact—those touches only a woman could bring—candy bowls and figurines and vases, pictures on the wall and rugs tossed on the floor.

I had bought a sofa and chair, a floor lamp, a dining table, and beds. But the place still looked barren. I even tried to get Clea to shop for me, and once in a while she'd go into a spurt and bring something home. Last time it was plaster apple and pear plaques for the kitchen, the fruit standing out from the wall like the backs of them had been sliced off. Just teasing, I asked her, "Where's the rest of it? The guy sold you half-eaten fruit."

Then she got mad. I stood outside her room and told her

we'd get evicted if she kept slamming doors. She wouldn't answer, not even the courtesy of a grunt. She'd become moody after that first visit to LaCote. Every night she shut herself in her room, playing records and writing in the diary she kept under lock and key. Everything would be fine one second, and then, pow, I'd be in the doghouse, not knowing what I did to get there.

I told Clea that I'd had just about as much as I could take, what with all that had happened in the past six months. She owed it to me to be civil. I'd always given her everything and deserved respect for that, if nothing else. Especially when she had so much more than most kids. So then she got polite to a fault, answering "Yes, sir" like she was in the Marines and eating like the King of England was at the dinner table. When I complained, she said, "Well, you're the one who wanted manners."

"You know this isn't what I was talking about."

"Then you should be clearer what you ask for," she said.

She brought me her textbook from English and showed me a story called "The Monkey's Paw."

"Read it," she said. "It's really good."

I thought kids like her should be studying better stuff, like *David Copperfield* or *Lorna Doone.* Anything but that trash about the dead coming back because the parents didn't say the exact words.

"It was obvious what they meant," I said.

"They weren't careful enough," she told me.

She sat with the book in her lap. Even in her baggy school uniform, her breasts and hips showed. With her hazel eyes and high cheekbones, I saw my own face done as a girl's, the way

Simon had looked like Nora as a boy. Disconcerting to see Clea so like me and yet so alien.

During her time of the month, she hid the pads in the bottom of the garbage so I wouldn't see them. She locked herself in the bathroom every morning and became only sound—water running, flushing, draining; glass clinking and a rustling that was almost silence. Then on those days, she hurried down the hall carrying the wrapped square like a little mummy into the kitchen. The lidded can opened and shut. Then she recrossed the living room as if she were coming from getting a glass of water or doing the dishes.

She kept other secrets from me in plain sight, the way she sat in the chair evenings and wrote pages and pages to that boy like it was her homework. She kept his letters underneath a cardigan she seldom wore, bundled in order and tied up tight. I could guess they were full of puppy love.

She should have been concentrating more on her schoolwork, so I set up rules. She had to come straight home from school unless she was in activities afterward. She had to straighten up the apartment and clean the kitchen on the days the cleaning lady didn't come. She had to study four hours a night and restrict her phone conversations to five minutes. She didn't like it, but it wasn't my place to be liked if that got in the way of taking care of her.

When I told her I'd invited Nora and Maggie for the Thanksgiving holidays, she had a fit. I said how we'd go for a big dinner at the Orrington Hotel and downtown the next day to see the store windows decorated for Christmas, but Clea sulked and argued until I gave in and agreed to go to LaCote.

We used to have a tradition when the kids were little. We'd drive into St. Louis the day after Thanksgiving to see the windows at Stix and Famous and Vandervoort's, all done up for the holiday season with mechanized figures and nativities and train sets so big they filled the large double corner windows.

We were like a Christmas card then—the kids and Nora peering at elves hammering toys or reindeer getting harnessed, and me waiting for them to come running back out of the crowd. "Did you see this? Did you see that?" Watching Nora with the kids skipping at her side, I felt like a shepherd, proud of how I'd made them all so safe and happy.

I wanted us to be that way again, but to do that meant Nora and Clea needed to learn that they belonged here with me. Where that boy couldn't sniff around my daughter. Where my son might have been safe.

The night we had the argument about Thanksgiving, Clea kept banging her foot against her chair and wouldn't look at me. I was so irritated that I wanted to say, "OK, go home for good with your mother and see how you like it."

I was angry at Nora for putting me in that trap but worried how she was managing. I called old friends regularly to see if the new agent was handling their policies to satisfaction. I'd say Nora wasn't up to moving yet but to let me know if she needed anything.

They said she seemed OK. They told me when Ozzie Kline came to work again and when he brought some of the boarders back.

"He'll take care of the heavy stuff for her while you're away," they all told me. "He'll see to what she can't handle."

"Ozzie and Nora have always gotten along good," Jack Rothermich told me right after Kline got back. "Have ever since high school."

I asked him about that. He laughed like I was being silly. "They just liked each other," he said.

"How's that?" I asked.

"Like kids do. Maybe he'll buy that place from you if you head up to Chicago for good."

Then I wondered if for all the time he'd worked for me, Ozzie Kline had been waiting for my property or my wife. Or if Nora's reason for clinging to the farm was that she wanted to be there with him.

Even before I hired him, she'd been disinterested in sex. Never initiating it, turning away when I reached for her or lying there like a cold fish. I never could understand what made her turn frigid like that. I'd heard of women who were cold and others who got that way. But I didn't understand how it could happen, except that there was something wrong with Nora that she'd inherited from old Grace. Some hereditary queerness that made her not like men.

I couldn't imagine she'd actually done anything with Kline. But who knew how complicated he'd made things by undoing what had been taken care of with the horses? Soon after, I wrote Nora to say that it wasn't safe for Clea to travel by herself. How even if we tipped the porter and asked him to watch her, we couldn't be sure she wouldn't be approached by some character. When the train had been late the first trip, I'd worried it had been in a wreck. The next trip, when she didn't get off right away, I thought she'd been abducted. I was just about to get the stationmaster to check when she came sashaying down the steps between two young hoods in tight jeans who looked like they'd come straight out of a pool hall.

When I took her bags, I asked her about them. She laughed.

Said they were trying to make time with her by bragging about the racehorses they owned at Cahokia.

"I asked them the names of their horses, and they couldn't even think fast enough to make them up," she giggled. "They said they *forgot.* Then I asked them if they knew Ozzie Kline, and they pretended to be thinking, saying 'Oh, yeah, the guy at the pari-mutuel window? That little old jockey with the limp?' I told them the blacksmith, the trainer. Everyone knows Ozzie Kline."

How could she have thought that just bragging about some middle-aged two-bit wrangler would keep her safe from these guys?

About that time, the dreams started. I never dreamed before. Not even as a kid. Just didn't have them the way other people did. Nora was forever drifting down to breakfast like a ghost, saying "I dreamed I was dead" or "We were all in a lifeboat about to be swamped" or "I was going to be born but climbed back inside my mother."

When Grace was alive, she encouraged her by pretending she could figure out all the foolishness. She'd sit there drinking her coffee and staring out the window, listening to all the details. If Nora said she didn't remember what happened next, Grace told her to make it up.

"What do you think should've happened?"

Then Grace would analyze this like it was the real dream, not that she could figure out the dream part anyway. But she'd say, "Why, you're feeling overlooked or anxious" or "You've changed your mind about somewhere you thought you were going in your life." She talked like all that voodoo was gospel and she was Hearst editorializing on bank closures and Herbert Hoover.

But late in the fall I kept having the same dream. It stayed with me, too, after I was awake, no matter how I tried to keep my mind off it. Nora, Clea, Simon, and myself were all in a two-story glass house with no floor between the stories. It was night, and the light from the house lit up the tree branches outside the windows. Night, but all the birds were cawing and screeching. When I couldn't find Simon anywhere, Clea pressed her face to the glass and pointed to a huge black crow with a brown thrush dead in its beak.

Crows do not kill thrushes, I thought, or carry them off. This one glanced at me with a black glass eye like it understood what it was doing, and Nora didn't seem to care that Simon was missing.

When I first moved up here around Labor Day, one of the agents at the office asked Nora and me over for dinner. I told him she was finishing some business in LaCote before she moved. A couple of months later he asked us for Thanksgiving, but I told him we were going back to Missouri for the holiday.

"Everything's OK, isn't it?" he asked.

"Oh, sure, sure, just a lot of details to tie up."

So he said, "Well, when she gets here, have her call my wife and she'll help. It's hard for the women starting from scratch."

"You don't know Nora," I told him. "She takes care of everything for me."

After he left my office, I sat there for a while longing for the Nora I'd told him about. The light from the fluorescents made the papers spread on my blotter and the metal filing cabinets hard-edged and over-real, unlike the Nora I'd described. I was overcome with an almost physical sense of loss for a woman that I could no longer locate or prove ever existed.

"There goes Neal Mahler," I could almost hear my employees say behind my back. "Had a wife and couldn't keep her."

I couldn't even explain why Nora didn't care. I'd provided well and been faithful, though I'd had chances to cheat. I knew how Simon's death upset her. But sometimes I worried that I'd catch her sorrow, the way I'd caught her way of dreaming. What if I had started thinking about him and then not been able to get out of bed or eat or work? Where would that have left us?

So I watched employees passing beyond the frosted glass of my office door, walking like figures in a blizzard past my name printed backward on the glass like it was Russian or Chinese. I tried directing my thoughts toward Nora like a stream of light from my head into hers 250 miles away. Lots of scientists believe that the mind has power. I concentrated on making her think like the Nora I'd described. *Nora, care. Nora, behave. Nora, don't do this to me.*

I pictured her the first time I saw her when we were both at college. I'd stopped after a class to light up a cigarette and savor the first drags of nicotine hitting my lungs after an hour's rest. The day was perfect Indian summer, and I stood there on the stoop feeling the smoke fill my chest and the sun bake the top of my head.

Some kids were playing touch football on the quad. Mostly guys, but also Nora and a few other girls still in their gym bloomers. Nora's shirttail was out and she had honey-colored hair, all loose on her shoulders and gold in the sun. I knew that sounded corny as soon as I thought it, but that's exactly how it was. One of the boys was teasing her by trying to smack the ball out of her arms.

"Girls can't play a man's game," he kept taunting.

Well, she backed off a bit, lowered her head, and charged him. Knocked him smack on his butt before he knew what was happening, hurdled him, and ran for a touchdown.

He marched down the field, picked her up, and plunked her in one of those oil drums they use for trash cans. Funniest thing I ever saw, her spitting and hissing as she tried to crawl out without knocking the barrel over. Another guy pulled her out and put his arm around her. One girl smoothed her hair, and the others gathered around. They all loved her, I could tell, and in that moment I loved her, too. Beautiful and spunky and full of life.

I still loved her for those things. But she needed to do so little and all this would have been over before it got out of hand. I thought of reaching for her in the night and unbuttoning her gown. Of how warm her skin would feel and how her nipples would harden under my fingers circling just over them. She'd arch her back and cry out, so small between my legs. She'd help me release and take all that tiring restlessness inside herself until I could fall asleep holding her.

But whenever I was back to visit and went to lay my hand on her arm, she turned away like touching me ever again would be too soon. When I tried to talk to her about Clea, she couldn't keep her eyes still and soon she was making excuses to go check on the horses or ask Ozzie Kline something. Then all I felt for her churned around looking for an outlet and at night spilled over into a dream spreading like a rash—of us riding double and Nora driving the horse right off the edge of the river bluff.

I tried to keep our conversations businesslike and ignore Ozzie Kline hanging around. But always when she looked up from the paper she was reading or came through the back door with her cheeks flushed, I knew how much I'd missed just looking at her. I wanted to graze her hair and touch her face so that she would close her eyes and part her lips slightly. I wanted to press my hands against her back. She'd told me how Arab horses have one less vertebra than any of the other breeds, and how that made their backs stronger. I wanted to touch each bone down her spine and make her the same way, with something less that would make her better.

I didn't know how to show her that I wished her well. So the week before last I said, "I've been thinking about what you said about money." Then I sat down and wrote a check for a little of the extra that she'd been asking for. She came and looked over my shoulder as I blotted the ink and stuck the edge of the check under the sugar bowl.

Then she saw me to the door and was more like her old self. She laughed and talked and asked me how my job was going. She told me about what she'd done that week and how Clea seemed better. Then the problems between us didn't seem so impossible, and I saw myself dropping those bread crumbs of money so in time she would follow me home.

But it didn't last, and the next time I called her, she'd gone back to the Nora who was prickly and difficult. Then I wondered how long she'd play this game and how often I'd be suckered into paying for her smiles. I began to think she was well enough to discuss selling the farm.

I wanted her to be happy. But as they say, there's "a time to embrace, and a time to be far from embraces." After I got us all settled in Evanston, I'd make her happy then.

Chapter Seventeen

Nora Mahler

LAST WEEK NEAL WANTED to know again about selling the farm and when I was moving. I told him that just to discuss the matter left me empty.

"Like you've come after me with a knife and I have to fight with so much energy that I'm good as dead when we're finished."

He shook his head. For once his eyes were tired and his face drawn like mine. All this was making us old and ugly.

"What are you talking about, Nora? I've sat at this table the whole hour I've been here and not even raised my voice."

"You keep at my throat," I said.

"If I really grabbed you, what would you do?"

Maggie looked up from the bowl she was washing at the sink and held her hands still in the water.

"Well, Nora?" he said. "Look around you. Where's this titanic struggle you're talking about?"

Even the chairs upright at the table contradicted me.

"I'm trying to give you time," he said. "But we have to move on together."

Then he just shook his head again and left without another word. I poured a cup of coffee, though my hands were trembling from the potful I'd already had. My mother scrubbed at a skillet, tilting it in the light to make sure she'd gotten off all the egg cooked to its surface.

"I can't tell you, either," she said without looking up. "But it's there."

"Sometimes I want to give in and get rid of this place, just to be done with this," I said.

She set the skillet in the drainer and wiped her hands.

"You need a lawyer," she said.

"For what?"

"I've told you. So you get what you deserve."

"Not now," I said.

I went out and sat on the porch swing. I couldn't tolerate the idea of contacting a lawyer, and just Maggie's suggestion made me anxious, the way impure thoughts were sins to confess and beg forgiveness for, just the same as the acts. As if even the thought of divorce was excuse enough for Neal to try and send me back to Arsenal as a way to get what he wanted.

But the day was warm and bright, and Ozzie was bringing the tractor up from the bottoms where he was harrowing flat the ground dug up by the flood. Since Maggie had asked him to move into the river cabin, he'd fixed the loose washers and wires and boards in the house that had gone unrepaired all summer, brought fresh sausage and applesauce he'd made himself, and planted armfuls of bronze mums. So many little luxuries I hadn't realized I'd been starved for.

I tilted my head back to watch the changing angles of the

swing's chain and the narrow boards of the porch ceiling and was pacified by their neat geometry. The emptiness was starting to fill, the way placing the first piece of furniture in a bare room wards off sadness, and I liked knowing Oz slept just down the bluff from me.

He came up to the porch and asked if I'd help him replace a kitchen pipe that was leaking. He laid out his tools and the new silver gooseneck on an old towel, slid his head and shoulders under the sink, and asked me to hand him the largest wrench.

I knelt beside him, his legs and hips stretched out across the floor. When we were eighteen, sometimes he sprawled on the grass the same way at a place called the Round, a grove out in the country with a small tributary running through it. Sometimes deer came out to drink, or a raccoon or possum waddled by if we sat there quietly enough. By moon the water was solid silver and on cloudy nights the trees a wall of black. We talked for hours and sometimes made love, so peaceful and connected it now seemed impossible that had happened in my life, even so long ago.

The wrench clanged, and he swore at his elbow hitting the side of the space he was cramped into.

"Hey, Nora," he said, curling forward enough that he could look at me out from under the sink as he rubbed his arm. "I ran into Tom Conner at the store. When I told him I was working here, he started laughing about the night he got us stuck out by Fox Hill. Remember?"

I'd lied about going to the library and we'd ridden around in Tom's car all night. I'd looked at the clock on the dash and it had said eight then, and again when I looked at it miles later.

We were out far on the other side of town, and Oz and I had panicked about getting home before my father caught us.

Tom told us, don't worry, he knew a shortcut back. He turned down a dirt road that soon became a path and then a pasture with deep ruts that the tires couldn't reach to the bottom of. He and Oz got out to push, leaving me to steer us through underbrush that stuck in the bumpers like strange Christmas trees.

"You had your foot on the damn brake the whole time," Oz said. "We were back there killing ourselves, pushing and getting nowhere, and when I went to check, you were sitting in the driver's seat just as proper. Your hands on the wheel like an old lady and your damn foot on the brake."

He leaned back laughing into the recess.

"I didn't know," I said.

"That a car doesn't go forward with the brakes on?"

"You didn't tell me what to do."

He sat up again, as much as he could without banging his head, his expression gone serious.

"I didn't want to get rolling too fast," I said.

"There's no such thing as too fast in the middle of a cow pasture, sweetie."

I shrugged, feeling guilty the way I would have with Neal and wondering at the old endearment.

"I thought you'd think it was funny."

I shrugged again. He pulled himself out from under the sink like he would take my hands. But he just reached out and ran his finger quickly across my knuckles.

"I was trying to make you laugh. I like your laugh and don't hear it enough."

"I thought maybe you were still angry."

"I wasn't angry even then, though you damn near gave me a hernia."

He grinned, and I giggled in spite of myself. From then on Oz and I reminisced about ourselves as we had been, and he took me back to places I'd run past too quickly when we were seventeen, ones I'd shut away from myself in the process of keeping them from my father. But since the shock treatment that slightly blurred the more recent times, those long-ago memories had been left clearer, like islands of land left uncovered by the flood. Looking at them stranded and separate, I wondered again how I had let Oz go.

The next Sunday he and I raked mulberry leaves out of the zinnia beds and pulled up the dead plants, knocking the soil from the root tangles and refilling the holes that pocked the ground. I remembered other falls with Simon working next to me, and earlier ones when I'd raked piles for him and Clea to jump in or made the outline of a house for them to play inside of. Brushing against those images made the bitterness of Simon's absence hardly containable. But the more Oz and I cleaned up, the more the bare garden turned pleasingly open, the way Japanese paintings are lovely in their spareness.

"How did we break up?" I asked him. "I don't remember."

I kept raking, trying to keep a blister in the curve between my thumb and hand from touching the handle. Oz stopped and looked over at me.

"You started going out more and more with Neal and your college friends, and finally you just told me to get lost."

I raked more slowly.

"I never expected you to stay, you know. You were always too far above me. But for a while I was like a puppy who couldn't get over that it was over. I couldn't stop running after you."

"You make me sound mean," I told him.

"You were just doing what you thought you had to."

He started raking again, the scritch and rattle covering up the silence between us. I tried to sort the vectors. My father had always said, "Don't ever let me catch you with him." His disapproval on top of all that frightening desire had been too much.

"Once during a battle I was captured," Oz said, keeping his head bent over his raking. "In all the smoke and confusion, I'd overrun my line. It was my own fault for not paying better attention and getting lost so far into enemy territory. I don't know why the German kid didn't kill me, except that he was so young, like Simon. I'd come around the corner of a farmhouse, my belly right up to the tip of his bayonet, and all he had to do was jab it in.

"But maybe he was scared, too, and wanted an excuse to get out of the fight, because he took me in the house and made me lie facedown. He put his foot in the small of my back and tied my wrists to my ankles. Eventually he went to sleep with bombs going off all around and our two rifles in his arms.

"I wondered what you were doing right then, right that second, all those miles away. If you were making love to your husband while I was trying to work the ropes free.

"When I got loose, I cut his throat.

"I couldn't take him as a prisoner when I didn't know how to get back myself to the line. I couldn't get my weapon without waking him and risking my life all over again. I took the knife he'd overlooked in my pocket and ended up standing there with blood running in my boots. Throwing up over what I'd had to do. Wondering where you were and why I wasn't the one with you."

He walked quickly away then to rake another bed on the opposite side of the yard. I didn't know what to say. I was shocked and sorry at what he'd gone through. Disturbed that I had come to his mind in that moment. But also strangely comforted by the thought that, if necessary, he could protect me with the same fierceness.

I remembered with a rush our old and passionate feelings so long disused I'd almost forgotten them during my years with Neal. How tightly and completely Ozzie and I had been connected.

Before he showed up every afternoon, I began going through boxes of mementos packed away. Old journals and pictures and even letters from him, illustrated in the margins with horses. Old words. "You will never know how much you mean to me" and "Do with my heart what you will."

Ribbons I'd won riding, before I started losing on purpose. Before a show Oz sometimes came to watch me working in the ring. He leaned by the wall or sat halfway up the bank of empty bleachers, his legs stretched out on the seat in front and his elbows resting on the one behind. Afterward he'd walk me back to the stalls, his hand slid around the horse's cheek strap.

If he came to me like that before a show, I rode not with my father reciting rote inside my head, but with the thoughtless confidence that Oz had given me. I won easily, not only in points but in myself, slipping through the ride as if I'd been carried on water. But that same feeling had come with whatever we did, in Oz's unconditional approval of my existence.

When I did well at school or made a joke or just stood in front of him, he was glad of me. After a while, when I lay with him naked and we learned to make love, he was reverent and careful of all that was happening between us.

For all the memories that he brought back, and for all those forgotten, I'd saved one especially that I kept playing over in my mind as I sat looking over the yard or lay in bed just before sleep. Not too long after we started going together, we'd gone sledding on an old metal Coke sign we'd found, he and I clinging to each other as we skimmed fast and out of control down the hill, ricocheting off trees and sometimes being thrown off before landing with our arms around each other in a bed of snow.

Walking back to his car, he stopped halfway and kissed me. We kept on, standing in the middle of that winter field until it began to get dark and the sky turned navy. He cradled my face, running his fingers over the lines of bone as if to learn me by touch, then pulling back to check his touch by sight. We seemed both fully separate yet with no difference between us, a twoness the way the nuns tried to explain trinity.

Wanting came loose inside us, the beginning of the lovely, dangerous aching we had for each other, as if we existed in the same skin, and after that we wanted more. Always more without an end we could imagine.

What I did with Ozzie, I never would have thought of with another boy. But I was never with him that I didn't feel whole and complete, with no guilt or expectation or fear. I had the sense he could tell me all the secrets I was supposed to know and take me to those places that, like the universe itself, kept expanding out into infinity but had no center for me to stand in except with him.

After Oz told me about killing the German boy, I went out restless every afternoon, as if the day could not start until he came back from work. I trekked the bottoms land where the lowest pockets were still filled with leftover flood. For the first time I tried to understand the difference between what I had picked for myself in Oz and then put aside for imagined survival with Neal.

But I felt the absence of Simon more keenly then, the huge space he had left around me. Wanting to fill it, I tried with those things parents do not tell their children, what I would have wanted to tell Simon in time, before that time was taken away. I imagined Simon with Janie, grown and married and having children. Simon as loving husband and father, the way I had once imagined Oz.

But I wasn't sure anymore that Simon would have become that so easily, no more than I believed now that Oz and I would have made it. Too many things I hadn't accounted for when trying to see the future.

So safe in Oz when I was eighteen that I thought safety would always be an easy thing to find. So dangerous also, like not having skin. I wondered if Simon had had the same and if he would have let it go because he'd seen me living without it.

Why didn't I know exactly how he had loved Janie? What he'd planned for them together?

Now just space to fill with words, certainly too late to tell. Desperate to hang on to something, I went over the past, looking for my mistakes that might have harmed Simon, for what I could still change to do better with Clea.

I thought about my father, whom my children never knew, and was shocked to resay his words and understand how they'd formed me. Women who did not dress well were "dutchy," those too shy "mousey," those too confident "loud." A divorcée was "that woman," and unwed mothers had "gotten themselves pregnant." Girls who sat close to their boyfriends or held their hands while walking down the street or otherwise showed they were in love were "loose" or "trashy." He left little space in which good women could exist, just as he left me little time by dating everything from two points—"Before you go to college" or "After you get married."

Every Sunday we drove to High Mass in his gray Pontiac, the chief's face in amber resin on the hood. In church we knelt under windows, red and blue like translucent Turkish carpets, and breathed the weighty incense. No matter that we were always early enough to get the first parking spot, the single women were already there as if they'd spent the night, reading their missals and telling their beads. My father said they had nothing to do but go to church, poor old maids.

Yet when one of the many mothers, pregnant or carrying the latest baby, herded her children down the aisle, my father said, "Well, she's been at it again."

"If everyone did that," he'd whisper, leaning close to my ear while placing a ribbon on the mass of the day, "what would the world come to?"

While our old monseigneur chanted off-key like a drunk singing to himself, I stared at the half-understood Latin in my prayer book and deduced that a good woman was like the rider my father was trying to get me to be. I saw anger in his face for those women who fell outside the narrow lane of his expectations, and later in the practice ring, when my elbows flapped or knees banged or heels came up, I saw him look the same at me.

"If everyone rode like that," he'd say, "what would happen?"

I kept trying until I wanted to cry, because the times when

he'd grin suddenly or put his hand on my shoulder or praise me to his friends were flooded with white light. I struggled and flailed and beat against the glass of his heart because I craved those moments like an addict, and praise from all others, even Grace, could not add up in chorus to one word from him.

Yet when I was nineteen and he died of a stroke, the one thought that shot out clear before any others got loose of the initial shock was that I was released. I thought of actually taking off like a wild Indian, hooting and hollering on my little chestnut mare, but suddenly I was like a cartoon character who'd run out past the edge of a cliff and had to scramble back on air.

In the weeks following I had no plans or wishes of my own and, after the first days of comfort, shied away from Ozzie Kline. I convinced myself that wanting him would bring me trouble, the same way I'd once believed when I was twelve that a woman could get pregnant just by desiring a man.

In part I'd married Neal Mahler not so much because I loved him or he me, but because he set the same firm boundaries as Frank Rhymer. Became them himself so that I sat inside the cage of his ribs like an overdue baby in no danger of birth.

Grace had had a premonition about Neal, the way she did with horses. She narrowed her eyes as if she couldn't quite get an accurate reading, and sometimes I swear her nostrils quivered as if she were trying to smell him out. Several times she asked why I wanted this one. I told her he was dependable and faithful and that he'd moved from Chicago and got his business going before he even thought of asking for my hand.

"Doesn't he want the rest of you?"

I scowled.

"Do you love him?" she asked.

"That's the only reason for marrying, isn't it?"

She picked an orange from a bowl and tossed it into the air, catching it without looking.

"Sometimes love is what we call what we're too afraid to name correctly. If you'd asked at my wedding, I would have said I was in love. That was how it was supposed to be, and I made it so. But really," she said, bending close, "I wanted to get away as much as I wanted him, and then a young woman needed a man to carry her off.

"Of course what I got was about as opposite as could be from what I'd expected." She dug her thumb into the orange and tore off the skin in jagged squares, opening the fruit and offering me a section.

"Didn't you miss him when he died?" I asked.

She sucked the juice from the end of a wedge while she thought.

"He was only twenty-seven. A cerebral hemorrhage, you know. Even if I hadn't known him, I would have been sad at a young father dead out of season. But mostly I was afraid for myself. I thought without him the children and I would have to eat dirt and then starve together anyway. Or I'd have to crawl home to my parents who'd say 'We told you so' for the rest of my life.

"But I didn't have time for much of that. I just started doing what there was no help for. At one o'clock the night he died I was standing out in the paddock, pumping the cistern to fill the big galvanized trough. The air was still muggy, the horses were crowding at the water, and I was crying because I was drowning in my own life.

"I remember that moment like it was sealed in amber, standing out there with all those horses milling around and the smell of their hides and breath and manure cooked up and hanging like a solid wall in the humidity. I knew I was supposed to put them in the pasture, but I couldn't imagine how that was going to happen. I'd helped before, but it was as if I'd forgotten how to do anything.

"Then I got tired of bellowing like an idiot and grabbed the nearest horse by its halter and pulled myself up. It was so dark I could hardly tell which one, but I kept riding in a circle, her mane wrapped in my fist, until they all swirled with me, circling the paddock in the dark. I don't know how long I rode like that, but I wanted to keep feeling them bump against me and hear their snorting and neighing like proof of life.

"That was my beginning, Nora, and it was hard. But once I got used to running the farm and the family, I liked the feel of it. Of seeing the wheat brought in and the horses in the paddock and children in the yard and knowing that I had made it all possible. I wouldn't have traded back then, not if I'd been promised wealth and servants and leisure."

She blew out hard like a swimmer coming up for air, then held out the last orange section for me.

"I got to love my life so much more than I remember loving your grandfather. He was a good husband as far as that goes, but he didn't know me, not really, and this life has been better, this one by myself, where I'm not always standing around and waiting for directions."

She licked the juice from her fingers and grinned.

"It won't be that way with Neal," I said.

She shrugged.

"Men are wonderful creatures, but we keep thinking they'll save us from things."

Then she kissed my cheek, her breath full of citrus.

I went ahead to prove I was right. I walked down the aisle by myself since I had no close male relative to escort me, carrying only my father's approval for marrying whom he would have chosen, for executing perfectly the expected dressage.

I didn't want to admit this or what I'd done to myself out of cowardice twenty years before. I wondered if I was fooling myself about Oz in the same way now. What if it was not him I loved or wanted, but an easy escape from Neal or some imagined return to a sweeter time?

Yet the moments with Oz seemed as soft and easy as I remembered and something better, too. One afternoon, on the way to check a fence break, I followed him down the path to the bottoms land, the way I used to onto a dance floor, and studied his back as I had almost a quarter century before when I'd run my hands over the boy that he'd been.

I thought how differently my life would have turned if only he had held me and promised, "Don't be afraid." Not of my father or myself or love. I was angry that he hadn't been strong enough to take my hand and guide me on our own path. I believed for a moment that I would have gone with him then if he had.

Then I wondered what we would do if we ever had that chance again.

Winter

And there, in the silence, at the mid-
point of the day, in a dirty, disgruntled winter,
the horses' intense presence was blood,
was rhythm, was the beckoning light of all being.
I saw, I saw, and seeing I came to life.

—PABLO NERUDA

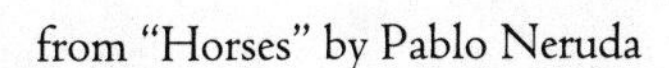

from "Horses" by Pablo Neruda

Chapter Eighteen

Clea Mahler

AS SOON AS I READ in English class, "Now is the winter of my discontent," I knew it fit me, stuck between a father who wished I was forty and a mother who thought she was sixteen. Maggie said she thought they should get divorced, but I didn't want to hear about it or know what was happening until it was over. When my dad and I came for St. Nick's Day, he brought all the Christmas gifts early, I think so he could show my mother how much he'd bought her and give her time to get him as much.

He asked me to look for her, and Maggie said she was out in the barn seeing to the newest boarders who'd come the day before. As I crossed the yard, the trees made a sound like water running and the wind blew my coat open. Stopping to button it, I watched through a barn window as my mother and Oz curried a little dappled Shetland tethered in the aisle.

They worked on either side, laughing and talking as they brushed him from shoulder to haunch. Oz reached behind to pat the nose of an Appaloosa, who had shoved his speckled face over the door of the stall, and a brown tabby barn cat rubbed up against his leg. Then my mother leaned on the pony's back the way men do at bars, and Ozzie leaned the same way so his forearm touched against hers. I couldn't hear what they were saying or even see their faces. But they stood so easy with the pony between them, as she would never with my father. Oz had kept bringing her horses, and she looked like my mother again, even better than the way I remembered her from before last spring.

When she'd gotten the first two horses, my father had said she wouldn't be able to take care of them. He said just wait, she'd get overwhelmed and give up. But that hadn't happened, and now she would never move. I knew that without asking. She would claim she couldn't leave the horses the same way my father swore he was needed at work, and I would always be batted between them like a shuttlecock.

I went back to the house and told my father that I couldn't find her. Maggie said she must have taken the horses out for a run. She kept on about how long they'd be gone, and finally he gave up and went out at the exact moment my mother came swinging out of the barn with Ozzie Kline. My father stood by his car, explaining how if he went to the trouble of bringing me, then the least she could do was be there. Ozzie said she had been there, and pretty soon all three of them were arguing.

I went to my room until Tommy came by. Later he drove us out to show off a fishing cabin near Grafton that his father had bought for cheap after the owner had been scared off by the flood. One on stilts, like ours where Simon and I used to go to get away from our parents. Where, when he got older, he used to bring Janie on nights when my parents were out.

Simon would coast down the drive with the engine cut and lights out, like I'd gone deaf and couldn't hear the tires on the chat. Then I'd watch from my window, Simon and Janie hurrying across the dark yard and finally switching on the flashlight at the top of the steps cut into the bluff. I never told, but I was always angry watching him disappear into the trees, like he'd somehow cheated by going and never mentioning later that he had.

Coming up on the Grafton cabin alone with Tommy, I felt like I imagined Janie must have with Simon. We pulled near the steps that led up to the door, and he left the high beams on for a minute. Snow flurries skittered in the beams, and beyond, the Mississippi was a dark and glinting shape moving past.

"Are we going in?" I asked.

"Don't have the key."

He cut the lights and put his arm around me. After a minute I turned around to face him, backward on the seat so I could lie against him and feel his heartbeat while he held me. I liked the difference between my breasts and the flatness of his chest. How beautiful and strange he was in that difference.

But looking out the window at that cabin so much like the one Simon and I snuck down to alone, I could not keep from crying over him. I had expected Simon to always be with me more than my parents or anything else in life. I knew he hadn't died on purpose, but it seemed he could have kept from leaving me.

I began making sounds I did not want anyone to know came from me. Inside myself I kept repeating, *Why did you leave me? Why didn't you love me enough to stay?*

When I tried to explain to Tommy why I was crying, he

thought I meant him. He kept stroking my hair and holding me closer and telling me he hadn't left, that I was the one who kept going back to Chicago, but there didn't seem to be anything we could do about that. He was always with me, always thinking about me and holding me in his heart, and someday we'd never have to leave each other.

The more I tried to explain about Simon, the more confused we got, with me sobbing and getting the words wrong, and Tommy thinking I was talking about something else. So we kissed and held each other and finally lay down together in the front seat, our feet bent up against the driver's door. His weight kept me from flying off and the only thing that mattered seemed to be getting close.

We were awkward in our winter clothing. Finally he tugged my sweater down and closed my coat. Took my hand and pulled me out the door after him and up the steps of the cabin with only a flashlight from the glove box to guide us. He shook the padlock, tried to pick it open with one of my hairpins, and finally took the big rock doorstop on the landing to smash at it. It held, but the latch pulled loose from the wood.

He laid the flashlight on an old kitchen cupboard, and it shone across the single room and threw high shadows against the far wall. A table and chairs there, an old chifforobe, a sagging double bed. An empty rifle rack, a clutter of rods and poles, an outboard engine dismantled on the floor. A feed-sack curtain hung over a string across one window only. The cabin was cold, though being out of the wind made it seem almost warm, and being with Tommy, I didn't care. We stood just inside the door, hanging on each other and kissing. Then he slid his hands inside my coat and pressed against the small of my back, the bare skin under my sweater warming his fingers.

My father would have said this was terrible, even this little Tommy and I had done so far. But Simon had loved Janie, I was sure of it, and my mother, Oz.

I thought of Maggie warning me to be careful, but her voice seemed to come from another place so far away that her words did not apply here. I didn't want to stop and ruin this. Didn't even think from then on. Was just carried warm and sliding into motion that erased the past months and especially that day of Simon's death.

Didn't plan on what Tom and I were about, but was only caught up by how his hips narrowed and fit between my legs hooked around them. How his upper lip curved and hand cupped my breast and chest pressed against mine. How he watched me closely and entered slowly so the tearing inside was the softest pain.

Then we were together so close that we lost consciousness of anything else. I no longer felt beyond reach or orphaned. Next to me, in me, was another who took me beyond the place that held what had happened to Simon and all the worries about my parents.

He pushed the hair off my forehead and told me he loved me. I said I loved him, too. I wasn't sure that I did or what being in love entailed. I knew I was grateful and no longer by myself, no longer stuck where I had been, and that seemed enough like love to count. Enough to tell him, yes, yes. I am.

The next morning I sat across from my mother eating grapefruit with a pointed spoon and Ozzie Kline reading the Sunday funnies. She told him I liked "Blondie" so he read me the captions, laying the paper down over the sugar bowl so I could see the panels. Then she asked about school and friends and even college, like we had to discuss my whole life that morning. He got in the act, too, and I wanted them to go back to staring at each other like nothing else existed. Then she asked how Tommy and I were getting along and what we'd done the night before. I kept my head down, afraid they would know by looking or take what was happening to them and apply it to me, just as I'd done to imagine them together.

Later they went out to the paddock, and I was left with Maggie staring out the kitchen window. She watched my mother work a horse on a lead while Ozzie sat nearby on the fence.

"You've guessed, haven't you?" she asked.

"What?"

"About Ozzie and Nora?"

"That they think they're in love?"

"Not think. Are. Just the way Grace said they were when they were yours and Tommy's ages."

Then what she'd said months ago about my mother's old boyfriend suddenly made sense.

"Not that they've done anything much about it yet." My grandmother smiled.

"How do you know for sure?"

She gave me a look.

"I just know from how they are with each other."

"You think they should?" I asked.

She shrugged.

"Nora's father was against him, and he would have been a hard man to have a family with, but now that it's just them..." She shrugged again. "The Chinese believe that an imaginary red thread connects those people who are meant to be together, and that nothing can ever break that line—not time nor distance nor circumstance."

"Do you believe that?"

"In this case I do."

"But what about Dad?" I asked.

"How could she go back with him, after what he's done?"

Then she gathered up the four corners of the tablecloth to shake it free of crumbs in the yard, and I was left sitting at the bare table. I wanted to scream, "What has he done that's so terrible?" But I knew the answers like animals I'd caught moving along the side of a dark road, though I'd barely seen their shapes. Then I was angry all over again. That my mother was in love when she should be taking care of me, and that by loving Ozzie then and now, she'd somehow been unfaithful to my father all those years between.

Maggie came back in and, as she was spreading the cloth over the table, said, "If your mother finally works up the courage to push for a divorce, you're going to have to decide which one of them to live with. All this traveling back and forth is ridiculous."

"I don't want either of them," I said.

"You have to live somewhere." She put her hands on her hips.

I wanted to say "With Tommy," but I told her, "I could live with you."

"And keep seeing Tommy?"

I grinned in spite of myself.

"I don't have a place of my own anymore. We'd have to stay here with your mother."

"Dad could buy you another house."

"He's the person who sold the first one, and the lesson for

you in all this is God bless the child who has her own. You better learn that."

She took off her apron and threw it on the counter like she was angry. I shrugged and felt like crying, and that afternoon was glad to see my father come for me. I didn't even go sit with the conductors on the ride home but told them I wasn't feeling well so I could close my eyes and think. I tilted the seat back and pretended to sleep, though the bursts of light as we came into stations hurt like fireworks inside my lids.

I wondered if my own mother had done with Oz, maybe in our cabin by the river, the same things Tommy and I had, but years before she knew my father and I was born. I could not get over that. I tried to imagine if Oz had been my father and how different I'd have been with half of me coming from him. When I tried to think which parent I'd pick to stay with, I ended up wishing for the mother in the story about King Solomon who would rush out to save me from being cut in two.

Then I tried not to think of anything but Tommy touching naked the length of our bodies, and how he closed his eyes when he came inside me. Then I concentrated on not being pregnant, on willing that not to happen. I prayed to Simon to take care of me the way he always had, and when that thought settled safely, I closed my eyes tighter, the wheels going a-clack a-clack.

I drowsed and tried to remember moment by moment the night before. Even so, soon afterward I couldn't quite figure how we held each other at certain moments. So I concentrated on my head and hand resting on his chest and my leg over his when we could still feel ourselves connected although we weren't.

Ozzie had once told me about phantom pain, the way soldiers could feel legs or feet that had been blown off. When I held still I could feel Tommy's body close and his arms around me, keeping me from every other thing that was going wrong. Phantom joy. I settled into it.

Chapter Nineteen

Ozzie Kline

Every day Nora waited on the porch with iced tea ready around the time she expected me. We had the excuse then to sit and talk, at first about what had been let go around the property and needed attention, then gradually just the plain talk of a man and woman who like to be together.

I couldn't shut up at first. I'd saved so much I hadn't realized I was keeping for her, even talking about what had happened during the war for the first time. I interrupted and went off on tangents and told the same stories twice because I kept confusing our real conversations with all those we'd had for years and months in my head.

She was my Nora and she was not. Sometimes it seemed that only a second had gone by in our lives since we'd been lovers. When I told her funny stories, like the one about Bandit and the skunk, she relaxed and laughed with the same exact expression as when she was nineteen. Other times we got in deep conversation, her leaning close and us going on so that

Maggie came out to see what we were doing. But too often Nora suddenly tired, like the breath had gone out of her, and she looked around like she'd lost her bearings, the way half-drowned animals lose track of shore.

You see them all the time during floods. Coons or possums or dogs. Cows, pigs, horses, fox, you name it. They're all just debris to the river, and they all paddle with the same dogged intent, their noses straining up and that scared white look in their eyes. When exhaustion hits, they flail with a kind of worn-out desperation before they slide under and lunge up again, more terrified than they'd been before. Sometimes I took the johnboat to get them, or reached with a tree branch to pull them to shore. But just as often they were too scared to be rescued. They rolled their eyes whiter and turned hard away like I was more dangerous than the river that they swam farther into.

Too often Nora got that same look like she was working to keep above the rushing of whatever she'd found herself in. Some days she got too worn-out to do more than keep to the house and sat all day in Grace's old study, the closed shades bright like yellow lanterns and an old afghan pulled up around her. Her smiles were quick and fake, her eyes hollow like she'd been looking at a world too full of nothing to hang on to.

Then I'd have to work to get her out of it. Sit and talk until she was better. Kid her so she would laugh and I'd know she was OK. Gradually she got in the habit of having me around, and if I was busy in the barn and didn't get to her soon enough, she'd come looking for me. At first she pretended she had to ask me about something like fences or the tractor. After a while she just said she needed to talk.

Then she went on like she'd saved up for me all those years

the way I had for her. Things I was curious to know and wished I'd been there for. How she'd had her babies, raised her horses, and seen Grace to rest. Things I almost didn't want to know. How Neal had put her down in cruel little ways, how even before the summer he had abused her spirit, though she was reluctant to call it that.

"It's just the way he is," she said.

"It's a bad way."

I told her he'd done too much to be excused, the way he'd demeaned her. I was shocked she'd let him, that she'd stayed with him until Grace's land and not herself was the issue.

One afternoon late when she was helping me string new wire on fence posts, hammering in the staples while I held the wire taut, she out of nowhere started talking about Neal. She kept the crown of her head bent over her work, the amazing variety of brown and blond and gray in her hair catching the light.

"About every three or four months," she said, "so regular that I could predict it, he'd come in from work and put his arms around me. After the kids were excused from dinner, he cleared the dishes and brought coffee, asking about my day and listening without taking his eyes off me."

She laughed short and hard.

"Then he'd start in about the horses, pumping me with questions to get me talking about what I usually kept out of his way. But like a fool I'd let him sucker me. Pretty soon he'd lean closer with a puzzled look on his face.

" 'Help me understand,' he always said, 'why all this means so much to you.' "

Nora smacked at the post with the hammer.

"No matter what I told him, how I liked being good at

what I did and how being with horses brought me joy and a thousand other reasons, he always said, 'But why?'

"Sometimes he went on like that for more than three hours at a time. It's stupid that made me crazy, isn't it? So stupid I've never told another person about it. He wasn't doing anything wrong, just asking simple questions. All wives want their husbands to understand them. But he kept on worse than the kids when they were two. Why, why, why, until all I loved and cared about was reduced to ashes.

"I could never make clear to him what was obvious to me. He's a smart man. But no matter how I explained or repeated or simplified, he looked even more confused and kept asking 'Why?' until by the end of the conversation I thought I must be crazy and there was no point to what I did.

"Seriously, Oz, I always finally cried. Then he'd look even more puzzled and ask, 'Why are you getting upset?' "

She smacked the post hard, then let the hammer drop to her side.

"The nuns always told us if we couldn't explain something, then we didn't know what we were talking about. Even though they never could explain God."

She reached to place a staple over the wire, and I put my hand over hers. I couldn't explain, either, exactly, why what Neal Mahler had done to her was twisted. I just knew all his talks had been beatings of sorts.

"It was him who was wrong," I told her. "Him, not you," and Nora looked up at me quizzically, like she couldn't decide if I was telling the truth or not.

Around the end of October, Maggie offered to let me use the river cabin to save the drive to and from town every day, especially late at night when I usually left for my rented trailer.

The cabin on its high stilts had survived the flood and just needed the steps replaced and a piling reinforced. She invited me to take my meals and baths up at the house and spend the evenings with her and Nora whenever I wanted. The cabin was only for sleep or when I needed to get away from them, Maggie said, and a coal stove kept it warm enough for that. I didn't mind being alone at night there. I rearranged the furniture the way it used to be twenty years before and lay in bed watching the shadows the way Nora and I had, sleeping with memories of us making love. I offered to pay, but Maggie said they owed me more than the rent for my labor.

"I'm just glad you're here," she said, and walked off like we'd been discussing nothing.

It didn't take us long to fall into a routine. I let myself in the house early every morning to get ready for work and sometimes ran into Nora, puffy-eyed from insomnia and wrapped in Simon's old red plaid flannel bathrobe. She'd give me a quick, tight smile. Sometimes while I was in the bathroom, she made toast and coffee and left it on the kitchen table. Every afternoon she was always waiting.

One Sunday afternoon in mid-November while we were in the yard throwing a ball for the dog, she said, "It's nice to have company."

"I've been here too long to be company," I said.

"No, I mean that you here with me is better than being alone." She cocked her head and tugged at the ball in Bandit's mouth. "Not like with Neal when I preferred it."

She didn't say much more about that ever, but I knew what she meant. I looked forward to our evenings and got attached to sitting around talking while she and Maggie cooked, and then cleaning up for them afterward. Sometimes we played cards or mah-jongg or listened to the radio. Other nights we read or looked at photos or just talked. Then I took a flashlight, walked across the dark backyard and down the steps on the bluff, and stood looking at the river as long as it took me to smoke a cigarette. Except for where I slept, it was like Nora and I were married and this was our life, easy and complete, with nothing I needed beyond the perimeter of her and her land.

At first when I came back, Clea didn't have much to say to her mother and grandmother, and in that pecking order, absolutely nothing to me. But she was out with her boy mostly and came back from him smiling. I didn't know how to get along with her the way I had with Simon, but was satisfied for the time being if she was just civil. Later, when Neal Mahler started coming with her, he swaggered around and glared at me sitting at the kitchen table, drinking coffee. I didn't have to do much but look up from the paper I was reading and nod for the muscles in his throat to clench. The politer I was, the madder it got him.

I always made sure to tell Nora how well Clea seemed and how Neal was more like a banty rooster than a man seeing about his family. That seemed to reassure her, like for years she'd been the kid who suspected the emperor was buck naked and finally had another member of the crowd agree.

I also started trying more seriously to get her to begin getting some of the boarders back. From the first night and every week or so after, I told her about the old friend of Grace's with the gray Arab filly. Yet she was more ready to talk about Simon than she was about horses, more about us young than about what she needed to do next.

But close to Thanksgiving, I gave up the soft approach and

brought in the first pair of horses almost without her permission. Nora was sweeping out a clean stall when I came up and leaned over the door.

"The Culbertsons have a problem," I lied. "I said we could help them out."

Then I made up some story about their old stable having an electrical fire, and thank God they got all the horses out, but now they needed an interim place to keep them until the damage was repaired. Nora looked up at me and didn't say anything. She kept sweeping the bare floor, and I didn't tell her the trailer was on its way. While we unloaded, she stayed in the house. I kept glancing at the windows to see if she was curious enough to watch, but just the clouds reflected back dim and wavy in the glass. I even walked the horses around the yard twice to make sure she saw them—a black Thoroughbred filly with a star and a sorrel quarter horse mare with three stockings and a blaze.

I left them in the paddock like bait and worked them within sight of the house. Two days later Nora came out, pretending to look for some old studbook of Grace's that I was sure was somewhere in the house. She drifted out of the tack room to the wide space between the stalls where I was currying the sorrel, walking up and down past us like she was out for a stroll.

"Check this, Nora," I said finally, lifting the sorrel's foot and feeling the bones. "Do you think the ankle should be wrapped?"

She couldn't keep away once I gave her the excuse. Then she was out there in that barn giving me so much advice, leaning over my shoulder and sometimes beating me to the work, that I wanted back some of the quiet I'd tricked her out of. I asked her to help me exercise the horses, and the workouts evolved into long rides down the bluffs and along the river.

We couldn't avoid riding within sight of where Simon had died. The first time I tried to hurry past, but Nora kept her mount to a walk and I had to circle back. Always I watched her closely out of the corner of my eye, but she never so much as turned her head, not until two days before Clea and, of course, Neal would be in for Christmas. As the trail bent the closest to the spot where we'd found Simon, she dug her heels into the sorrel's side and turned her hard through the matted grass and skeletons of scrub trees.

Nora rode in a circle around the spot she had obviously picked as exactly Simon's. Turning the mare to the center, she pulled up, slid off, and let the reins hang.

I stopped outside the trampled ring of grass, not certain what to do. She dropped to her knees and called, "Oz." I hesitated, but she called again, insistent this time, and I crossed the space like a trespasser. She wasn't crying the way I'd expected, but had a hurt and puzzled look, her hands out flat in the grass like she was looking for a lost ring.

"I feel him all around me," she said. "But I don't know how to get to him."

I knelt, and she leaned back against me.

"Oh, Ozzie, how could this have happened to us?"

I didn't have an answer, no more than I had for anything else in my life. Simon's death and most other loss seemed a series of flukes, interrupted only rarely by moments of choice. Like the chance I'd had with Nora before, and the one I had again now.

But going out to her was like stretching across space to where she kept the center of herself, so far out that I pulled thin to the point of breaking. Even with every muscle braced I trembled. But I had always wanted Nora close with me. I wanted that enough to risk myself, I thought.

Right before New Year's we hiked down the bluff to check the fence line after a storm. For ten minutes I thought about putting my arm around her, and finally did, the way I would over the back of a mare. She fit perfectly in the crook, and after we'd walked a quarter mile touching, I pulled her to me. She looked up, her eyes smoky, and ran the tip of her finger in a semicircle from my forehead to my jaw. Her arms slid up and around my neck, but suddenly she pushed off and jerked away. Just like that, so I didn't even know what had happened.

"What are we doing?" she said. "I'm still married."

She walked a few paces off and half turned to look at me.

"He's broken all his promises," I said.

"It doesn't matter what he's done."

"No man treats a woman the way he's done you. All vows are null and void, Nora, once a man kicks you like a dog."

She got angry at that, and the more we argued, the more that drowned and panicked look came over her again. I hadn't saved her from that, not with all my efforts, and now I couldn't even make her see reason.

Love wasn't a thing to argue about anyhow.

Then I knew we'd only been playing house, and I'd invented her and anything good I'd ever thought about us just as surely as I had my perfect family for strangers in diners. She was still Nora Rhymer with too much power over men and not enough sense to know what to do with it. If I overturned the world to get to her, we'd do no better in time than she had with Neal Mahler, and a family would be broken behind us.

I left her standing there, mouthing the defense of her marriage to my back, and went up to the woods behind the house to smoke and turn over the same thought. How I'd fooled myself into thinking this could ever really be as good as I'd imagined. She came to get me, and when I wouldn't look at her said, "Don't be like this, Oz."

I lit another cigarette and watched the smoke unwinding into the air.

"Please don't be mean," she said.

I didn't say anything but after dark packed up my gear and moved out of the cabin. That night I slept in my truck, parked facing out over the river down by Grafton. The cab was cramped and cold, but I deserved that for ever thinking she could want me the way I wanted her.

But I felt good, too, about facing up to that fact. Like the part of me that had been spilling out and pooling around her feet was back inside where it belonged. That we could be together had always and only been a stupid hope, and now that I was done with it, I was flooded with the same relief I'd had finding myself alive and whole after the worst battles.

I'd help her with the horses until she was on her feet again or she followed after Mahler, that much I'd do. But the horses were all that would be between us, all that I could ever expect within reason from this woman I used to feel too much for.

Chapter Twenty

Maggie Rhymer

Up until Simon's death I was never much of a mother. When Nora was born, Frank had shamed me from nursing her by constantly harping on how modern bottles had removed the need for a woman to go around like an immodest cow. By the time I was out of childbed, Grace was keeping her in a bassinet by her own bed, and I resigned myself early on to being not needed.

But on the farm I'd always longed to escape as a reminder of my deficiencies, I discovered the surprise of standing my ground. There was no one else to stop Neal or defend Nora or comfort Clea. So I began the lessons I had put off learning as a young woman.

From the moment I put my arm around Clea at the burial, I began to see myself in her. The outsider in the family, the stranger who found all things foreign. At first I did nothing, this child not my business. But soon I began to see her in danger, just as I had Nora at the mercy of the shock treatments.

Grace had always told me it was no good to let Nora turn herself inside out to please Frank, but I dismissed that as her jealousy. Now I watched Clea do the same to please her father and get back at her mother, and I wanted to undo with her what I'd let go with Nora. I helped Clea get to Tommy, and in exchange she allowed me to at least mention what she didn't want to hear.

I hoped these little touches would do better than silence. But she, like Nora, seemed to be straddling the balances of a scale, throwing her own weight to compensate against the heavier side. She told me she couldn't leave her father who needed her, just as Nora put off her divorce with the excuse that she couldn't survive financially.

I asked Nora why Oz had suddenly moved out of the cabin. She was peeling potatoes at the sink and pushed the hair out of her eyes with the back of her hand.

"It was too cold down there at night," she said, but when I asked Oz, he said he just felt like moving.

Working together, they were gruff and blunt. Around the house, they took turns talking like they'd made a deal not to be in conversation with me at the same time. But I'd catch them looking at each other when they thought the other didn't see, and I thought of what Grace had told me shortly before Nora got married.

"Parents," she said, "watch to see if their children decide to be safe or take chances to get what they want. Most of us are at least relieved when they pick safety, but there's a danger in that, too, and consequences we can't always see. I didn't want that for Nora, but I'll bow to her decision, just as I did to yours."

Then she asked me to thread a needle for her, her sight

getting so poor that she couldn't bring the eye into focus, and she joked that her arm had gotten too short for sewing.

I asked her what she had against Neal.

"I never trust a man who doesn't like horses."

"You didn't like Frank, and he was a great horseman."

"Frank?" she said. "He just didn't like women."

Then as always when my mother became cynical and cryptic, I wanted to argue against her. Yet in that great vacuum left by Simon's death, the space filled with Grace's breath, and her words came out of my mouth. When Neal told me he was only concerned with Nora's happiness, I said bull. When he said he meant well, I asked why he didn't do well. I prodded at Clea and outright badgered Nora.

"If the divorce will take two years, what are you waiting for?" I told her. "Start the clock running now. You can always change your mind if things get better."

She told me she wasn't strong enough yet to fight Neal, and I was half afraid she was right. When I asked Ozzie to talk to her, he looked up from the filly's hoof he was filing and said I was sounding more like Grace every day. I knew, I could hear it myself, that part of her I'd always cringed and run from. But finally I understood what she had been about.

None of us should know how our children die, as Grace and Nora did. Or our children's children, as I had found out. But those deaths compelled me to keep what was left from being lost, particularly since no one else around seemed ready to do so.

I went back to the lawyer's to reassure myself about our rights with the farm. He said that matter would have to be settled among the three of us, as our names were all on the deed. The only thing that would affect parity would be if one of us died or was declared incompetent.

Then I wanted to know if there was anything we could do to get Clea back without a bloody battle.

"Since they're still married, a judge might leave it up to the daughter to pick her place of residence, and if push came to shove, the mother's preference might have more weight."

He played with his pen as he read over the notes.

"Still, it would be unpleasant, and if they can get back together, that would be the way to go. Or if the daughter could make her own decision without the courts getting involved."

"Isn't there anything about mental cruelty?" I asked.

"Oh, sure, but that would be hard to prove about Neal Mahler, what with his reputation."

"But what about what he did to the horse?"

"What about it? I heard it just dropped dead. That's what Neal's been telling everyone, and how the shock of it was just too much for his wife on top of the other." He shook his head. "I felt so bad for her when I heard that."

"What if he shot it?"

The lawyer looked up and blinked in surprise.

"Was it sick or break its leg or something?"

"I mean, what if he just shot it?"

"Well, I'd have to know the extenuating circumstances, but that would change the case, no doubt."

I could hardly sit still for the rest of the interview, and when it was over, went directly home. I waited all day for Oz to come by, then for Nora to take out one of the boarders for a run so I could catch him alone in the barn. He was packing a poultice on the sorrel's foreleg and looked over his shoulder at me—my old self, still wanting a man to confirm what I knew for sure.

"Oz, what happened to Zad?" I crouched down next to him.

"The bastard shot her. You know that."

"Do you know for sure?"

"Sure as I recognize a dead animal with half her head blown away."

"You saw that?"

"Didn't see him do it, but I heard the shot and buried her."

"You're sure that's what he did and could testify?"

"Why you asking, Maggie?" He stopped fussing with the horse to look at me.

I told him what the lawyer had said.

"It'd be my word against his, which in this town isn't a fair contest, but yeah, I could testify. It's Nora you have to convince."

He wrapped another strip of poultice and held it in place, his hands tight around the mare's leg. I went inside then and phoned Neal. At first he was friendly, as if he expected that I'd called to throw my lot with his, and talked about how he and Clea would be down again in a couple of weeks. But as soon as I said, "You lied about what happened to Zad," he denied it.

"You told everyone she just died."

"It was none of their business and just too hard to explain. I was protecting Nora from everyone bringing up a sore subject and upsetting her all over again."

"Is that what you were doing?"

"Listen, Maggie, I don't know what burr you've got under your tail, but I think you were unhappy with your own husband

and so you're trying to split up Nora and me now. Leave her alone. No one likes a meddling mother-in-law."

Then I wanted him in front of me so I could wrap the phone cord around his neck and beat him senseless with the receiver, and I was even more angry over my impotence to do that or anything else that made a difference.

"You listen, Neal Mahler. You back off Nora or I'll dig up that horse and drag her down Main Street, and then I'll have you arrested for destroying my daughter's property. Just ask her lawyer."

I hung up and sat there shaking, not knowing if even the logical part of what I'd threatened him with was possible and feeling foolish for my childish anger besides. But I knew that if anything could scare Neal Mahler, it was the fear of being exposed for what he did and lying about it afterward.

I kept thinking, too, of a trip I'd taken to India years before. I'd been traveling out in the rural areas where tourists rarely go and stopped at a town so small I don't even remember its name or if it had one. The children and dogs were so thin their ribs showed, and the whole area reeked of sewage and dirt. When I arrived, the adults were gathered in agitated groups. My guide, who spoke perfect English and a pidgin form of the local dialect, had gone over to see if we could buy some vegetables that I could wash and cook in bottled water. He said all the commotion was over some woman in a neighboring village who'd committed suttee.

Of course that had been outlawed over a century before by the Raj, he said, nodding his approval, but in the more primitive areas isolated cases existed of wives throwing themselves on their husbands' funeral pyres. I couldn't understand why anyone would do this, but he said it was considered a holy thing which guaranteed the woman would be remembered as a goddess. Besides, a husband's male relatives were responsible for feeding the widow for as long as she should live, and she was under great pressure not to burden them in any way. For the rest of the trip I had watched smoke coming over the trees from the village fires and wondered about women who destroyed themselves so as not to be a bother.

Now I sat twisting the phone cord and thinking of how Neal did remind me of Frank. The same arrogance and trick of diverting an argument off course. Maybe I was just getting even by proxy.

When Nora came in, she kicked off her boots and stood at the kitchen window, looking out at the leaden winter sky.

"Snow's coming," she said.

"I talked to the lawyer again," I said.

"Why'd you do that?"

"Because I can't stand to see you like this."

"Like what?"

"This." I waved my hand in her direction.

"I'm fine. It's just that Ozzie gets in these moods. He's fine one minute and the next acts like he can't stand to be here."

"You're the same with him."

"We're fine," she said.

"I'm fine, you're fine, he's fine."

I got up and left the room, tired of repeating what I thought she should know and pointing out what she didn't want to see, and then getting nowhere anyway. It was her life and none of my business, just as Neal said. But if Neal had said it, then it must be suspect. I turned and went back to the kitchen.

"What do you think will happen if you just stand there? Maybe this will all go away? If you can't be with Neal, divorce him. If you want Oz, tell him. Sit down with Clea and ask her to stay with you. Do something, Nora, or you'll lose what you have left."

"Do what, exactly?" she asked.

"Some horse trading, as Grace used to say. Take my half of his co-op. Barter it for his share of the farm."

She leaned back against the counter, rubbing one stocking foot against the other.

"You'd do that for me?" she asked.

"Of course."

She stood studying me for the longest time, her arms crossed over her chest.

"What if we couldn't keep this place going?" she said. "What if we didn't make enough money?"

I shrugged.

"Cross that bridge when we get to it."

"But if we get to it and can't cross, I will have lost everything."

She turned and looked back out at the sky, and for the rest of the day we kept away from each other. The next morning I woke as though I'd dreamed an answer from Grace. I hauled out all the old tax forms and account books, glad for once that Neal hadn't been able to keep himself from writing down each expense. I tallied and calculated, pulling the arm of the adding machine as if I would yank it from its socket.

I called the lawyer and got an estimate on alimony and child support. I quizzed Ozzie about how much profit came from each boarder and how many we could handle and how much we could charge for training. I went back to the house and combined the figures, finally arriving at a sum we could survive with. Then I added fifty dollars.

The numbers sat neatly on the page like the bull's-eye of the target. The missing piece Nora claimed she didn't know. The only words we had to answer when Neal Mahler tried to throw a discussion off course.

I signed the paper like a contract that couldn't be taken back. I put the figures on Nora's bed with a note explaining the plan.

"This is exactly what we need, what's fair. I can talk to Clea or Neal or Ozzie for you. I'll even help exercise the horses if you'll teach me to ride all over again."

Then I shut her door and leaned against it. Willed her to do the rest.

Chapter Twenty-One

Nora Mahler

I carried Maggie's numbers in my pocket for a week, wondering if they could be accurate. If I got the farm, free and clear, I would need Oz to help. But then what would happen between us? I felt safer with him angry, as if that distance gave me space to take a breath and think. I was as afraid of him as I had been at nineteen, terrified that his love would engulf me the same way memories of Simon did. Too much, too much. So, not able to deny or take hold of either, especially both together, I kept the two riding on the periphery of my self.

For the time being, as long as I met him each morning at six, leading the first mount to the exercise paddock, the reins loose in his hands and our breath thick steam in the early air, then the day fell into its groove and could ride to the end.

Bandit scratched at my door each morning at five and pushed it back until it banged against the bureau. He clicked across the floor and stood patiently with his chin flat on the bed and lifted one eyebrow and then the next until I patted the mattress for him to jump up. I dressed and took him out and stood hugging myself in the cold while he smelled out a place to urinate. The sky was still dark and the birds sang to find each other. I never felt like getting up, but by the time I was standing in the dawn yard, the feelings that would have weighted me to the bed had fallen away.

Soon Oz's pickup came bouncing down the drive, its lights yellow columns in the grayness. He came in to sip coffee from a fat mug like the kind in truck stops, and we leaned against the kitchen counters. Standing under the bulb over the sink, bright and harsh compared to the soft sky which lightened outside, I felt caught between day and night, between my old life and this new.

Oz didn't want to talk to me, but if I only discussed the horses, he answered me as long as I kept to that. Then we left the mugs in the sink and went to the barn, and by the time he left for work, I'd started in on training. Then Maggie had lunch ready and I was over the noon hump and going easily along the downhill slide of the day.

Neal also seemed to have found a schedule on which to shape the weekends when he didn't visit. He wrote me every Saturday and mailed the letters at exactly the same time before the post office closed at noon. I pictured him putting on his jacket and walking the half block from the apartment to the mail slot, and neighbors several stories above looking up from lunch and setting their clocks by his passing.

His words were cajoling, threatening, reasoning, commanding. A flood of markings in his thick slanted hand. I tried to push through them, his Palmer cursive as incomprehensible as scimitar blades of Arabic or boxy temples of Korean. I pictured him as some lord sending missives to a far outpost, with customs and conditions so foreign that his idea of them would be laughable were he not basing his orders to the barbarian on that.

I tried also to remember him at the time I was in love, but that incarnation seemed as unreachable as the meaning of his letters. All that had survived was the memory of the crazy heat that made me call him twice a day and drive by the house where he rented a room and pace like a caged cat if he were late for picking me up. But I no longer knew if I had wanted him or just to be a wife.

Yet if I had wanted him, then maybe I would again, though desire seemed locked behind the most recent summer and what love I had had for him a memory erased for good by the electroshock.

I almost said I could see the summer like a movie, myself kicking through the paddock to the circle of Zad's blood or lying drugged in my darkened room. But the images remained vague and filmy; more than them, the smells came back to me. Stale air and metallic fluids. Sour sweat. And, from Neal's head pressed sideways against my face, his day-old hair tonic and the waxy mix of oils in the curves of his ears. More often than the memory of him forcing my legs or leaving bruises on my arms, the smells returned and overcame me.

I would have liked to go back to him, or at least to the man I imagined I'd married. I would have liked to do what he wanted and continue our history to the end. But I could not find those people I'd thought we were—the hopeful, careful girl and the young man who wanted her. And because I could not, I was left with only this—the beaten woman and the man who would beat her again, if only to remind her that she must lie still to please him.

How did we get from lovers to this? I could not even guess. With a million small slashes, so many that most went unremembered. Yet how to reweave what had come so unraveled? A task so monumental that I'd lost connection with it, and the idea of being Neal's wife was only a stray thought, like those I had about alchemy or God, and just as foreign.

So I found myself like Eve with no childhood and a strange man before her. This was no Eden and the end of the world seemed to have come before the beginning. Yet Oz had found a gray filly bred by an old friend of Grace's and one so rich that she wanted the right owners more than top dollar.

He'd told me the whole story. How Mrs. Bader's son was a banker who couldn't tell a horse's ass from his own, and how she had this gray filly who was the granddaughter of the mare she'd loved above all her horses, the way I'd loved Zad. How she couldn't train her because of old age and her leg that hadn't healed correctly after a fall three years before. How because of her respect for Grace and desire to place the filly with someone who would take care of her properly, Ozzie had pestered her unmercifully until she agreed to trade us the horse on the promise that we never sell her and that she be bred to the lines Mrs. Bader had picked out and that all her foals be sold to people who cared well for their animals, the money going back to her from the sales as we became able to afford it.

Though Oz showed no break from his surliness since our fight, he and I took the pickup, and on the way to the Grafton ferry and her farm in Illinois, we passed through the flat stretch of land wasted by the summer's flood.

Most of the standing water had finally dried up so that the sky no longer reflected in the muck as if caught there. But the fields were stubbled with dwarf shocks, draped with what looked like lank, muddied hair. A corn crib caved around a punch to its center, down the road from a collapsed tractor shed. Cold bright January. Oz squinted into the sun as he reached over to adjust the heat. He was driving fast, and the land streamed behind his profile, a graying lock of dark hair falling over his forehead. I felt set down out of nowhere and kept repeating in my mind:

We are going to get a horse. A gray girl pretty as Zad. I am with Ozzie and we are grown. What has happened in the twenty years since I last made love to him seems only a dream. We are going to get a horse, a smoky filly born out of wind.

Yet even this seemed unreal, more so when Ozzie slowed down and turned off the main road onto a rocky dirt lane.

"Look at that," he said, and lifted his chin toward a house or what was left of one. "I knew a family who lived there once."

"Who?" I asked.

"A woman. You didn't know her and she wasn't here for long. Lived here with her kids when she couldn't afford any better. Couldn't make it after her husband left her with no money, so she eventually went home to her folks in Arkansas."

I didn't think much of this until the slow thought came seeping that this had been a lover of Oz's when he came back to work the year before Simon died. Stupid to be shocked that he'd had lovers. Of course he'd had, a single man for all this time.

Then I, too, was curious to see the house as if I'd find clues to what had happened between them or see their faint ghosts eating or talking or making love.

The house was a ranch style with the river's mark halfway up. The windows had been blown out by water forcing through, the yard stripped bare and scattered with debris. Inside, the sludge was several inches deep on the floor, a few old boxes and odds and ends of furniture crushed and washed up against a far wall, and the moldy dank of rot so strong I held my hand to my nose to breathe in the film of Jergens on my skin.

"Looks bombed and abandoned," Ozzie said.

"She wasn't here when this happened, was she?"

"No, left a few months after I started working for you the first round."

He walked to the center of the room and stood looking all around, his back to me and hands on his hips. I wondered what he was remembering of her, and I was jealous that he could picture a lover in this ruin. Petty to be jealous. I could have had him if I'd wanted. All those years we weren't in touch I'd been afraid to think of him and what I'd given up. But now I was angry I'd missed all the life he'd had in my absence and that he hadn't loved me enough to give up the others.

"Did you live here?" I cleared my throat.

"With three little kids running around and raising hell?" He grinned and rolled his eyes. "No, just spent the night every once in a while."

"What was her name?"

"Carol. Carol Doucette."

"Was she nice?"

"Yup, she was always trying to please. Did that to a fault, though. If I took the kids for an afternoon or fixed something around the house, she'd have to do a hundred things in return to pay me back."

I picked my way into the room, across the shelf of hardened mud.

"For instance?"

Oz looked over his shoulder at me as he peeled a strip of wall from the lathing underneath.

"Oh, cooking, mending, you name it. But mostly when we went to bed together, she treated me like a king. Massages and rubdowns. Anything, anything at all, though I kept asking her what she liked."

He came over and stood near. He wouldn't touch me or even look at me without a hardness in his eyes. I wondered if he was telling about her to hurt me.

"She always said she didn't need a thing as long as I was happy."

He went to a window and looked out over the barren yard.

"That made me nervous." He turned and looked around the room. "Like she would just keep running out of herself until she was empty. I kept trying to change her, not because she and I were ever going to stay together, but because I wanted her to get something for herself. But she was like water, you know, running over me and away in all directions, having no shape of her own. I kept thinking she was trying to fill me, to use me like a bowl and take my shape.

"I tried to get her to stop, but that just made her mad and she finally left to go back home. She kept saying I wouldn't let her love me."

He stood so close I had only to step forward to touch him. A moment to make up what I'd ruined, but I could not bring myself to move.

"Were there others?" I asked instead.

He shrugged.

"What do you mean? Others I slept with or had a beer with or what?"

"Others you loved," I said.

"Not really."

"Not the one you married?"

"We were just kids and that was only for six months. Who knows what I would have thought of that in time? But as far as I can tell, I didn't love any of them, not in the way you're asking. But then again, I loved them all, if for nothing else but how they struggled with their lives."

He looked at me closely then turned away again.

"Ready to go?" he asked.

As we drove down the road, I looked back at the house—dirty, faded yellow with the windows ragged eyes and the yard and floors one long mud plain. Once children had slept here while Ozzie Kline made love to their mother, under covers that became too warm in winter or in front of fans that blew hot night air over them in July.

Now like the dead. I hadn't gone to the cemetery since Simon had been buried, didn't want to see it or anything else quiet and still and ruined. I stared at the fields flying past, the road bisecting the winter land and us headed to the horizon. If this were a picture, that road narrowing to the vanishing point, then we were on our way to driving literally from sight and falling off the edge of the canvas like ancient mariners.

"What did she look like?"

Oz shook his head in bewilderment.

"Why?" he asked.

"I just want to know."

"It doesn't do any good to describe a person. You'll still see her the way you imagine."

"Just try."

"Well, her hair was light, light brown," he said. "I used to tease her about it being dirty blond, and she'd get mad."

I saw him picking up a tendril of her hair and absent-mindedly studying it.

"It was real short and curly and she'd brush it a hundred times each day to straighten out the kinks."

"Eyes?"

Ozzie rested one hand loosely over the top of the wheel and laughed.

"Blue? Green? Gray? I don't know. All of them, maybe."

"Size?"

"Dress size? Height? Weight?"

"Any of those, approximately."

"Fourteen hands."

"Like a horse?"

"Yeah," he said. "I used to be able to look right over her head the way I could a mare's back."

"Figure?"

"Not fat or overweight."

"Plump?"

He stopped the truck, idling in the middle of the road.

"What are you doing?" he asked.

"What are you doing?" I said. "We're stopped in the middle of Highway 94."

"Look around, Nora. What's out here but us?"

The whole flat plain was deserted except for a tractor hauling hay up to a far barn.

"It's not safe."

He took his foot off the brake, and the truck rolled so slowly that he could look at me and steer with only an occasional glance to the road.

"Why do you want to know so much?" he asked.

"I just do."

"You were married at the time."

"I'm still married," I pointed out, suddenly glad of that familiar refuge. Even with its pain, it seemed somehow safer than entering this new territory with Oz.

He floored the gas and we snapped forward. The bright sun and rows of plowed fields clicked past. The speed of the truck accelerating to eighty and Ozzie's anger made me queasy.

"Stop," I told him. "You're acting like you're sixteen."

"And you're not?" Oz said.

"Acting like my father said you would."

I was sorry, took a breath, and started over.

"I just want to know about her so I can know about you."

"What about me, Nora?"

"What you did until you came to work for us. What you saw in her."

He let the truck's speed drop back to normal and drove on as if nothing'd happened. We didn't say anything else until we pulled up in the yard of the woman with the filly. Oz yanked the keys from the ignition and pushed open the door. Just before he got out and slammed it behind him, he leaned close across the space between us in the cab.

"What did I see in her?" he said. "I thought for a little while that I saw you."

Then he walked off to the paddock and leaned against the fence to watch the horses. I followed after, conscious of my gait as if he had eyes in the back of his head. I stood a little away from him and stared out without really seeing, so much did I just want to look at him.

"See her?" he said finally, and for a moment I thought he meant the woman who'd lived in the flooded house.

Then the filly tossed her head over the back of another. The fine wedge-shaped head and wide-set eyes, the small ears and dark flaring nostrils, she was a beauty even among the other sweet-faced Arabians in the herd. So caught up that he forgot how angry he was, Ozzie took my arm and pulled me to where he was standing, as if that was the only place I could see.

"Look at her," he said.

I could look nowhere else. Then I was angry all over again at Neal who'd made me so poor that I couldn't afford anything more than mean survival. The food, the heat, the taxes, the insurance, but beyond that, no things owned for the sake of love. And I was angry at Oz for dragging me out here on the fantasy that somehow we would go home with this horse.

"I'll never be able to afford her," I said.

"We can barely afford an old fat pony, evil tempered from too many children kicking his sides," Oz said. "But that filly's not going for money alone, and this is your interview to see if you've got what she does cost."

Then Mrs. Bader called from the porch, stopping on each step as she picked her way down to wave and hallo to us. She walked with a cane, a gnarled stick twisted in wide curves like Bernini's pillars in St. Peter's. One of her black shoes, the laced chunky heels all old women seemed required to wear, was built up with a platform on the bottom. Oz waved and turned back to the horses.

"Shouldn't we go to meet her?" I asked.

"Not unless you want her to feel like an old cripple," he said.

So I waited an eternity for her to cross the yard and another while she fumbled the cane to her left hand.

"Nora Rhymer," she said, pumping my hand. "I haven't seen you since you were a kid."

The sound of my maiden name was shocking as if she'd addressed the dead. I'd almost forgotten Nora Rhymer and all she was, until she was called and came present like a daughter.

"Grace stopped off with you once on her way back from a trip to visit your grandfather's relatives in Quincy. Why, that was so long ago that you were only a moody, rude twelve-year-old."

I opened my mouth and shut it, shocked again at this image of me.

"The only thing you seemed to like was horses. Remember that?" she went on. "I saddled up that red roan cob we had and you rode for two hours around that paddock." She lifted her cane in its direction. "Happy as a dog with a bone as long as you were sitting a horse."

Vaguely I recalled her as a woman who sat poring over studbooks with Grace, so preoccupied with equine breeding that she didn't seem much interested in me or other humans.

"That old horse learned something from you, too. Even if he was wearing a martingale, he had this trick of throwing his head back, and if you weren't thinking about it and leaned forward to adjust the reins, he could practically knock you out of the saddle. Never did it for the next few weeks after you rode him though."

That day was only returning the way a drunken night comes back slowly in pieces. There had been something quirky about that horse, but I couldn't remember now.

"Well?" she asked. "What did you do to him?"

I shrugged, and Mrs. Bader eyed me as if she thought I was withholding something from her.

"Enough of this," she said, waving her hand. "Oz, cut that horse out and let's look at her."

He let himself in the gate and went toward her with the rope held in easy loops. The horses stood in a group now at the far side of the enclosure. Oz went toward them crooning the way people soothe babies and testing the weight of the noose in his hand. The filly raised her head over the back of the bay mare next to her as if she knew he was coming for her. She watched him with huge gray eyes, whinnied low, and raised up her front hooves, enough so the mare moved away and Oz stepped in to slip the lead over her head.

They came toward us, her neck arched and mane flying. She pranced sideways, a bit shy and skittish. But she was lovely—solid gray, light like fog over a morning river.

Oz led her up and Mrs. Bader cupped her hand around the filly's muzzle and then rubbed her forehead.

"The Arabs believed a filly like this was a mark of Allah's blessing."

The filly nickered and stretched her nose out, the same way a cat does to be petted.

"Arabs think they're people," Mrs. Bader said. "All those centuries of living in Bedouin tents and being fed camel milk instead of water. Spoiled rotten. Those horses were treated as well as the children and better than the women, you know. It's in their blood, and if you give them a chance, they'll try to sit in your lap like a baby."

Oz ran his hand over the filly's withers and chest, down the delicate legs to her broad hooves.

"Can't take my word that she's sound?" Mrs. Bader asked.

Oz grinned.

"I just wanted to touch her. Look at this." He ran his hand down the swell of her foreleg and knee to her fetlock. "There's nothing prettier than an Arab's leg."

"Except for their big feet," Mrs. Bader says. "I like their feet. Kept them from sinking in the sand and being drowned in the Sahara. Their hooves make me think of Minnie Mouse with her skinny legs and those big feet in high heels."

She stroked the filly's cheek as if the animal herself had been responsible for her lovely feet.

"Well," said Mrs. Bader. "Enough of this beauty contest. Try her out. Her gaits are rough, I'm warning you, so keep her in the paddock. She's barely old enough for riding, and I've been so gimpy that I haven't been able to train her right. I thought I could if I rested up, but my old legs can't take it."

Oz led the filly off. I wanted to say something observant to impress Mrs. Bader, but all I could think of were stupidities drifting around shouts of how I wanted this horse. I wished that I had never seen her, never knew that she existed or was available, never hoped for anything wonderful for myself.

Oz circled back with her, and Mrs. Bader held the reins as he gave me a leg up. For a baby not yet trained with all she would know, the filly moved like water. Her ears were pricked as if she were waiting for what I would ask of her, and she picked her feet up crisply. I watched the rhythm of her shoulders and followed the line of mane rising over the crest of her neck. She settled into a rocking canter, and I would have kept riding for hours, longer than I had the red roan when I was twelve. I would have joyfully worked her until we both dropped. I did not want to give her up when I might not—would not—have her again.

But I was also so conscious of not displeasing Mrs. Bader that I came back quickly and then was careful not to let a grin spread across my face or delight escape in any sign. I could not afford an old lame pony, let alone this, I kept telling myself. So I handed the reins back to Oz and told Mrs. Bader, "She's a wonderful mount."

Then the old woman looked at me again as if she didn't trust me. "Didn't you like her?" she asked.

I murmured on about the filly's potential and natural stride and soft mouth. Mrs. Bader went "Mmm" and started back to the house, calling over her shoulder, "Come in for coffee if you have time."

We sat in her kitchen smelling most prominently of spice and yeast over a faint touch of leather and manure, she and Oz gossiping about local horses with me barely listening as I replayed every moment of my ride.

Suddenly Mrs. Bader leaned across the table toward me.

"You didn't ask her name," she said, placing the tip of her index finger down on a spot in front of me.

I shrugged. Stupid now to ask.

"Not the silly long name I had to put on her registration, but the one she's really called."

I nodded like an imbecile. Mrs. Bader sat back heavily in her chair as if she couldn't decide if there was any point in telling me.

"It's Malaak," she said finally. "That's Arabic for 'angel.' Not those fay little creatures with harps, but ones who walked the earth and taught humans what they should do."

I smiled tightly, sure whatever I said would be as stupid as not having asked in the first place.

Mrs. Bader raised one eyebrow.

"Are you all right?"

"Yes, of course," I told her.

"Not sick?"

"No, I'm fine, really."

"You seemed better as a kid. More spirit."

When we stood up to leave, Mrs. Bader hobbled close to me. "Your grandmother and I corresponded for years, and she always gave me the encouragement to go on with what pleased me, no matter what I had to do to get it. I never told her how I looked up to her. I thought telling you would make up for that, but I suppose it doesn't."

Then she pointed at the door.

"The steps are too much for me a second time. Can you see yourself back to the truck?"

I watched the filly out the back window until the road curved and she swung out of sight. As soon as we turned onto the main highway and accelerated up to speed, Oz smacked the steering wheel.

"Why did you act like that?" he said.

"Like what?"

"Like you didn't like her."

I stared at the dented-in glove box. Cold air blew out of the vents and collected around my feet.

"What difference does it make?" I told him and began to cry, although I didn't want to. "It doesn't mean a tinker's damn whether I liked her or not."

The tears burned and my head throbbed as the truck carried me away from the horse lost in that great space that had already swallowed Simon and Grace and Clea and Zad and all that I would keep close to me. I had a flash of Simon riding the new filly, how she would have pleased him. But the thought frightened me so that I quickly erased it. Then it seemed that life was only loss and it did no good for me to love that which would be forbidden or taken away or was beyond my means.

Oz drove the truck bouncing onto the shoulder, slid across the seat, and put his arms around me. I leaned against him, glad he was holding me. But all I could think of was *I want,* and the maw of the universe I seemed to be falling through was only the mouth of a monstrous baby demanding satisfaction. *I want my children and my life and this man to love me and that gray horse.*

Then the fact that I had none of this and no way to get it washed over me again and I cried harder out of sheer desolation.

"Shh," he said.

"It's no use," I sobbed. "What does anything matter?"

"Nora," he whispered, stroking back a strand of hair, "you're feeling sorry for yourself."

"Why shouldn't I?" I pushed him away.

"You could've had the filly if you hadn't been such a jackass."

"How?" I demanded.

"I told you. She wants her adopted so she doesn't have to worry if she dies or her son puts her in a home."

Oz held my shoulders and shook me with each new point.

"She wanted you to love the filly as she did, and you acted like you didn't care."

Then I started crying again, harder than the first time. Oz pushed me away and made a U-turn in the middle of the highway, and headed back going eighty-five. After he stopped the truck in Mrs. Bader's yard, he pulled me from the cab and led me still crying up to her door. Through the sheer curtain we saw her coming slowly down the hall, carefully placing the cane before each step until I wanted to scream at her to hurry. When she finally conquered the lock and opened the door, Oz didn't even wait for her to ask what we wanted. He yanked on my arm and said, "Tell her."

I stood there snuffing up tears and moving my mouth like a sock puppet and making incomprehensible animal snorts and sobs. Ozzie yanked my arm again.

"Tell her, damn it."

Then I took a breath and began with increasing speed and hacked out phrases in no special order about how this filly was filled with grace and how all parts of her fit in harmony and how I would give my arm or leg or other body part to have her, to only ride or train her, for that matter. I felt like an idiot, spewing away with my face swollen and my stomach twisted like a wrung-out sheet. When I finished, Mrs. Bader looked up at me with brown eyes so dark and round they reminded me of Bandit's. She kept staring as if Ozzie Kline had brought a deranged child who'd cut the heads off all her marigolds.

"In honor of Grace," she said, "bring the trailer on Tuesday."

Then she herded us in and gave me a glass of water and ran cold water to splash on my face. My sinuses were afire and all energy scraped out inside. But in a wobbly sort of way, I also felt mighty and blessed and reborn.

For weeks I crept out to the barn several times during the night with a flashlight to check her. I don't know why I was so silly, pulling on boots and a heavy coat over my pajamas and crossing the dark yard in the wind. But it was the same as when the kids were babies and I'd wake and tiptoe into their rooms, the floor icy under my feet. Sometimes they were sleeping so deeply that they seemed stone-still dead. I would stand with my heart in my mouth until they stirred or whimpered or took a breath deeper than the invisible ones that had frightened me so.

I went to see the filly in the same spirit—to marvel over her existence and assure myself of her life and to think how Simon would have loved her, which made her all the more dear. I would close the barn door behind me, shutting out the nip of wind, and walk like a cat to her stall, the light beam first catching the velvet gray of her haunches, then her in waking, her head swinging around to see what I might want.

Each time, I stood hugging her neck, the warmth rising between us. I pulled off one glove, held my bare fingers under her nose and felt her breath, would blow out a cloud of my own to see it mix with hers. I closed my eyes and ran my hands over her, down the rise of her withers, across the broad flat of her back, and up the second rise of her haunches. I sang her lullabies and canticles and we leaned into each other.

Running back to the house through the cold, I often thought of Christmas, of waiting tense and awake until I was sure my parents were asleep, and then sneaking down the steps and standing just at the living-room door across from my packages and toys laid out under the tree. I didn't know why I had had to do this each year before I could sleep, just as I didn't know why I had to keep going to the barn. But I did, and nothing gave me joy as the filly turning to study me through the shadows.

"I am still here," she seemed to say. "I am, and at least in the square of this stall, the world is perfectly right for the moment."

In the mornings, Oz led her out before the others, and I watched them, like a father with his daughter. I thought that if I could have chosen anything in the world to see first thing each day—besides Simon's face again—that sight would be Oz running beside the filly and talking to her as if she understood each word.

The thought came dropping slowly that this good thing had happened—now, it seemed—so easily. I had asked for what I truly wanted and not been struck down nor confined nor made guilty or afraid. I was standing in the clear, cold air and filling with joy at the sight of Oz with the filly. Getting used to the idea that I could have what I wanted and keep from what would hurt me simply by listening to and carrying through with my own desire.

Watching the filly's tail plume out and mane dance with her movement, I realized with a shock that I had never felt exactly like this before. Never, except in small portions and quick moments—either stolen with Oz when we were kids or with my own children later. And never with the expectation that this feeling of safety and rightness could make up the permanent breath of my life.

When I looked around at the landscape that was home, the winter fields and Ozzie with Malaak, I wondered why I hadn't.

I wondered. Who had stopped me, except myself?

Chapter Twenty-Two

Neal Mahler

At the lawyer's office down in the Loop, the walls were paneled, and the chair and couch dark burgundy leather. The oriental carpet, the mats on the pictures, the drapes, and even his tie, all the same wine color. I felt orderly with the lawyer jotting notes for my file in its clean manila folder, just as I had with the undertaker when I'd gone to make arrangements for Simon. Soothed, in a way, like they'd just handed me a drink and told me everything would be taken care of without another thought.

"She's thinking about divorce," I told him. "Or her mother is, at least. I'm not sure how seriously, but I want to know the score."

The lawyer was prematurely gray. On his desk, a photo of his wife standing behind their two children, her hands on their shoulders. He said I should be seeing a lawyer from home, but I told him I wanted to be as discreet as possible, besides being Catholic which made it against my religion to divorce.

The Church would only grant an annulment, which the Vatican wasn't likely to give and I didn't want anyway. But Nora didn't care about her religion anymore, not since her father died, and I wanted to know how I could stop her from even threatening. A carrot for the donkey, so to speak, a stick to convince her.

"Sure," he said, leaning back and making a steeple with his fingers. "There's ways to work this."

He told me what Maggie had. That as long as I still wanted Nora and kept denying the irretrievable breakdown of the marriage, no judge would grant a divorce for at least two years. Not to mention that unless Nora took messy legal action to stop me, I had the perfect right as Clea's father to take her where I wished.

"The point is to keep throwing complications at her—plans for property settlement and interim support, that kind of thing, that will wear her down in negotiation and make her give up before the two-year waiting period."

Desertion, he kept saying. The woman's deserted her marriage and family.

"We can use that and anything else to stop her."

When he paused with the pen slightly lifted, I said, "Don't forget that she had a shock treatment besides the confinement and drugs."

The lawyer shook his head.

"Poor thing."

He leaned back, tapping his finger against the side of the yellow legal pad. "Any extenuating circumstances I should know about? Adultery or even suspicion of such for either of you? It's best you tell me to avoid any unpleasant surprises."

I told him of course not. He advised me to keep Clea and

cut back even more on Nora's support, to starve her out, so to speak.

Driving home, I kept thinking about the announcement I would put in the LaCote paper. *I am no longer responsible for debts incurred by my wife, Nora Mahler.* No longer responsible for whatever foolishness she was up to.

Rush hour streamed up Lake Shore Drive, past the Field Museum, Shedd Aquarium, and tony apartments along the curve of the lake. I passed two maids, their white uniforms hanging out below their short coats, heads bent into the wind, walking a poodle and a cocker. A few kids huddled on the beach, and as cars filed north to Evanston, headlights shone white in my rearview mirror, a double strand of diamonds against the ruby taillights going south. Just like a necklace laid against the throat of the city. Nora would have liked that picture, and I made a note to tell her next time we talked.

Then I started thinking about the lawyer's question. Even as I kept telling myself she wouldn't have done that to me, the flashes began coming. She and Kline riding across the pasture, their opposite legs almost touching. Me driving up after work and catching them in the doorway of the barn talking. Him hanging over the fence and watching her ride, like a woman going in circles was something to study.

Most of all, how he'd acted after Simon died. How he refused to return the boarders or take our horses to auction at a time when any normal person would have done what I'd asked if for no better reason than not to upset me. How he sneaked off to bury the damn horse when I'd expressly told him not to, and the surly way he gathered up his belongings and took off, pulling out so fast the truck fishtailed. Then the dog. Stealing the dog. I should have called the sheriff for that one, but at the time I'd thought good riddance to both of them.

Now I wondered. The wide avenues with houses and apartments sitting across lawns like women waiting quietly for their families—they mocked me as I drove on to my place that my wife hadn't even seen. I couldn't believe Nora would cheat, but I was nagged by the possibility. I thought of instances before we were married when she hung around my neck and pushed her hips against me. Saying good night under the porch light when her mother might have been awake, or in the parking lots of dances where anybody could walk by and see her, kisses turned suddenly into something else. I always let her go on for a few minutes more than I should have before I grabbed her by the wrists and held her away so she wouldn't feel my erection. I told her she had to wait until we were married because I didn't want us to get out of hand and do something we'd regret.

I confessed to the priest every week how just thinking of her could bring on a physical reaction. But I didn't tell him how I wondered if she'd been passionate with other men. Eventually I asked her if there'd been anyone before me. She'd looked me straight in the eye and said, "Never anyone like you."

I told her how our love was made all the more special by waiting, and I dreamed of reaching in to touch Nora deep in the satin and net of her wedding gown. Of taking her with all the fury I felt building up, her under me in her beautiful dress, the veil spread out like snowy fields behind her on the pillow.

But on our wedding night, she was fidgety and restless. She didn't want to eat, though I'd ordered her a steak at the resort restaurant. Out of nowhere tears rolled down her cheeks and everyone looked at her, sitting there crying on what should have been the best night of her life. I kept asking if she was all right. I told her that if she really was ill, we could wait until she felt better.

When we went back to the room, I thought to turn off the light and wait under the sheet for her to come out of the bathroom. At first she was stiff, but as we kissed, she loosened up a bit. Her nightgown exposed no more bare flesh than a strapless formal, but without the wires and linings it was almost obscene, how close I was to her with only that thin silk between us. I kneaded the back of her neck and rubbed the flat between her shoulder blades. I whispered for her to relax and trust me, that this was what we'd been waiting for and now nothing we did could be wrong.

Then before I could get myself situated and decide how I would approach her, she put her hand on me. Reached inside my pajama bottoms, grabbed me, and more. I was so shocked I turned away and she lost her hold. We lay there in the dark, and I stared at the light coming through the drapes. She asked if anything was wrong. Instead of answering, I rolled on top of her and finished the job quickly. I closed my eyes and drove myself to the end like she wasn't there, then fell asleep so I wouldn't have to talk to her.

The next morning I pulled back the sheets and looked for the blood that I'd been told should have been there. When I went in to shower, I checked the back of her negligee hanging on the door, just in case it'd been under her. I argued with myself that she'd been more like a baby reaching for a toy than an experienced woman, but for two days, I made sure we kept busy. The lodge had a pool and shuffleboard and nearby golf. I even offered to go horseback riding with her, but she looked up from the grapefruit she was eating like I'd lost my mind.

"They're all trail broke," she said, as if that explained everything.

Finally I took her for a drive around the area. After about an hour, I asked her about the blood and if that meant she was not intact.

"It's very common for young girls who ride to lose their 'intactness,' you know."

"How do you know that?" I asked.

"It's in a book my mother gave me. A pink one put out by Modess. Would you like to read it?"

After that, we dropped the subject and adjusted. It wasn't that she made excuses. She didn't have "headaches" like other women I'd heard of or become a shrew with a rolling pin like in all the cartoons. She was distant and polite, and most often when I was above her, it was like she'd gone off to someplace alone and left only her body for my use.

The situation remained like that, though once I asked her where all her spark had gone. It took me months to get up the nerve and find the right moment. Then she looked at me like I was talking Greek.

"You know," I said. "How once in a while when we were dating you acted different."

She laid the book she was reading down on her lap.

"I'm either myself, or I'm not," she said. "You seem to prefer the not."

"That's gibberish," I told her.

"You know what I mean," she said.

I got so disgusted that I left the room, slamming the door so she'd know I was angry. I stayed at the office until long after I was sure she'd gone to bed, then came in without turning on any lights upstairs. The spot on the barn always shone against our window and left enough light to move around the room. I pulled the covers up just enough to climb under them and got situated slowly so the motion and creaking wouldn't wake her. Then I lay there and watched her sleep, her hands crossed on her chest like the Little Flower.

This sweet Nora, her hair tousled and her profile like one on my mother's cameo, milky face against a deep blue stone. I wanted this Nora to act as I'd dreamed about her and love me so much that there wasn't room inside her for another thought. To plan her day around our life together and work as hard for me as I did for her.

I shifted next to her. She was warm from sleep and peaceful like a little girl. I lay like that for more than an hour, satisfied with our closeness but sad, too, how when awake she wouldn't let me touch the way I wanted without walls coming down around her. I didn't understand how I could be sought out by others and ignored by this woman I loved and wanted above all.

I couldn't help myself from cupping my hand around her arm and moving my hip tight against hers and my leg over her thigh, close like we should've always been. She woke up and looked at me sleepily through half-closed lids.

"What are you doing?" she asked.

"Just lying here."

"Why?"

"I wanted to, that's all," I said.

"To touch me?"

"What's wrong with that?"

"It's sneaky," she said, her words mumbled and slurred so I could hardly understand them. "You touching like that."

Then she pushed my arm away and rolled over. In the morning she acted like nothing had happened, and I passed off her words as sleepy nonsense.

But after that I looked at her in a different way, seeing what I'd missed before. Oh, she was civil; she did her job and sometimes even seemed satisfied, but it didn't take a genius to look at her and know most of it was surface. In her eyes, always the eyes, I could see other thoughts moving, the way a dog that's pinned lies still except for its eyes looking for an empty spot to run.

But whenever I asked what was wrong, she always told me "Nothing," and there was no question that we would stay together, what with the children and all. I'd always been taught to make the best of any situation, and after that night, I put hope behind me.

What we had was good enough, and I just didn't think about the rest if I could help it, not until the lawyer stirred it all up again. I used to think that if Nora didn't want me, she wouldn't want anyone. But now I wondered what had happened to that hot little item she used to be. That part of her didn't just disappear, and maybe I was so trusting that I didn't notice what was going on right under my nose.

All that time with Kline alone. I didn't know until a year after we hired him that he and Nora had had a thing about each other when they were younger. After a Kiwanis meeting one night, a few of us had gone to Earl's Bar. The waitress was an old sweetheart of one of the guys, and he started talking about how pretty she'd been as a girl. Then this got the whole lot of them going. They were all locals, except me, and had gone to high school together, and the more they drank, the more nostalgic and sappy they got.

One of them, Lowell, said how funny it was that he could remember so clearly things that had happened when he was a kid and not even be able to tell us exactly what he'd done that day.

Then he turned to me.

"Hell," he said, "I remember Nora as a girl almost clearer than I do myself last week."

He talked about how smart and pretty she was and so far above them that most guys didn't even consider asking her out. I knew he was right—one of the reasons I'd married her was for that pride in being able to get her when most other men wouldn't have had a prayer. Then he said he remembered one night at a sock hop after a basketball game. How the gym smelled warm and sweaty, and the lights were turned down. Lowell and a bunch of the guys were sitting on the hard-as-hell bleachers and watching other kids dance, especially Ozzie Kline with Nora.

"They were both handsome kids," Lowell said, "and the way they were looking at each other that night, I was sure they'd end up together, though nothing ever came of it.

"Still, I can recall that moment. I don't know why I've saved it, maybe because it was so pretty and sweet."

Then he stopped like he'd said too much, and the other guys started kidding me about how I was a lucky bastard to have gotten Nora Rhymer, while Kline was lucky that she'd even danced with him that once.

"Yeah," Lowell said, "the rest of us had to be content with mortal girls for normal guys."

Then he winked. I wondered why Nora hadn't said anything to me about Kline, but decided he hadn't meant enough to mention. Probably she didn't even remember that dance, the way I'd forgotten most of the girls I'd dated. I didn't think much about it until the lawyer brought up the other matter. I walked around the apartment that night while Clea was out at the library. The drapes were open and the night overcast. I could see into lit apartments across the way and watch couples reading the paper or eating dinner, just like the side of the building was missing like the fourth wall of Clea's old dollhouse. I kept catching my reflection in my own windows, the black shape of myself in the room with the lamplight blaring. I imagined Nora with her back to me and hugging a pillow like a damn life preserver. Or under me with her eyes looking into the dark over my shoulder at nothing.

I saw others looking in at this, too, and went back through the rooms, closing the drapes and thinking that even if Nora and I went on together, estranged and distant, it was better than suspicions about Kline breaking us up. I didn't want anyone in LaCote to see me as demoted, especially by a nobody, or to think I wasn't man enough to keep her.

So I made more trips back to LaCote on the excuse of checking out the area offices or bringing Clea for visits or picking up odds and ends we still needed to move. I was careful to see as many old acquaintances as possible, to take them to Earl's and buy a few rounds and catch them up on the news. How Nora had never recovered from Simon's death. How she was still so unbalanced that she couldn't take care of Clea. How I was afraid to insist she move for fear of sending her over the edge.

"What can I do?" I asked, holding my palms to heaven. "I tried to get her medical help before Maggie stopped me. I tried my best and everything else with her."

"Leave her alone and she'll come home," one said. "Wagging her tail behind her."

Then they told me, those men, how I could only do what I had to do and see what happened. They said women sometimes got strange and that I shouldn't be punished by having to pay for what wasn't my fault.

"She made her bed," another said, "let her lie in it."

I felt safe then, like I'd gotten back free to base. I dropped by the houses of old clients, especially women so unlike Nora that I was sure they'd take my side. I visited my pastor at the rectory and one of my old professors who was president of the college. I jotted down names in the little notebook I kept in my shirt pocket, and when I got around to seeing those people, I sold my case like a whole-life policy. They nodded, their belief making my side of the story gospel, and I felt satisfied, the way I did filling sandbags during the last flood or settling claims right on the spot after that twister set down.

But when I saw Nora, that peace went away. I told myself that if she didn't want me, then I certainly didn't want her. When I went by to give her an expense check or to discuss Clea, some business matter like that, I was nervous and couldn't get my voice to hit the right register or find my natural posture, especially if Kline was sitting in my chair and having coffee like he lived there.

I wanted to forgive her. Wanted to get her back and start over like nothing had happened. No, more. Offer to change in little ways so we could be happier. I watched her moving around the kitchen, the familiar way she rinsed cups and stacked them in the drainer or measured out the coffee and dropped an eggshell in the grounds, and I was overcome with missing her. I wanted to do anything to be able to look up from my breakfast or paper and see her moving around me in everlasting orbit. She had been mine, this place had been mine, and now they were not. I knew I hadn't taken her wants into consideration, but that would all be different when she moved to Chicago, and I thought of telling her so.

Sometimes she saw me to the door and stood waiting for me to go through. I thought about taking her in my arms while we were alone in the hallway and kissing her with such force that she couldn't speak. Thought of carrying her upstairs and making love sideways on the spread where I'd laid her. Of being so rooted inside that she would never think of leaving me.

The last time as I was leaving I quoted the Book of Ruth as a way of saying good-bye, hoping the words I found so moving would touch her.

"Remember the Bible," I said, "the part about 'whither thou goest, I will go'?"

" 'Thy people shall be my people'?"

"Yes," I said, and stepped closer to her. "What every husband wants to hear."

She moved so the edge of the door was between us.

"You better go read that over again," she said as she pushed me back with its closing. "One widow said that to another widow, long after their husbands were too dead to hear."

Then she laughed, the first time I'd seen her do that since before Simon died. Like I'd just told the best joke, and her laughter rolled across the pasture so sharply that one of the grazing horses raised its head.

I slammed down the steps and drove away, only satisfied when I'd accelerated to feel all eight cylinders and the horsepower flying that Buick down the road. Rage came up pure and strong and reached speeds as fast as the car's. Somewhere in my mind I could hear the lecturing voices of every nun and priest I'd ever known. Turn my other cheek. Divide my only cloak in two. Give love and mercy without question.

But Nora was an exception. What would happen if I took her back like none of this had happened? Moved back to this place that she refused to leave like some brainless soldier defending a leveled castle? If I let her get away with this, no telling the end of it, and before we could go on, I had to get things straight between us.

Driving down the road to town, the winter wheat bright green and flying past on either side, I found my resolve and slammed on the brakes. The car skidded sideways and stopped crossways in the road. I sat there a minute, a little stunned, dust rising in the sun streaks, each particle visible. Then I backed up so far the tail hung over a ditch, and made a U back to the farm.

Chat banged against the undercarriage like shots as I pulled into the yard. Kline's truck was gone, and standing on the porch, I thought, *Why should I knock on my own front door?* The downstairs was empty, a chair pushed back and coffee cup still on the kitchen table, an unfolded afghan and open book on the living-room couch. I went up the steps two at a time and found Nora coming down the hall from her room. She pulled up short when she saw me, like she'd run into a burglar about to rob the place, and sucked in her breath so loudly I could hear her.

"We have to talk," I told her.

"What more is there to say?" She stepped back against the

wall, her shoulder nudging one of the photos hung in double rows all up and down the hall, the black-and-white photos of horses her family had owned.

I came up close to her. Over her shoulder, a black horse, his neck arched and eyes rolled white. Brushed until the coat shone like a dull mirror. Frank's Tennessee walker that Maggie had sold before he was cold in the grave. Nora jerked back from me and knocked the picture crooked.

"You haven't listened to what I've been telling you," I said.

She looked up in that big-eyed way of hers and ran the tip of her tongue over her bottom lip.

"I don't know how to be with you anymore," she said.

"I love you," I told her, but she tried to twist her arm out of my hold.

"I want to stay here, Neal. Why won't you let me do that without trouble?"

"It'll be different between us." I held her tighter. "You'll see."

I held her between myself and the wall, pressing against the solidness of her breasts and hips. Then more than keeping her still so we could talk, I craved her touch. I kissed her so I could feel her breath in my mouth and pushed against her to get the sensation of our bodies so close that there was no question or possibility of separation ever again.

She jerked her head back and the glass on the photo cracked into a web. I tried to work one hand up to feel for blood, but every time I loosened my hold, she twisted for an opening, turning her body to wedge her shoulder into my chest or her knee between my legs. I kept yelling at her to hold still and listen. I kept telling her how I loved her.

But she was wild, and I held her pinned against the wall.

The cylinder of her windpipe fit neatly in the V between my thumb and hand, like a faraway target in the sight at the end of a gun barrel.

The more she struggled, the more I leaned into the point of the V. I wanted to make love to her standing right there in that corner, with that same force I'd used to hold her still, so that she could see how much I loved her. I wanted this moment to be the turning point that settled our disagreement once and for all.

Then Maggie came up the stairs and just stood there staring at us. The minute Nora was still, I loosened my hold, tossing her sideways like an animal that'd bite the instant it was free.

"Why the hell do you want me when I don't want you?" She backed away from me against the far wall. Then she shut herself in her room and fumbled with the key.

I didn't try to stop her. By this time I was shamed that I'd let her see me like this. Was surprised myself by how she'd made me act, like she was water and air that I didn't know how to hold in my arms.

But I'd also seen another layer below that, one disgusting like a sick dog in heat, that had showed itself when I'd told Nora how I wanted her. I promised never to be vulnerable with her again, lest that underside open once more.

I wanted out of the hall surrounded by pictures of dead horses that she seemed to care about more than me, pushed past Maggie, and left the front door open with heat rushing out. I trembled as I started the car and drove down the lane, shaking as much from my anger as from the draft over my feet.

I imagined her that night not being able to sleep. She would step barefoot on the cold floor and know she'd done what couldn't be taken back. I wished for her to know in that moment how alone she would be without me, and I wanted her to bitterly regret all that she'd given up and all I could still take away.

Then I slammed the car in gear and drove away from that house so fast that the speed lifted me and let me forget what had happened just minutes ago. I kept going, all the way through LaCote and down Highway 94 on the other side, all the way to Weldon Spring and on to Valley Park. Driving as fast as I could, that speed coming out of the engine and back into me. But, still, something was over, something finished. Like a death, though I didn't know of what, not the name or the shape.

Yet the driving helped take me away from it, and I didn't go back to my motel room until well after dark, crossing the Missouri with the lights of LaCote stretched wavy and long in the water.

Chapter Twenty-Three

Nora Mahler

THE NEXT MORNING I called Neal at the motel where he stayed when he was in LaCote.

"I want a divorce, and I want the farm."

"Catholics can't get divorced. You know that, Nora."

"Then you stay married and I'll get divorced," I told him.

"That's your mother talking," he said. "You don't mean it."

"I do," I told him. My reply came out the way school-yard arguments do. *You can't. I can. You will. I won't.* As much reflex as anything. But once the words sat outside myself and Neal's silence told me he half believed them, I left them there.

Neal and his lawyer began calling twenty times a week to prove they could keep the case in litigation for the two years they promised. At first Neal asked for everything—Clea and his apartment and pardon from alimony and a third of the farm without argument. I was tempted to give in, just to have it over. But Maggie kept repeating the sum she had calculated.

"Neal's just seeing what he can get away with," she said.

"What will he do if I fight him on this?"

"He can't do anything worse than he's already done. Ask for what you want and see what happens."

So I asked for Clea, except at Thanksgiving and one weekend the other months. I asked for the farm in trust for her so that it could remain whole without Neal accusing me of trying to steal his share. I asked for the money Maggie had told me to.

Neal and his lawyer argued that I'd give up security and cause upset if I went through with this. They pointed out the postwar boom in marriages, the pages and pages of new brides in the Sunday *Post-Dispatch.*

"The whole world's getting hitched. Why are you the only woman who wants a divorce?"

Holding the receiver that their voices came out of like snakes, I wondered. All this turmoil for what? A few acres of Missouri, half on a floodplain, kept because my grandmother told me to hang on to what was dearest to me.

"You're trading your family for a farm you don't farm?" Neal asked. "How can you do this to us, Nora?"

Neal and the lawyer reduced the argument. One plus one. Nora against Neal. They told me there were horses in Chicago, as if I didn't realize. Riding stables and bridle paths and farms outside the city to board a mount. I could ride, Neal told me, until my butt fell off.

When I tried to explain my side with logic and syllogisms and evidence, the kind they were always telling me to use, they fell silent as if I were speaking gibberish.

"I can't have my land in Chicago, and I'm not going there," I said. "I'm not ever going to be with you again."

But they lapsed into puzzled silence as if I'd lost my mind. I suspected again that I had, when the obvious to me was so incomprehensible to them. Neal told me I was being unreasonable with my demands and that I needed to think more about what I was asking of him, especially since I'd been the one to desert him.

I gave in and said I would wait to file the final papers. He reminded me that each delay ran up the cost of fees and each phone call was charged. But what was fair? What did I really want? The farm and the horses, yes. Clea, though I was anxious about how to mother her now. But more. Something I couldn't quite define, like being let out of a box.

After a February day when Neal had called three times, argued for an hour each, and hung up on me twice, I woke in the middle of the night and walked the dark hall, the floor icy under my bare feet. I stood in Clea's room, the winter moonlight in slanted squares across the quilt. I stood there missing her and wondering if I would get her back, not only in the house but in spirit. If I would know the right things to do for her.

Neal's arguments against me knotted like twine I couldn't find a loose end to start untangling. *Deserter.* I rolled the word on my tongue. But how could I have deserted him by staying in the place I'd lived since the day I was born?

I knew the flaw in his argument was the assumption that my true place was wherever he wished me to be. If I would not go where he wanted, then I had left him. If I did not follow after, then it was the same as if I had packed up and gone off on my own.

I could explain the untruth of his syllogism, though he didn't seem to understand. But I had been unable to shake my guilt over not being the good woman Neal—and my father, the Church, and the town—had expected me to be. The one who would not betray them with wishes and wants of her own.

I had failed at loving him, at keeping my promise to stay with him through any kind of circumstance until one of us died. I was incompetent where every good townswoman and farmwife was successful. At staying married. At teaching her children to survive.

But I was getting used to Neal's absence, and I liked him gone. To empty him out of me and have for my own use the energy it had taken to guess what would please him. For once, in spite of my guilt, I held on to the thought that I counted as much as he. But I also understood suddenly why freed slaves did not leave the plantations or displaced persons their camps or peasants their villages in the path of war.

Standing in the middle of Clea's room, I was conscious of the cold like glass pressed hard against my skin. What if she decided to stay with Neal? What if he kept her? I wanted to cry, but what was the point? Rocking back and forth, my hands dangling loose, I cried anyway. Over misused love and years of my life handed to Neal in trust that whatever I gave of myself was worth the trade for our marriage.

At least Neal could care enough to talk soft as I would to a horse or dog I had to put down. But he shifted from threats about money to awkward enticements of sex to attacks against me. "*You won't like what happens if you go through with this,*" he spat.

For the next couple of weeks I was so worn-out that I began yearning almost constantly for relief. Especially for my old intimacy with Oz, which had given me the right to lean my weight against him whenever I'd wanted and just rest. Each time I passed him in the kitchen, his shirtsleeves rolled up past the diagonal line of muscle from wrist to elbow, I thought of how he used to hold me.

One afternoon, to get away alone, I drove out the River Road on a whim to the old Kurtz quarry. Dug years before and filled since with seepage and rainwater, it was where everyone swam before the big pool in the park was built after the war. Grace had started taking me there when I was barely five, teaching me first the dog paddle and then the Australian crawl amidst the boisterous, splashing teenagers who gathered on summer afternoons.

I stood on the outcrop, looking down on the gray rock cut flat like walls and the lighter gray of the water, rippling in the cold wind and the eerie out-of-season quiet. From the beginning, I'd begged Grace to let me jump from the ledge, twenty feet above the water, the way I'd seen the older boys do. She made me wait until I could swim the widest point of the quarry and back to her.

Then I'd stood at about this same place, looking down on the other kids and her, their faces smiling and upturned and calling to me high above them. I'd jumped without a thought into the weightlessness of falling, and in spite of how hard I'd smacked the water and how far I'd had to swim back to the surface, I'd climbed up twice more before we went home.

After that, I always jumped at least once every time she'd brought me to the quarry, though I wasn't sure anymore where I'd found the daring. The older kids told their friends, "Watch the little squirt. She jumps like it's nothing."

Simon had been the very same way when he'd been old enough to come here. Climbing up the rocks and jumping until I got tired of watching. Clea had never wanted to try, but when she was nine, Simon kept telling her how wonderful it was to fly into the water. She'd finally let him take her hand and lead her up. He stood on the ledge, showing her how to point her toes and hold her hands over her head to enter smoothly. Then he gave her a hug. Just like that.

I didn't know where he'd learned to be so sweet and careful with people. But he kept smiling and talking until she ran off into the air. He jumped after and came up laughing next to her, the two of them far out in the center of the water, both so happy with her bravery.

I stood there a bit longer, missing the summer heat, the shout and noise of the other swimmers, missing Grace and the kid I'd been, the one who liked plunging through air and into water. I needed to get away from the image of Simon standing poised on the rock, his trunks drooping low on his hips and his skin shining with wet. Simon shouting, "Mom, watch what Clea can do."

I drove home, the flurries of a coming snow dancing away from the windshield as if they were too light to settle in for a landing, the sky low and gray and leaden.

Chapter Twenty-Four

Ozzie Kline

Sometimes in a certain light Malaak would turn her head and I'd think she was Zad. The expression was the same, the coloring similar, and as I came into the stall I'd get the eerie feeling that I'd dreamed all that had happened and still had a chance to change what had gone wrong. To keep Zad and Simon alive. To defend Nora and not fall in love all over again without hope.

But Malaak was not Zad. She was smaller and lighter, her proportions different, and eyes wider set. She held her head to the side and danced at an angle when she was excited. She was less even-tempered: one minute wild and mean, and the next, pushing up against me like she was too shy to be on her own around the other horses.

People who don't know animals think they all look alike. When I was a kid, we had two cats around the place, both tabbies, and my father always asked how I could tell them apart. "For starters," I'd told him, "the gray one's bigger than the brown." But then most guys in my unit thought all Nazis looked the same, though I could describe in detail the faces of the ones I saw and killed.

Being able to tell the difference was what kept me so connected to Nora in ways I didn't want to be. I knew the way she moved and her expressions. I'd paid too much attention and listened too carefully; her memories were as vivid and set inside me as my own, the strongest of which included her anyway. When I tried to push her out and was as hard to her as I'd been to anyone, I ended up shutting down a part of myself as well.

I didn't like to do that. It was too much like the guys who shot themselves in the foot to get sent back from the front. So I just kept away as much as possible. If she was going to leave Neal Mahler, she was going to have to do it by herself, and until if and when that happened, I was just the hired hand who tried not to talk to her more than necessary.

But sometimes she sucked me in until I couldn't help but answer her. Like last week I came driving up the lane, and she was standing in the yard between the house and barn and turning in a slow circle. When she heard the truck, she hugged herself, and when I got out, she smiled over her shoulder at me.

"Look, Oz," she said, "you can see where the wind ends, where the edges are."

Thinking she was going nuts on me, I stopped and followed where she pointed. The branches of the mulberry over her head were still, but the treetops out farther along the edge of the bluff swayed and rocked in turn, the strange wind moving down the line of them and around to those on the far side of the house. It circled until it hit the first ones again, the noise like high surf, and then it kept on moving.

I turned with her to follow the passing confusion of the trees. She kept smiling over her shoulder at me. Then for a minute I felt wrapped again in one of those crazy, stupid bonds between Nora and myself. How we both noticed in the same way and took delight in inane and pointless pleasures. I was embarrassed for standing out in the middle of that wind and turning with her like two kids trying to make themselves dizzy enough to fall down. Was angry for how easily she'd gotten me to slip into this game with her that I no longer wanted to play.

When I said I was going to the house for coffee, she shoved her hands deep into her coat pockets and hunched her shoulders.

"Ozzie?" she said.

"What?"

"I can't stand it when you're mean."

"What are you talking about?"

"I expected it from Neal and even got used to it. But I can't from you."

"Why's he getting off easy when I don't?"

She shrugged.

"It's just different with you, that's all."

I wanted to say it was different with her, too. But then I started to think of all the ways how, and if she knew that for sure, how she would be able to crush me at her feet.

"I said I was going to get coffee, understand?"

She held her head to one side and looked a little like she was going to cry, but I turned away anyhow. I had work to do. That's all I'd promised her.

I skipped the coffee and instead put a halter and lead on Malaak and took her to the training paddock, as much to give myself time to think as anything. She was balky and leaned against me the way a dog who doesn't know how to heel will sway into your legs and trip you, though, in a way, I liked her weight against me.

Mrs. Bader had warned me how she'd try to get away with anything and keep testing for any weakness.

"You'll have to be like Jacob wrestling with his angel. Watch out that she doesn't break your thigh."

When I took both hands and shoved hard against Malaak's side, she looked sideways like to ask what the hell was I doing, being so rough.

"I want you to behave, damn it, so we don't go through this contest every day."

We stood there quiet, the only motion her ears pricking forward. So quiet I heard my heart thudding and felt her breath warm on my hand that I'd cupped around her nose.

"Come on, brat. Make it easy on us." I put my arms over her back and leaned against her so she could feel and know me. Just stood like that, wondering if Nora and I could ever get used to each other in the same way.

When I went up to the house for supper, Nora and Maggie looked up for a second when I came in but didn't stop arguing while I washed my hands, the soap lathering gray with dirt.

"You talk to her, Ozzie," Maggie said. "I'm not getting anywhere. She needs to file the papers and get Clea back."

"She doesn't want to come," Nora said.

"Oh, yes, she does," Maggie answered. "As long as she doesn't have to face her father to do it."

I dried my hands slowly and ran one nail under another to

get out a strip of dirt. I wanted to say I was only the wrangler who had nothing to do with Neal Mahler's marriage or anything for that matter except those horses in the barn. Maggie smacked her hand flat on the table and marched over to stir a pot of stew on the stove. She buttered slices of bread, poured the stew over them in bowls, and set them on the table.

"You realize," she said as she sat down and snapped her napkin open in her lap, "if you don't get moving, the next thing you'll lose is that horse."

"No," Nora said.

"Yes," Maggie said. "Yes."

We ate in silence, Nora stirring around in the stew like she'd dropped a piece of jewelry in there and Maggie banging her spoon with every pass against the side of the bowl. A winter kitchen with black windows and the rooms beyond disappearing into the dark past spills of light. I took another piece of bread to mop up the gravy and concentrated on wiping clean the blue onions curling on my dish.

"Why don't you go on another trip?" Nora said finally.

"Where do you want me to go, especially with no money?" Maggie asked.

"Where would you like?"

"The other side of the world. I'd like to take a shovel and start digging in the damn zinnia bed to see if it's true that I'd come out in China. I'd like to dig and dig so by the time I got there, I'd have forgotten everything here."

Then she got up, set her bowl down hard on the counter, and walked out. Nora and I listened to her moving around above us. Her footsteps and a door closing and the bed creaking. Then I got up and cleared the table. I kept my back to Nora while I washed up the dishes.

"What should I do, Oz?"

I held the stew pot under the water for twice as long as I needed to rinse it.

"I'll tell you what I used to tell the new men sent in as replacements on the front. That we all have two impulses—what we want and what we fear. Usually it's better if we take what we want, but more likely we end up acting out of fear. During a battle I always wanted to be somewhere else, but I was afraid of being a coward more than I was afraid of being killed. So I went ahead and did what I was told. That works and it's enough, if it's the best you can do at the time."

I turned the pot upside down in the drainer and walked out without finishing up. Crossing the yard, I was glad of the cold wind that swooped in and made my balls pull up inside me. Glad of the discomfort that kept me in mind of how the world really worked.

I puttered around the barn, rearranging tack that was already in place and finally leaning against Malaak's stall to just watch her. Nora let herself in the door with a blast of cold air. She crossed her arms over the stall door and laid her head on them, her hair spilling silver-gold over the heavy sleeves of her coat. She stood quietly like a child watching me for so long that I looked away and stared again at the horse.

"What I want," she said at last, "is for us to live here forever with Clea and Maggie, if she wants, and to fill the pasture with Malaak's children, and for you to sleep every night with your arm over me. That's all. Only I don't know if that's possible or how to get to it if it is."

A shadow cut across the diagonal of her face, leaving only one startling blue-green eye in the light.

"You just want me because I'm convenient to fill up Neal's space," I told her.

"Oz," she said, "you are the most inconvenient man I know. You can't support me and you won't fight for me and when you get spooked, you take off at a moment's notice. But you're who I feel myself with."

She shifted her weight, and Malaak did, too, like she was copying. Her hooves hit like wooden bells against the stall floor and her tail swished three times.

"I can't explain it right," Nora said. "With you I open from the inside, but with Neal I keep pulling smaller."

"You're crazy," I said because I didn't want to hear what she was telling me.

She jerked her head a little like she'd been stung, but then stood straight with her fists jammed in her pockets.

"I made myself forget how different I am with you, but now I know again."

"You're nuts," I told her.

"No," she said.

I went out quickly to the pickup. The engine wouldn't turn over right off and I was afraid before I got it started she'd follow me out and put her hands flat up against the window. I was a little ashamed of calling her crazy, but I wanted the space of that word put between us.

Yet driving down the lane with distance opening into a pit, my heart sank when I looked in the mirror and didn't see her running after me or even standing in the open door of the barn to watch me drive off.

I couldn't sleep that night. The winds howled for hours under the belly of the trailer like they would lift and flip it over, this tacky little can with drafts leaking in around every window and the whole place banging and rocking in the storm. I lay flat on my back with the covers pulled tight up to my neck like I was some neat little sardine in a keyed tin. I tried to think of nothing and ignore the clock since I knew how crappy and tired I'd be in the morning, but Nora's words came seeping through. *"What I want..."* She couldn't know that, no more than some fairy tale she'd dreamed up to keep from thinking about what she had to do with Neal.

Didn't I know that trick myself? How for twenty years I replayed my old memories of her and slept with her ghost naked in my arms. How when I was lonely I pictured her so clearly with me—asking about my day and throwing her arms around my neck and sitting across the table at meals and answering what I'd said to her—that this dream Nora I'd made into my constant wife took on a life of her own. Yet she was only a trick of the mind to keep me company and had less to do with me loving or being with the real Nora than a reflection has to do with the person standing in front of the mirror.

I knew from experience what Nora was blind to. How easy it was to be perfect with a reflection. How many mistakes and hurts would come when I tried to do the same with a woman. I got up, lit a cigarette, and stood barefoot in the open door, the cold puckering my skin and the wind blowing the smoke back in my face. The first snowflakes were coming in swirls that turned back on themselves, the way a flock of birds will suddenly fold and collapse in on itself before opening out again into a new flight. I was right, I knew it. No matter how much we wanted each other, I would be no better and maybe even worse with her than I had been with others I hadn't loved nearly as much.

When my feet got so cold I could feel the bones, I shut the door and put on two pairs of socks and a heavy robe. Then I stood at the window a little longer, watching the first patches of white collect in the hollows of the ground and the grooves in the tree bark. I seemed the last man awake in the storm, and then for a second it seemed safe to admit without all the arguments against it how I wanted Nora and ached without her. The thought came at me like wind so hard that I couldn't catch my breath, and a second of it was all I could take.

The next morning Nora acted like she hadn't made her big speech to me the night before. She came in the barn with a list of supplies she was getting from the feedstore and asked if I wanted to add anything she'd forgotten. She held the paper out with two fingers at the top so I could read it, wobbly, without even taking it from her. Then she went off in the truck, the snow too cold in the tracks to rise much behind the wheels.

A few minutes later Maggie let herself in, stamping her boots and smacking her arms to warm them. She studied her white breath like she didn't quite believe it was coming from her.

"How do you stand it out here?" she asked.

"You get used to it," I said.

"Colder than a witch's tit."

She stood just inside the barn with her arms crossed over her chest.

"What happened between you two last night?"

"Happened?" I asked. "Nothing."

"I can't even guess what you said to make her cry like that."

"Nora doesn't cry."

"The hell she doesn't."

I led out the black filly to brush her, and Maggie blew a long exasperated cloud of breath.

"Don't you love her?" she said. "It seems you do. Maybe if you'd make a move for once, you'd get Nora moving, too."

"This is none of your business."

She took a step toward me.

"Every time I've tried to stay out of your way, or Nora's or Neal's or Clea's, I've watched you all cause hurt to one another."

She took a deep breath.

"Such hard lessons since April, Ozzie Kline. I've only added to the damage by assuming everyone knew what they were doing and letting them go on. I want to stop being like that. It's all I know how to do at this point."

I didn't answer. She smacked her hand against her leg.

"You're a fool, Ozzie Kline. Or a liar, or a coward, or just plain deaf, blind, and dumb."

"Probably a little of all of those," I said, running the brush down the filly's back and studying my handiwork. Finally she stamped her foot and went out, leaving the door open behind. I had to stop to go close it and cursed her for being a meddling old woman.

Twenty years before, she was the one who'd acted deaf, blind, and dumb so she wouldn't have to tangle with Frank Rhymer. That's when she really could have helped Nora and me, and I didn't appreciate her butting in now.

But when Nora pulled up and I worked beside her unloading the bags of feed and blocks of salt, I couldn't help but look at her from the corner of my eye. The cold pinched her nose and ruddied her cheeks. I wanted to pull my glove off and touch her skin. To move so close I could feel the warmth between us.

I felt starved and punished, keeping myself from her. I swore at Maggie for making me feel guilty over letting this happen, for throwing in my face what I couldn't deny was the truth.

Nora swung a bag off the tailgate and started to the barn. She staggered a little with the weight, the snow crunching under her uneven steps. But when I put out my arms to take the bag from her, she turned her shoulder and kept going. With every sound, sharp like twigs breaking, the wind in my lungs and winter around, the thought of living the rest of my life like that made me not want to live at all.

When Nora came out for another bag, she looked up at me, her eyes teared from the cold.

"You on strike?" she asked.

"Just resting," I told her.

"I just want to hurry up and go get warm."

"I'll finish."

"Just take your share, OK?"

I whipped a bag off the truck and carried it too fast inside. I couldn't help it.

When the last bag was stacked, we stood catching our breath. I was sweaty from the work and undid my jacket, lit a cigarette, and offered one to her. We leaned against the tailgate and watched the smoke hang in front of us, not able to tell it from our breath.

I could feel her coldness radiate, the way I could the cold in the metal of the truck from a foot away. Then I was afraid that for once it was finished between us, and I was more afraid of that than I had been of anything.

I kept hearing Maggie nag at me. I wondered if the chance was really there and if I was smart enough to make it work.

"You mad at me?" I asked.

"Nothing to be mad at," she said.

"Then why you acting like this?"

She cocked one eyebrow and looked up at me quizzically.

"I learned it from you."

"I don't like it."

"Neither do I."

I exhaled in little breaths until I was sure I was blowing air and not smoke.

"What do you expect?" I said. "First you act like old times, and then you start yammering about how married you are, and then you give me this big speech about wanting me to sleep with my damned arm over you every night. What am I supposed to make of all that?"

She ground the butt under her heel.

"I want you so much that I think I'm crazy," she said. "I'm also angry that I'm such a coward."

She crossed her arms over her chest and leaned against the sacks again. I couldn't look at her, shamed as I was for being a worse coward. We stood there staring out at the bluff.

"What if you wouldn't be alone?"

I could hardly stand to say those words. She looked up at me quickly, out of the corner of her eye.

"What do you mean?"

"Just that."

"You mean if we were together?"

But I wasn't ready to go on, not with Nora so unlike her dream self who never pressed for me to explain or act. But I had made a proposal, of sorts. Now instead of worrying that we were acting out a make-believe, I worried that we weren't.

"You think that over," I said, "and we'll talk about it tomorrow."

Then quickly I turned and walked to my truck. I heard her calling after me. "Damn it, Ozzie. Think over what, exactly?"

Going back to my place, the back end of the truck sliding over the snow, I kept telling myself we could finally be together, we could do this. Still, I lay awake again that night so restless that I got up three times to get the blanket from where I'd kicked it. I kept trying to figure how I would take care of her. I wondered how we could make enough money to survive. Even when I slept in fits, I twisted so the covers tied me like spider silk, and I dreamed long dreams about her coming to me disappointed because I'd failed her in some simple way.

But all the night I also kept imagining holding Nora, skin against skin and touching whenever we wished, wherever we pleased, with nothing at all between us, not even our bodies to keep us from reaching inside.

Not the old fantasies that for years had kept me as close as I ever came to content. But the joyful, fearful anticipation of the real her with me.

Chapter Twenty-Five

Nora Mahler

All evening I was restless, wondering if Ozzie had actually meant what I thought he had, hardly daring to believe we might have both come to the same question at the same moment, for once in our lives. I dozed off and woke a little after midnight, pacing the house as I did the night I was in labor with Simon, the early pains low and heavy in my back. I'd wakened Neal who told me to get him up when I was ready to go to the hospital. But I was too uncomfortable to lie down and walked the rooms, thinking that soon I would be a mother carrying new life in my arms.

I had liked nursing and rocking Simon, just the two of us together in the night. The way he curled his fist around my finger, nuzzled my breast, or made hums and coos after feeding. Sometimes he woke and just wanted to play. Kicking his feet, so small that I could hold both in just one hand when I wanted. Reaching up as if being able to touch my face was the most pleasing thing he knew.

Even when he was older, long after most kids wanted to have nothing to do with their mothers in public, he'd claim me. Like during Little League games—right up to the time in sixth grade when he started to get bigger than I was—he'd walk over to where I was sitting in a lawn chair on the side of the ball field and sprawl in my lap for a minute to talk about his last play. Not like a momma's boy looking for protection, but a friend who liked to share my company.

How Simon and I both enjoyed the world more with the other in it. How we loved to show each other what and how we saw, thus making that world newer and larger and more various for us both.

At first, as usual, I doubled over with missing him. But the memories came to me differently that night, the images overwhelming in their brightness and warmth. As much as they were still reminders of what I had lost with Simon, they were also pure, clean moments of affection and beauty and love. Mine to keep forever, and forever to draw spirit from.

I knew then. By trying to save myself from the pain since he'd died, I'd also denied myself his joy. I was angry for letting go of what would sustain me in order to avoid suffering that was unavoidable. I wanted to claim whatever of him I could still have.

I got dressed quickly, pulling on whatever I found in the dark, a hodgepodge of flannels and sweaters, and went outside. The old engine took three tries to catch, but then I was driving down the deserted roads, hardly daring to think where I was going and yet headed there like an arrow.

I parked and stepped over the chain looped across the cemetery entrance and started down the rows of markers, glowing white whenever the moon surfaced from clouds streaming by.

I hadn't been here since Simon was buried and couldn't find the plot at first. The names I read in passing were familiar. The parents and grandparents of schoolmates, boys killed in the war, babies a day old, and an eleven-year-old who'd died from polio the summer before.

I recognized the maternal family names as well, the local custom being to identify married women by maiden names, as Maggie had been a Hartson and I had been a Rhymer. I thought of a whole other town under my feet. *Our Town,* not hanging in the sky somewhere, but in boxes set in earth. I walked carefully down the narrow aisles between the mounds and almost went past the stone marked SIMON MAHLER.

Almost incomprehensible that Simon was contained there, the plot too small and still and quiet. I knelt and traced the dates, touching them to help me understand. I put my palms flat through the layer of snow to the ground as if I could feel his shape through the earth. I talked to him, or what part of him was left there, and told him how I missed him, though I didn't know whether to address the sky or ground or space inside myself. Then I cried because I had been helpless to keep him.

I stayed until the sky grew light and I was so numb from cold I could hardly stand. I didn't know any better why he had died or how to feel less pain over that. But I was sure of his existence down to my bones as if he filled all the spaces inside me with solid good. He had been in fact, and would always be in memory and spirit.

By the time I got home, Oz was out in the paddock with Malaak. He stood with his arm over her back and watched me walk toward him.

"Where you been so early?"

"Out."

He shrugged and lifted the saddle off the top fence rail. I watched him buckle her bridle. I studied his shoulders, their broadness that I loved to look at in that present moment just as much as I had when I was sixteen.

Like my memories of Simon would in time, my memories of Oz had already carried me through the starved places of my life. But unlike Simon, this man was still before me. Close enough that I could reach out and place my palm flat between his shoulder blades. I could still come to him, and it would only take the same kind of fearful dive I had taken in the second when I'd asked for Malaak. I wanted to try, at least.

"Want to ride her out today?" he asked. "I think she's ready."

"This morning?"

"Good as any." He cinched the girth, and she shifted her feet in the snow. I came closer, and he held out the reins.

"You do it," I said, thinking that surely I had misunderstood his question from yesterday if all he had on his mind this morning was Malaak.

"Why me? She's yours."

"Ours," I said, suddenly feeling the bond of the horse between us and such sadness that he and I, even when estranged, were so close to each other in ways I had never been with Neal.

"C'mon, Nora," he grinned, tossing the reins at me so I caught them out of reflex. "What the hell are you waiting for?"

I shrugged. He adjusted the stirrups, his arms and chest brushing my leg, and tugged at my boot heel to set it right.

"Oz," I said, watching his hand run the length of rein to make sure it wasn't tangled, "what about yesterday?"

"We need to do this first." He patted Malaak on the rump. "Have a good ride."

At first I was woozy from exhaustion and the vertigo of being so high above the pasture moving beneath us, the tufts of grass poking through the white. I was tentative, this first time she and I had room to move outside the confines of the training ring. But as I settled into her rhythm, I forgot anything but our motion. She was quick to respond to what I asked of her, so eager that I barely had to suggest the speed and direction before it was accomplished. I took her through the gaits and nudged her into a gallop. Then with her mane whipping my hands and the land moving under us through the sight of her ears, I heard Maggie's words again—*What more do you want to lose?*—and I knew I could not give this up.

When Oz grabbed her reins and I slid off, I wanted to throw my arms around his neck to thank him for giving me this, for finding her and training her well and staying with me.

"Well?" he said.

I couldn't stop grinning or let go of the handful of her mane that I'd grabbed. Then he walked around her and fiddled with the bridle, looked at me for a long while over her back, and shifted his weight.

"You don't know how I am, how it would be with me."

"I already am with you."

"We did this OK together, didn't we?" He nodded at the horse.

Then all the force I'd felt driving back from the grave boiled up again. For all I couldn't help, I was sick of all I had lost through excuses and inaction and stupidity. What I'd done out of fear instead of want.

"Yes," I said. "We did this better than OK."

He studied me as if trying to judge whether I was telling him the whole truth.

"I've got some business to see to," I told him suddenly. "Wait for me to get back, all right?"

I turned and walked back to the house, past Maggie looking up over the morning paper, and down the hall to the phone. When Neal answered, I took a deep breath.

"You can do whatever you want and prolong the misery any way you can, but as soon as my lawyer's office opens this morning, I'm filing the papers for sure, and I want what I asked for."

"Nora," he said, "are we going through all this again?"

I hung up on him and went upstairs. I sat on the side of my bed and just trembled like some animal that's been out too long in the wet and cold. But somehow this was better, this pain on its way to someplace instead of misery biting its own tail. Better, even though I was far from done with it and could not imagine what tricks Neal would pull on me next.

I was at the lawyer's by ten and done by eleven. Then I called Clea's school and told the principal there was an emergency. She came to the phone breathless.

"What's happened? Did someone die?"

"No. Just the opposite. I want you to come home."

There was a long pause.

"Why are you telling me this now?"

"Is it OK with you? I'll take care of the arrangements, and you can see your father anytime you want. But I need you back."

She didn't answer.

"Clea? I've missed you."

She cleared her throat.

"Me, too."

"OK then? Do you need time to think?"

"No. It's OK, I think."

After I hung up, I turned and saw Maggie standing in the doorway behind me.

"Is she coming?" she asked.

I nodded, and we both smiled suddenly as if we had just remembered how. Then I went to the barn. Oz stood up from mucking a stall, his head cocked to study me.

"Want to take me to St. Louis for a movie?" I asked.

"You OK?"

"I just want to get away for a while," I told him.

He came in the kitchen at four, freshly shaven and smelling of Old Spice. As he drove across the Missouri River and down the Rock Road, he talked nonstop. How Malaak liked to work a carrot from his back pocket and nipped at his rear if he came with the pocket empty. How she arched her head like Delacroix horses carrying red-tasseled sheiks. How she followed him around, trying to lick his fingers.

We went down the same road Neal had driven me on our way to Arsenal Street, as if that June day had gotten stuck in time and waited for me to come back to it. Oz kept glancing at me, but I stared out the front until my eyes ached from concentrating on the pavement disappearing past the hood. When he pulled into a parking space down the street from the Fox Theatre, he asked again, "Are you OK?"

"I think so."

He helped me over snow piled at the curb, and I stared at our reflections in a shop window as if to get used to the sight of him and me together. The twilight shadows and sky were an early evening blue, and I felt awakened on that street with no idea of how I'd come to be there.

"C'mon, what's happened?" he asked. "You're different."

That he'd noticed was as strange as the snow glowing neon blue in patches where the streetlights missed. That same eerie shimmer as rosaries or crosses that glowed in the dark.

He took my arm, not steering the way Neal would have, my elbow like the rudder on a johnboat, but touching to stay close. The buildings and light poles and passersby, the cars and street speeding to the horizon, all overwhelmed me as if the past months had made me forget depth and volume. I slid my hands inside the sleeves of my coat to feel the roundness of my arms and I leaned back against him.

As Oz got our tickets, I looked up at the rows of bare bulbs on the marquee and then away so they floated over Grand Boulevard. I couldn't stop looking at all I'd kept away from since Simon died. At couples walking down the street, the men with briskly tilted hats and overcoats flying open over dark wool vests, the women in square short furs. At the blind man selling pencils, and two seedy bums, and a shopgirl with too much rouge.

I felt a pang that this was the first winter Simon had missed, the first snows that had come without him. So many people going about their business and my son not in the world to feel the clean smack of air each time he went outside or the warmth when he came back in. I could not picture Simon in his new state, but at that moment thought of him as part of the winter blue brushing past my hand.

Standing with Oz in the rush-hour city, I felt just as nebulous—neither myself nor the monster Neal railed against nor much of anyone at all. Only emptied and waiting for what I could make of myself next.

Oz and I went up the steps of the theater lobby, my hand on the brass rail like a fat gold anaconda, past the caryatid women holding the heavy vault of the room on their heads. We were the first into the theater, all gilt and marble like a pagan temple, with seats like rivulets of red plush flowing away to the proscenium. Oz folded my coat with his and sat square in his seat, his legs so long and splayed out that his knee grazed mine.

"I filed the papers," I said.

Oz stared up at the golden lion heads on the walls and six Krishnas in their alcoves.

"Good for you," he said.

He moved his arm against mine on the rest.

"I don't know if I can do it," I said. "I don't know if I can hold on until it's final."

We both stared at the red curtains covering the high screen.

"Like being ordered across a field," he said, "when mortars are flying and machine guns firing. For a second you can't move, but once you get going, the worst is over."

He lapped his finger over mine.

"It'll be all right."

I could have changed where this might take us by simply moving my hand, but the lights went down, and in the blind moments before my eyes adjusted, there was just his touch. I felt silly for how much importance I put on this tiny gesture, like we were seventeen again and our lives depended on the other.

I heard my father warn that Ozzie Kline was a two-bit nothing and that I could do better. But I didn't care what he said. Oz moved his arm around me, and I scolded my father. *Old man, I was right the first time.* Then I imagined Neal's mouth opening and shutting like a guppy's and being as beyond his reach as I was from Frank Rhymer's.

I didn't pay a second's attention to the movie, it being just an excuse to sit close to Oz and get used to him with me. I could not stop looking at him in the flickering light. The nose bumped from being broken in fights and hair flattened from his cap, the features so familiar and yet so new.

Afterward, we walked from the theater into the night, now deep black and filled with snow flying at us like stars, and the streets and the sidewalks covered over with fresh white. I scooped up a snowball and pelted Oz in the middle of his chest. He looked at the white burst marking his sweater, then chased me down the street.

When we stopped at the truck, I threw my arms around his neck so briefly that, if we wished, the hug could be taken as only exuberance. But he pulled me close, and our breathing made ocean noises in the space between us.

He kissed me hard, and all that I had been holding tight at my center ran out like warm oil. Our old want lifted me out of Neal's reach and beyond the deep center of Simon's death and all the smaller losses in the last year that I had allowed or had no choice in. It carried me back to the time before real hurt and loss, and to reach that place if only for a moment made all the difference.

We rested our foreheads together, so close that it seemed we might read the other's mind, and I craved for Oz to make up in the next hour all the touch we had deferred. I slid my arms inside his coat, and we flew like the snow streaming white and beautiful out of the dark. Oz as he had been and yet himself now, with love and hope and comfort as sweet as the pulse beating in a baby's head.

"What do you want of me, Nora?" he whispered.

"This." Though I hadn't known how much.

"Sure?"

I nodded, too scared to speak.

We drove through the storm as if in a parade with a few other cars and some truckers creeping toward the Missouri bridge. The headlights caught the snow driving down irresistibly, and the wheels skimmed sideways as if the road was twitching us off. When we finally edged our way up the farm lane, the truck in low gear and pulling through the drifts with effort, Oz parked close to the barn and said, "Let's check the horses."

The sound of his voice surprised me, as if we hours ago had passed the point of needing to speak. I followed behind while he slid open the door and pushed Bandit back so that he couldn't go in with us. With just the light from the outside spot leaking through the window, I could barely make out the silhouettes of the horses' heads lifting over their stalls and Oz disappearing into the tack room. Hay and manure and horse mixed in a lovely, familiar soup. I picked my way over to Malaak to rub her nose and feel her breath on my hand. She pushed against my coat, looking for sugar or carrot, and I felt as I did when I'd check on the kids and one of them would wake up enough to roll over and hug me.

Then Oz came back, carrying an armful of horse blankets and a kerosene lantern that swung bright shards of light. He hung the lantern on a peg, pulled fresh straw into an empty stall, and arranged the blankets.

"What are you doing?" I stroked the filly's cheek.

"Making our bed." He took my hand and pulled me after him.

"Here?"

"Yes, in our own place."

The straw bed had rises and hollows different from mine until my weight pressed them right; the blankets were rough but soon warm. Oz shook out another and pulled it over, the stall enclosing us. Once more I thought of Neal and the safety he threatened me with.

"Ozzie, I'm afraid," I said.

"Nora," he said, propping himself up on one elbow, "if the entire German panzer force was coming at me this minute, I couldn't be more terrified."

I didn't know whether to laugh or be overcome by his tenderness, so I pulled him to me and brushed my lips against his. We kept on holding each other, just as we had at sixteen and were first overcome with awe at our closeness. Then we shifted so we touched at every possible point, and for a while I wanted us to stay like this forever, caught at the midpoint between wanting and having, until it seemed as if I would break if we did not go on.

When he moved his hand up over my ribs and breast, resting for a moment, I stiffened, afraid of how my body had changed since we were young.

"I'm not the same," I told him, stopping his hand with mine.

"Neither am I, and that's the way it's supposed to be."

He ran his fingers from my temple along the line of jaw and down my body in ways I would have flinched away from Neal. I touched him, remembering the shape of the boy still familiar in the heavier weight of the man.

We fumbled buttons, untangled arms from sleeves and necks from sweaters, hardly able to undress as quickly as we wished. He lay over me, my toes pointed to reach his feet and his hardness against my belly.

"I have never let another travel inside me where I've let you," he said.

Somehow I had always known that. Knew also if I did not get up then and run into the house, so fast away from him that I streamed naked across the winter yard, I would pass into the beginning of what would come next in my life. I wanted that new start, even as I felt time moving away from me and taking what I would keep as well as what I was better off without.

Thinking of Simon, I moved my hand into the cold outside of the blankets as the wind shifted and turned the snow back into crisscrosses past the window.

"I miss him," I whispered, and was surprised at the tears running back and turning the edge of my hairline cold.

"I miss him, too," Oz said, and rested his forehead against mine. "As much as I've missed us."

He braced his elbows to keep me from his full weight, and we lay quietly like that until he reached up to wipe dry the wet from my temples. Then, even in sadness, I wanted him, pulled his mouth to mine, and lifted my hips to move against his.

Again, as it had been between us years before, I could not stand to be separate from him, not only from his body but his self so close and with me, as if any small space between us was too much.

"Ozzie," I said, "come here and stay."

He pulled back to look at me, and I held his face, marked with crow's-feet and a scar over his eyebrow, his expression boyish with both hope and hesitation.

"Are you sure you want this?" he asked, and I nodded.

"More than I did the first time."

"We won't be able to take it back, not this time," he said.

"I know. I want it that way."

Then we pushed tight as we could against each other, the physical only the acting out of that other connection between us, immense and all-encompassing as blue air. We watched each other, as we always had before, not like with Neal where I closed my eyes to go away from him.

Oz, his eyes soft with pleasure and love, watched me so carefully that even when I closed mine in coming I could feel his sight inside the sweet darkness, felt him there with me. As I returned completely, he smiled, happy and satisfied with where I'd gone in myself. Then his eyes closed as mine had while he lost himself in me.

On the edges of myself I regretted my old life passing, since even pain becomes reassuring in familiarity and love is treacherous as birth. Inadvertently I caught myself as if I'd been falling in a dream. He tightened his arms around me, pressed his face against my neck, and I was surrounded by the peace we'd always had with each other when we'd allowed it. But now it was joined by the relief of again discovering our pure selves—as we had been and had become, as we were only when we were together.

Malaak stirred, her warmth heating up and sending out her special smell into the cold. We could breed her in the spring and every spring after, could rest here together after delivering her foals, just like this, and celebrate. Could breathe in the tang of birth blood and afterbirth and mare's milk and hold that breath inside us.

Ozzie would understand that when I told him. Would have perhaps thought it himself.

He kissed my forehead and rolled on his back.

"Look," he said. "See her?"

Malaak had lifted her head over the side of the stall to watch us, and the lantern threw her shadow large against the wall, her ears like black mountains with a divide between.

"Someday I'll teach Clea to ride her," he said. "If she wants."

I liked that and tucked in the curve of his arm, my hand flat and quiet on his chest, my fingers slid through the curls of hair there. We lay still until we both grew sleepy from our warmth in the center of all that cold. But beyond our quiet, I felt the wonder and excitement of his arm around me, of my leg over his, of us together. These simple things, so difficult to come to, so long in finding.